With the sound of her own blood pulsing in her ears, Kyril pushed Kathryn down against the bed, gazing intently into her eyes. Slowly, she lowered her face to Kathryn's and began to kiss her again, her body moving over Kathryn's in time to the rhythm of her tongue in Kathryn's mouth. Together, they rolled on the bed, disrobing, caressing, writhing against one another.

Kyril slid her lips over Kathryn's chin, to her exposed throat. The skin there gave off a fragrance sweet with the promise of the blood that surged in the huge veins and arteries beneath....

Other Books From Rising Tide Press:

Shadows After Dark, Ouida Crozier
Return to Isis, Jean Stewart
Isis Rising, Jean Stewart
You Light the Fire, Kristen Garrett
Corners of the Heart, Leslie Grey
Love Spell, Karen Williams
Danger in High Places, Sharon Gilligan
Faces of Love, Sharon Gilligan
Edge of Passion, Shelley Smith
Romancing the Dream, Heidi Johanna

Shadows
After Dark

Shadows
After Dark

Ouida Crozier

RISING TIDE PRESS

Rising Tide Press
5 Kivy Street
Huntington Station, NY 11746
(516) 427-1289

Printed in the United States on acid-free paper

Publisher's note:
All characters, places and situations in this book are fictitious and any
resemblance to persons (living or dead) is purely coincidental.

Publisher's Acknowledgments:
The publisher is grateful for all the support and expertise offered by
the members of its editorial board: Bobbi Bauer, Beth Heyn, Harriet
Edwards, Pat G., Adriane Balaban, and Marian Satriani. And a
special thanks to Harriet and Adriane for their excellent proofing and
criticism, to Edna G. for believing in us, and to the feminist bookstores
for being there.

First printing August, 1993
10 9 8 7 6 5 4 3 2 1

Edited by Lee Boojamra and Alice Frier
Book cover art: Evelyn Rysdyk

Crozier, Ouida, 1947
    Shadows After Dark

ISBN 0—883061-50-4

                    Library of Congress #: 93—083669

ACKNOWLEDGEMENTS

I wish to acknowledge the following people in the completion of this manuscript: All those who have come before, writing and filming in the vampire genre; Kate Allen, for her belief in my work and her invaluable critical support; members of my writing group: Pat, Randy, Stan, and, in particular, Justine Stahlman, for their critical comments and their support; others, including my former partner, Lynn Liptak, who have given input or just, in general, put up with me. Dawn and Dan for the use of their computer. Thank you all.

AUTHOR'S NOTE

I have attempted to portray the course of the AIDS epidemic as truthfully as possible, but any errors in doing so are solely those of the author and should be attributed to no one else.

For those who are unfamiliar with the details of its beginning, it is important to note that many gay men and lesbian women, and most straight people, thought that victims of this plague were to be only gay men. In the early eighties, few dreamed it would spread as it has, and no one anywhere knew how it spread. We have learned so much in the ten or so years we have been studying AIDS, though not enough, never enough, for the thousands whose lives have been prematurely ended by the deadly virus. And were it not for the gay and lesbian communities across this country—who organized very quickly in the face of this grim threat to fight it—even less would be known about HTLV-III than is.

Prologue

Kyril stood in Szaj Nagy, the Great Os, at the Place of Interface, watching the misty sworls that characterized the oupirian side of the Boundary between dimensions. It was evening. Shadow and soft light, cast by the ever-burning flames in their sconces on carven pillars, flickered on stone walls. She sighed, holding herself, a tall, dark-haired creature, brooding on the faint images seen through the misty curtain. She was conscious that soon she would become yet another of those images— a Visitor from her dimension to the Other.

As she gazed at the swirling eddies in the Interface, her mind drifted back to her talk earlier that day with Guardian Tyrell. Kyril had known that Tyrell would agree with her decision to return to the Other dimension. Tyrell knew as well as she that—while there was at present little to hold her in their world—it was imperative that someone seek the answers to her tragic riddle and return with them.

Kyril started at the sound of a footstep behind her, the reverie broken. She swivelled, her arms dropping to her sides, the cape she wore fanning out around her.

"Tyrell," she greeted quietly.

Tyrell placed her hands on Kyril's shoulders. "My Daughter." She paused, her dark eyes searching Kyril's. "Have you readied yourself?"

Kyril swept her gaze over the ebony features of her friend and spiritual Mother, seeking to absorb one further, sustaining memory. She slowly inclined her head in assent.

Tyrell turned Kyril back to the dimensional Interface, one hand remaining on her shoulder. There was a silence as both contemplated the dim world on the far side of the swirling Boundary.

"It is time," Tyrell breathed.

Kyril turned and they embraced for a long moment. "I bid you farewell," Kyril said, stepping back, her voice catching on her sadness.

"I shall await you each time Csatlós visits us in her travels across the sky. Until you appear, I shall know that you have not yet succeeded in your quest." Her dark eyes shone with unshed tears. "May all the Creator's holy creatures be with you, my dear. Good-bye, Kyril."

"Good-bye. . .Mother," Kyril whispered, refusing to admit the tears to her eyes.

She gathered herself and the bundle she would carry with her through the Interface and crossed the short distance to the edge. With only a pause, she raised her head and stepped——

——Out of rock into luminous night where the wind blew a song through the trees and crevasses of the high mountains in which the Door was located. Slightly disoriented from the dimensional transit, she sought to clear her head, breathing deeply of the thin, cool air, remembering its scent and the crispness.

Glancing over her shoulder, she could see the shimmering of the energy barrier which was the only visible aspect of the Boundary from this side. Kyril knew Tyrell stood there, watching, even though she could not see through to this dimension. She waved once, then wrapped her long cape about her as she scanned the glittering stars for her bearings. She struck out southwestward, her long-legged strides devouring the distance. There was no path here, no trace of human habitation, but her keen eyes enabled her to pick her way easily among rocks and roots and nature's debris. She deftly shouldered aside branches and small trees, and her boots softly crushed the carpeting of fallen leaves and needles, flooding the night air with fragrance.

With all the gifts of her oupirian senses, she could see, hear, and smell nocturnal creatures disturbed by her passage. Some—the smaller or more timid—scurried away in fear; others—a wild boar, included—paused to listen or sniff the air for her scent. Her private knowledge that she had no scent they could catch, that it was the noise and vibration of her movements that gave her away to them as easily as their scents told her from yards distant who, and what, and where they were, briefly amused her. They had nothing to fear from Kyril: oupirs no longer preyed upon four-legged, winged, and furred creatures in this dimension. Instead, when they Visited, her kind derived sustenance from the one species that wantonly used and abused this planet and its resources. Over the countless Cycles of Seasons during which Kyril's people had watched, this avaricious species had exterminated more of their own number, for every imaginable or unimaginable cause, than had died by fang or claw or natural cause since their ancestors had lifted their heads from the primeval muck or descended from the trees of this world. They referred to themselves as *homo sapiens,* but the appellation Kyril would have chosen was that of *savage.*

She paused at the top of a gorge cut by a rushing river which fell in cascading sheets hundreds of feet to an invisible floor below. She thought of the human beings she had known, thought that if they had been aware of her real identity, they would now mock her, rail at her about returning to this place which she clearly regarded as inferior to her own. *So*, she asked herself, *why **am** I here*?

She moved on, keeping her eye on the treacherous path she now followed. The query was rhetorical. That she sought the solution to a mystery she had charged herself with solving was, in truth, not the only reason she was again venturing among *homo sapiens*. The answers she needed were connected to a loss she had no real wish to confront—and a once-met human. In spite of what Tyrell might expect, she already knew that, if she were unable to solve the mystery with which she had charged herself, she could not return to her own world to commit herself in Guardianship at the Os. There was nothing there for her. The thought of this human tugged at her: Perhaps here, in this dimension. . . .

With a heavy sigh, Kyril paused at another craggy turn, gazing upward at the silvery orb that cast its soft light over the sharp peaks of the mountains: full moon in the Carpathians. Enjoying a remembrance of the folklore and mythology of the world in which she now stood, she grinned to herself.

A distant howl came to her on the night air, echoing eerily off the rocks, and she laughed aloud, the mocking hilarity a wry counterpart to the mournful howl. Pulling her cloak tighter about her neck, she strode through a night soon to become dawn.

Spring 1983

1

T he keening of the circling gulls was a bittersweet sound for Kathryn Hartell. She paused in her meandering through the edge of the surf, watching as they darted and dove among themselves. As a child, she had loved seagulls until she had learned that they appropriated the nests of other birds for their own use, and sometimes killed the young there. Now she viewed them askance, her feelings a mixture of nostalgia brought on by their cries and a quiet horror at their mindless betrayal of childhood innocence.

She began walking again, her gaze fixed always on the ocean, her layered blonde hair lifting in the late afternoon breeze. She loved the feel of the wind on her skin, in her short hair, its constancy a match with the endless roar of the surf, the ceaseless breaking of waves and their lapping on the shore. She splashed in the shallow tide pools, and wriggled her feet in the soft sand, the present overlaid with countless memories of being a child on a beach such as this one, summer after summer, through all the years of her growing up. Some part of her stretched, reached, yearned to recapture the magic of those heedless, innocent summers, when the future was but a careless dream, and the present of such an intensity that she sometimes ached, deep inside.

When her mother had died the previous fall, Kathryn had flown to Florida from Minneapolis for the funeral, then spent several days helping her brother and sister-in-law go through her mother's things and ready the house for sale. The evening before she was to have returned to Minneapolis, she had stolen a few moments to drive down to the beach in her mother's car. At first sight of her beloved ocean, she had burst into tears, choking with an emotion so deep that it found expression in silent words from that reaching place within her: *Mother!* she had greeted the grey-green waters, *I am home!* Later, when she had tried to put that joy, that sense of homecoming, into other words, she had failed. The ocean had always seemed an awesome thing, never ending, changeless yet everchanging. An ageless phenomenon through which she felt rooted all the way back to the beginning of time. Via tears, she had re-connected with that part of her which had survived all the years between the end of innocence and the immutable moment in time that was her mother's death, a death which had left her totally unshielded in the face of the universe. Never had she felt so alone, or so free.

Now, six months after that death, she prowled the white sands of that same north Florida shore, feeling in a quiet limbo between the intensity of those childhood summers and this changed and changing spring of her thirty-eighth year. She had come to finish up matters of the estate, and for a much needed vacation, but she could not shake the past, and its presence made the present slightly surreal.

Kathryn stopped again, bending over a curious piece of flotsam half-buried in the sand. Straightening, she turned and looked behind her at the setting sun. She knew her sister-in-law would be getting supper ready, but she wanted to stay, to wait: for something to change, to fall into place, to be finished, purged, released. She was not sure what—or how— she only knew that it must, that something MUST be different, that something must emerge to make the present solid and real, to end a seemingly endless, empty past, to quell persistent memories. . . .

With a deep breath, she shook herself, thinking that she always got like this when she allowed herself to be hypnotized by the rolling sea. A grudging glance at her watch told her she must go.

"Mindi!" she called against the wind, clapping her hands. "Mindi, here girl!" Forty pounds of wet, sandy fur came running, eager as always to get on with the adventure of living. "Good dog, good girl!" Kathryn praised. They jogged the half mile back to their car, where Kathryn persuaded the auburn-haired dog to shake herself clean of the worst of the sand before climbing into the back seat. With one more long look at the water, she took her own place and drove off.

☾ ☾ ☾

Kathryn lay on the bed in her motel room near a window that overlooked the surf, and through which the ceaseless seabreeze whispered and sighed. She revelled in the soft touch of wind on her naked body. In her mind's eye, her fantasy lover rose over her, adding her caresses to those of the breeze and Kathryn's own hands and fingers. She stroked her breasts and belly with one hand, the fingers of her other gently circling her clitoris as she visualized a tall woman with dark eyes and hair, whom she had met nearly two years ago. The features of her fantasy lover's face were indistinct, having dimmed in Kathryn's memory. What had not dimmed was the attraction Kathryn felt for the woman, and she easily let go of outer reality and slipped into a vivid re-experiencing of their encounter.

❆ ❆ ❆

She stood in the smoky half-light of the bar, part of a sea of shifting, milling forms. Disco speakers thumped an insistent, augmented bass under the treble of the vocalists and the voices of those who strove to make themselves heard above the din of the music. People danced, cruised, stood against the walls, watching, searching, hoping. Tonight there was a restlessness in the crowd of women, which Kathryn shared. In the last year, she had found herself drawn more and more to the bars, until she was going nearly every weekend. She always arrived with her anticipatory excitement, always left with disappointment echoing in some part of her. Her hazel eyes flicked over the crowd, seizing upon momentary glimpses of faces in the flashing lights. She sought some mutual recognition, some answering flicker of desire, some beautiful sorceress who would know her at a glance and cast a spell on her which would ensure life-long commitment and happiness between them. Someone who would fill her aching emptiness and enable her to give herself as she had never given herself before.

She finished her rum and ginger and pushed away from the wall near the edge of the dance floor where she had taken a position with her friends. Threading her way through the mass of bodies toward the bar, she waited in line, got a refill and began making her way back. As she neared her companions, she saw that someone was standing in her spot. The woman turned and their eyes met across the gyrating bodies between them. Kathryn was stunned by the jolt that shot through her. Everything suddenly faded but the woman. There were no words spoken, but they moved out onto the dance floor together, and it seemed an endless time that they danced, Kathryn mesmerized by her partner. The eyes, dark, recessed in a pale face framed by black hair that floated in thick waves across her shoulders as she swayed to the music. Kathryn's desire rose, enveloping her in a heat that had little to do with the warmth in the bar. She thought it must be apparent to anyone who would look. As if that were true, the woman moved closer and put her hands on Kathryn's hips, synchronizing their movements, transmuting the dance into something intensely sexual for both.

When the dancing ended, and the flashing lights stilled, they stood, not touching, in the sudden seeming-quiet. Then, the woman took Kathryn's hands into hers, her eyes never leaving Kathryn's, and held them briefly before turning away and fading into the fast-clearing crowd.

Kathryn was left with the ghost of a hurriedly whispered name, and unfulfilled desire.

❨ ❨ ❨

As the memory of that night blurred, Kathryn cried out to the moist evening, clutching at a pillow, imagining the woman's mouth devouring her, her hands and body possessing her: "Kyril! Oh, Kyril!" she called, over and over again until her shudders subsided and she lay, at last, quiescent in the fading twilight of her room.

Over the months that had followed that night in the bar, Kathryn had struggled to push the woman from her mind, to ignore the torrent of emotion and desire that Kyril had evoked. But her unconscious had refused to let go. Periodically, she dreamed of Kyril, and her image arose again and again, unbidden, in sexual fantasies. When she was being honest with herself, Kathryn had to admit that she still hoped to find Kyril in some unguarded, unexpected moment, the way that people tell of their discoveries of life's treasures. Drifting now towards sleep, Kathryn reached out toward a Kyril who wandered somewhere in an unknown part of the universe, asking, inviting, entreating her to show herself in Kathryn's life again.

2

The tall dark woman used her papers and allotted funds to book passage on a transatlantic flight to the United States. Her passport bore the identity she assumed when a Visitor in this Other dimension: Kyril Vértök, citizen of Hungary, resident of Budapest, professor of medicine. As she stood in line to check in at the airport terminal, she reflected that in their centuries of journeying in this world, her species had developed a tremendously broad power base, having eventually infiltrated every major organization in every major country in the world. Their foresight and organization made it possible for oupirs to come and go easily in a global society where so much depended on encoded records of identity and residence. In this world, money *could* buy almost everything one needed, at least in a material sense.

Once on the plane, Kyril dozed. It had taken her longer to make her journey to Budapest, and then on to the airport, at Ferihegy, than she had planned. There had been a major rock slide on one of the highways in the foothills and their bus had been delayed an entire day while the road was cleared. She had deemed it unwise to attempt to feed in the sparsely populated farm country, instead waiting until she reached the anonymity of the city. She was tired, and momentarily sated.

As they became airborne, the droning of the engines lulled her deeper into sleep. For a while, she slept heavily; then she began to dream. She was in Kornägy, her own world, seeing the thin form of her lover lying in a hospital bed, a victim of some wasting disease. The image was so vivid that the sleeping Kyril could almost feel Lanaea's pain like the palpable thing it had been in waking life. She saw the furrows etched in the ravaged face, a face from which nearly all beauty had been erased by incessant and prolonged suffering. Again she fell on her knees beside Lanaea's bed, clutching Lanaea's hand and forearm until the skin around her fingers paled, as if her grasp could keep her mate from slipping into death. And then came the immeasurable time until Kyril had realized there was no more pulse under those rigid fingers, and she had raised her head to see the final peace of death on Lanaea's face. Tears, hot and scalding, flooded her cheeks, but no cry escaped her as she swallowed her pain. She would allow it later, in the privacy of the home she and Lanaea had shared. She stared at the stilled face, its lines forever etched in her memory, the etching overlaid with images of the living, breathing Lanaea at her peak of health and joy in their life together. She was so absorbed she failed to hear the soft step behind her and started at the gentle touch on her shoulder. She looked up to see a medtech and panicked, thinking that they had come to take her beloved Lanaea away from her. She threw herself over Lanaea's body, sobbing, "No! No, you can't have her! No! No!"

With a jerk, she awoke to find herself in the airplane, its lights dimmed, darkness outside the windows. She wiped at the tears on her face, consciously slowing her heart and breathing, forcing herself to relax as she tried unobtrusively to ascertain if others had been disturbed by her dreaming. By habit, she sat alone, always purchasing two or three seats side by side so that she would not have to be in too close proximity to human beings. Although other passengers were sleeping and seemed unaware of her disturbance, she could hear the flight attendant coming forward. The woman stopped next to her and bent down. "Are you all right?" she inquired in a quiet voice, her hand resting lightly on Kyril's shoulder.

Kyril nodded, smiling briefly, wanting to be rid of the touch. "Yes, thank you," she replied. "I was just dreaming. Really, I am fine now." The heat radiating from the woman's hand, the rich human scent in Kyril's nostrils, her awareness of the throbbing pulse in the bare neck, inflamed a renewed hunger.

The woman straightened, appearing doubtful. When Kyril shifted her gaze to the darkened window, she finally moved off, back to her station.

Glancing at her watch, Kyril calculated they would reach JFK in less than an hour. She had planned her flight for a night landing, and she sighed, laying her head back against the seat, accepting that she would have to feed again before she caught her flight out the next day. She supposed the gnawing emptiness was due to the exertion of her mountainous trek, coupled with the enforced abstinence during the journey from wilderness to the fringes of what, in this dimension, was euphemistically referred to as civilization.

She passed the time during their approach to New York by reviewing her knowledge of the layout of the city, mapping out a strategy for the hunt. There were numberless vagrants and transients adrift in the sprawling, filthy metropolis at all hours of the day and night, and she knew she would have no trouble locating prey.

With the memory of Lanaea's death again fresh inside her, she turned to wondering how Lanaea could have contracted the disease that had killed her. From long experience in this dimension, the oupirian species had learned that their bodies could consume, without harm, almost any human sickness along with the blood they obtained from their human prey. Their medical sciences had developed immunizations for those diseases to which their systems were not impervious. Thus, whatever it was that Lanaea had fallen victim to, Kyril was certain that it had crossed the Boundary with Lanaea after her last Visit—even though they had been unable to discover any previously unrecorded organisms in any of the fluid or tissue samples they had taken from her. Kyril had volunteered to journey back to this dimension, ostensibly to unravel the mystery of the unknown danger. As a physician, she was well suited to such a task.

After she buckled her seatbelt for the final approach, Kyril closed her eyes and allowed her awareness to turn to the other reason she had returned: the human female whose existence drew her almost against her will. She reached out, actively trying to apprehend the woman's presence in this dimension. There was *touch,* so slight it might have been illusion on her part. But with it was an echo of an intense longing that served somehow to reassure Kyril. She could not, she reflected as the lights of JFK began to show through the cloud cover, put into words what she felt for this human female. Whatever it was, it had been with her constantly, on the edges of her awareness, since Lanaea's death. Soon, it must have attention.

Two hours later, she stepped out of a taxi near the Hudson River, in lower Manhattan. She had left her luggage at the airport, in the hands of the airline personnel, then changed from her silk jacket and skirt into an indigo jumpsuit and stowed her carry-on gear in an airport locker. Although she had been to New York before, it was a continued source of amazement that even at this late hour, the streets throbbed with life—a veritable jungle of human beings in all sorts of enterprises, teeming through the concrete canyons and byways, swarming in the towering sky scrapers and over the face of every flat surface there was.

She paid the driver in American currency and made as if to enter the bar to which she had directed him. She paused in the doorway and lit a cigarette, watching from the corner of her eye as he drove off. When he had disappeared, she struck off down the sidewalk, the leather of her soles marking the rhythmn of her long strides. The glare on the street was an annoyance to her light-sensitive eyes, so she stepped into the edge of an alleyway. As she was fleeing the light, she glimpsed a man of indeterminate age and features lounging in a doorway across from the alley.

Deliberately, she strode back into his view, catching his eye, then turning away from him, inviting him to follow her.

Discarding her cigarette in the gutter, she grimaced as she exhaled—she hated the taste and smell of them, and only affected them as an element of camouflage for the places in this Other-world in which she wished to move unnoticed.

In the relative dark of the alley, her movements became feline in their stealth. She swiftly took in her surroundings, noting that the alley abutted another building and alleyway, and that the only windows that opened onto it were very high ones near the top of the building against her back. Her eyes strained against the penumbra created by the lights of the megalopolis, but she could tell that there was still a cloud cover. The bricks behind her were dark with moisture, and light glinted on wet patches in the concrete of the street. If she listened well, she could distinguish over the roar of the traffic on the FDR Highway a shushing sound of water against a pier. She knew where she might lose her victim if she could get him there without being seen.

She glanced back at the opening to her alleyway and saw that the man had come across the street and was poised a few feet into the brick warren. He was trying to see her. She stepped from the shadows into his view.

He started. "Oh—hi . . ." he said uncertainly. "Uh, what are you doing in here?"

"Waiting for you," she said in as sultry a voice as she could manage. She felt revulsion rise in her: She hated men with a passion born of her utter disdain for their endless centuries of slaughter, rape, and pillage. She never killed coldly, and never women—it was always an act of vengeance against the males of this species. She struck a pose she had seen the prostitutes affect, playing the role to its maximum.

He came forward, swaggering a little, feeling more sure now of her intent, responding to her body language with his own, in the never-ending game of seduction. "Well, how about coming out into the light where I can see you better?" He grinned, the expression a smirk on his unshaven face. His breath washed at her with the odor of stale cigarettes and alcohol.

She stepped away from him, luring him deeper into the alley. "Let's go down by the river."

He hesitated.

"It's not far, is it?" she coaxed.

"Well, no but—" he broke off uncertainly.

She read the hesitation in him, the energy field about him radiating his every emotion. She shifted her stance, beckoning him. "I know a place—very private," she tantalized.

"Well, okay," he assented, glancing around him at the murky urban canyon. "It's got to be better than this place." He shuddered. "This place gives me the creeps."

She led him toward the back alley. Kyril hoped that it gave onto another street. As they turned the corner, she looked well ahead of her to where, indeed, there was an opening to a street which looked as if it might front on the river. Against her inclination, she took his hand and pulled him with her. He stumbled once or twice in the dimness before they came into a better lit area approximately fifty yards from the wharves.

Turning away from the light, Kyril glanced rapidly over the wharves, searching for a likely spot for the privacy she had in mind. "This way," she indicated, stepping out again.

"Hey! Wait!" he protested. He caught up to her and tried to swing her around with a hand on her arm. She neatly sidestepped his grasp and pivoted to face him. She could not see his face well with it backlighted, but she sensed his surprise at her agility and apparent strength. They were of a height and he had obviously expected that he was the stronger of the two.

"Whaddaya wanna go there for?" he objected, pointing at the sheds on the docks.

"I told you, I know a private place," she replied smoothly, readying herself to take him if his resistance mounted or he tried to bolt.

He stood staring at her, finally noticing her accent. "Are you a foreigner?"

She nodded, waiting. She shifted, and pulled out a cigarette, leaning towards him for him to light it. After a moment's hesitation, he fumbled in his jacket pockets for a match. She drew on the cigarette smoothly, seeing clearly into his eyes above the glow of the small fire. She knew now she would have no further trouble from him. Playing sultry again, she flirted, holding out her elbow for him. They strolled across the river front pavement, the peaceful lapping of the water a strong contrast to the overhead roar of the constant traffic.

When they had reached the water, Kyril stopped and flicked her half-smoked cigarette into the dirty film of oil that rode the river She turned to him and put her hands on his shoulders, leaning forward in a teasing kiss. His response was evident in his sudden intake of breath as her lips approached his. He reached out and pulled her closer to him, his arms encircling her, his hips cocked forward to meet hers. He slid his hand down her back and pressed her belly into him, grinding against her. She could feel his hardening penis through the fabric of their clothing and took it as her signal to break away from him.

He seemed less surprised this time, and readily followed her into the shadow of a storage shed as she pretended to fumble at the front of her jumpsuit. She let him take her in his arms again as he tried to pin her against the wall, his hand seeking her breast. His tongue intruded into her mouth. Controlling her desire to gag, she pulled her lips away and raised her head, offering her neck to him. He fastened his mouth on the supple, cool flesh there and she shifted, rolling him sideways and around so that she now was on the outside, he with his back to the wall. She opened his zipper with one hand, allowing his penis to break free. As she stroked him, he moaned, lolling his head back, loosening his grip on her, his eyes closed in pleasure. With a triumphant look at his unguarded face, she lowered her head to his neck and placed her mouth over his right carotid, her other hand on the left, gently pressing.

Suddenly he jerked and tried to pull away, but Kyril, her grip like a vise, immediately had him pinned against the wall. His muffled moans were lost in the overhead roar, and his struggles quickly ceased as she held him, her body pressed against his, and drained him into unconsciousness. As he slumped, she lowered him to the ground to finish her meal. At last, she rose from her crouch, cleaning her mouth on the handkerchief she pulled from a pocket of her jumpsuit. She surveyed the corpse for a moment, taking satisfaction in the thought of having wiped one more blotch from the face of this earth. His vitality surged through her and she was renewed, her energy seemingly boundless—it was always best when the prey was at the height of some exhilarating passion. His adrenaline was her high.

She glanced around and, seeing no one, stuffed the handkerchief into his pocket and slung his body over her shoulder. She moved swiftly to the river's edge and let the burden slide quietly into the murk. Her evening's work finished, she retreated into shadows, threading her way back the few blocks to the lighted, busy streets. She caught a cab to a hotel where she slept the very few hours left to her before she had to return to the airport to board her flight to Minneapolis—and the tall, ash-blonde human woman with hazel eyes whose image beckoned to her out of restless dreams.

3

Kathryn gazed out the window behind the desk in her office in the department of Biochemistry at the University of Minnesota. It had been an unusually early spring, and flowers were blooming and bobbing in the early May breeze. Students bustled from class to class under the pure blue sky, or stopped in clusters to talk, everyone coming alive in the invigorating sunlight. She sighed, stepping back from the view and eyeing the pile of paperwork on her desk. No matter what anyone said to the contrary, when you took a vacation, you always paid for it when you returned in piles of folders, countless slips with phone messages, and extra hours in trying to wade through it all.

Shifting a handful of papers to one side, she stared listlessly at the unopened mail her research assistant had so carefully arranged for her. She fluffed at her hair restlessly and tapped the desk with her reading glasses. Ever since her return to the Twin Cities the middle of the previous week, she had been aware of a quiet inner agitation. The time away, she felt, had been good, but something remained unfinished. She and Mindi had taken several long walks in a park near their house, during which she often caught herself in an attitude of searching—as if for a certain dark-haired woman, or for something else she could only vaguely define. This, her first day back at work, had an equally unsatisfying tone to it already. In two hours, she had accomplished nothing but moving things around rather aimlessly on her desk and walking a series of circles back and forth from the desk to the window. With an exasperated exclamation, she shoved back from the work, leapt from her chair, and strode forcefully toward the door. Flinging her lab coat at a file-cabinet, she yanked her jacket from its hanger on the coat tree with a vigor that left the metal rattling. Maybe a walk in the sunshine with everyone else would help.

"Susan, I'm going out for a while," she flung over her shoulder at the young woman behind the tiny desk in the outer office. In the two years that they had worked together, Susan Johnson had become accustomed to her supervisor's occasional impulsiveness and she scarcely glanced up as Kathryn flew out the door.

Outside, Kathryn shoved her hands in the pockets of her skirt and threw her head back, breathing deeply of the fresh air, basking, like the others, in the lovely warmth. When she had moved to Minneapolis to take the research position at the University, she, a born and bred Southerner, had not expected what she had witnessed and immediately dubbed "Minnesota Madness": a sort of frenetic enjoyment of each and every day of warm weather from its first tentative and brief appearance in (with luck) February or March, until it was rapidly squeezed out of existence by the crispness of fall in September or (again, if lucky) October. Having spent five winters here, Kathryn found that she, too, now lived through the long, cold days of Minnesota's nearly six month winter waiting for the first promise of spring. She had decided, like the natives, that the cool, relatively dry spring/summer/fall season made enduring the long, grey winters worthwhile.

As classes resumed, the campus cleared, and Kathryn found herself more alone. She slowed her pace and looked around, seeking a place to park herself for a while, to think. She sat in the gentle heat and contemplated a dream she had had the night before. It was of her persistent shade, Kyril, in an airplane, her face wet with tears, in wrenching pain. Kathryn's response to the vivid image had been intense and she had awakened abruptly, half expecting to find the woman in the room with her. She had spent the remainder of the night in restless dreams, with Kyril's indistinct face, hidden in shadow, floating in and out. A curious sense of Kyril's presence had accompanied the disembodied dream image, and when she had awakened before her alarm shattered the early morning silence, she had felt the longing that had visited her so frequently of late as if it were a tangible element in the room. Kathryn knew it was this longing and the dream imagery which interfered with her concentration, kept her distracted. As she sat in the May brightness, she recognized that she had to do something to get the woman out of her mind, once and for all. The problem was, she did not know *what* to do. Perhaps she could discuss it with her therapist. She had intended to call her when she returned, anyway. This would give their meeting focus.

Kathryn sat a bit longer, lulled by the sun, bemused by the dream images of her fantasy lover. When a bevy of students once more emerged onto the campus, she roused herself and wound her way back to the laboratory. Following a phone call to her therapist to arrange an appointment, she tackled the waiting papers with more resolve. At quarter to five, Susan stuck her head in the door and said good night. Kathryn smiled tiredly and waved at her, then stretched and put her own pen down. Gathering her things, she meandered to the bus stop and sat staring blankly as the familiar scenery passed outside the dirty windows on the ride home. There, Mindi greeted her, as always, as if she had been away for weeks instead of a mere few hours. Kathryn hummed to herself as she prepared Mindi's supper, then frolicked with her in the backyard before she went in to fix her own meal, bathe, and change for an eight o'clock meeting. Because of her interest, and because of her background as a biochemist and researcher, she had been asked to join the board of advisors to Project AIDS, an organization of gay and lesbian people who had been lobbying for funds for research into the causes and treatment of the newly defined acquired immune deficiency syndrome, AIDS.

Mindi, who went nearly everywhere her mistress could take her, pranced eagerly to the car, then paced excitedly back and forth in the back seat as Kathryn drove through the deepening twilight. While she drove, she considered the proposal that would be discussed at tonight's meeting: the formation of a small clinic under the umbrella of the Project, whose function would be clinical research with victims of AIDS. A substantial sum of money had been offered anonymously from a private source to fund the hiring of a limited staff and to supply the necessary medical and research equipment. The problems, as Kathryn saw them, were that there was no guarantee of a continuing source of funding for such an enterprise, and that there were already efforts to pursue the same line of research in other parts of the country. She wondered if the donor would consider giving the money to another, already established agency.

She parked her car and entered into a once elegant Park Avenue mansion which now housed an assortment of offices. Two hours later, the eight women and men who constituted the board still were unable to reach a consensus on what to do with the proposed monetary gift and finally adjourned in a stalemate.

Eager for the fresh night air after the smoky stuffiness of the board's meeting place, Kathryn burst out of the huge door of the old Victorian-style home. Mindi jumped up at her approach, barking and wagging all over. Laughing at the welcome, Kathryn tossed off the discord she had carried with her from the heated discussion. She lingered at the wheel only a moment, briefly considered going to a bar. Then, with a glance at Mindi's waiting face—knowing she wanted a walk—gave in to practicality and went home. She did not truly think she would find what she sought in the bars.

(((

Later in the week, Kathryn sat in her favorite chair in her therapist's office. As she ran her fingers through her layered ash-blonde hair, she tried to untangle the jumble of thoughts and feelings she had been struggling with over the recent weeks. "I've been so restless. I can't sit still, I can't concentrate—or stay with anything."

She glanced at her therapist, a small, dark haired woman of fifty who was a transplanted New Yorker. "You remember the woman I told you about that I met in the bar a couple of summers ago?" The therapist nodded. "Well, I dreamed about her the other night. Eileen—it was so *vivid,* as if she were there, with me, in the room—as if I could reach out and touch her." Kathryn paused, glancing at her hands, which were poised in front of her—reaching.

She sighed, sitting back again, dropping her arms. "I can't figure out what this is all about," she finished quietly.

"What feelings go with your restlessness?" Eileen prompted. Her liquid brown eyes probed gently, but insistently.

"Longing—wanting—yearning for completion." Kathryn felt tears rising in her throat. "Can't I ever have what I want—in a healthy way?"

"Is this woman what you want?" Eileen challenged.

"How can I know that? I don't know her! No, it's— She's a symbol. A symbol of what I want: to feel an irresistible attraction for someone who is, to me, beautiful, . . .who is near my age, . . .a professional woman, . . .a *strong* woman, independent—yet someone who can both accept me as I am and share herself with me." Kathryn paused for a moment.

"I don't think I want to 'devour' someone anymore, nor do I want to be 'consumed.' I *do* want a peer, an equal—someone with whom to share power in a relationship, and with whom I can, ultimately, share my life. Someone I can give myself to, completely. I feel like I've waited so long, Eileen—all my life. And sometimes, I get so lonely." She fought the tears again that made her voice waver. "You know I have friends, acquaintances—people to do things with." She shook her head slightly. "It's not enough. I want a partner, a mate." She searched the face of this other woman who knew her so well. "I've asked this before: Does it seem so much to ask, to want?"

Eileen smiled gently, shaking her head. "No, no it does not, Kathryn," she said softly. Her eyes held Kathryn's. "It does not seem too much."

Kathryn did not voice the next question because she knew Eileen did not have the answer: *Then when? When?* she cried out within. *When will my waiting and wanting be ended?* Giving in to them at last, she closed her eyes on her tears, and felt the ache reverberating deep inside her.

4

May became June. Clear, bright, breezy days with temperatures in the seventies, and complementary nights of lows in the fifties or sixties, were interspersed with days of overcast skies and rain: typical Minneapolitan young-summer weather. Kathryn managed to lose herself for a few weeks in her work at the University and with the AIDS project. The board continued battle over the grant and came to no resolution. Having no further dreams of Kyril, her longings receded and business became the focus of her waking hours.

One cool, quiet, early June evening, Kathryn took Mindi down to the park near her house for a walk. She had gone biking with a friend earlier, and now wanted the peacefulness of a walk at dusk. As they reached the lake, Kathryn let Mindi off the leash and she bounded away, relishing her freedom. Kathryn watched the dog head for the nearest bush, sniffing its myriad and, to Kathryn, unknown scents. Oftentimes, on walks such as this, it was with a nearly physical sense of vicarious satisfaction that Kathryn watched her investigating everything within range of her sensitive nose.

Tonight, however, she strolled along, only peripherally aware of Mindi, herself inhaling the night air scented sweetly with new-mown grass and cottonwood bloom. She gazed at a stand of enormous elms, marvelling as always at how old they must be. How sad she found it that the same culture that could develop the technology to send someone to the moon could not, or would not (she had never been quite sure which), develop a cure for the Dutch Elm disease which had ravaged Minnesota's elm population. She turned from the aged titans to discover Mindi beside her, very still, her attention fixed on something behind them. She lifted her gaze to a tall, dark- haired figure poised next to another tree some fifty or sixty feet away. Glancing curiously at Mindi's unmoving pose, then back at the silhouetted form, Kathryn felt the sudden start of goose flesh rippling over her body. A second later came the recognition. She gasped and stared at the figure who had begun to move toward them.

The sinuous walk, the lanky limbs, the dark eyes in a pale face all came at her as an overlay on a memory now two years old. She stood as rooted as Mindi, watching the black-clad apparition advance. When it was close enough for Kathryn to see the tentative smile on the full lips, Mindi sounded a warning growl deep in her throat. The apparition paused. The lips parted.

"Kathryn." The voice was quiet, controlled.

Kathryn stared into the now-remembered face of her fantasy lover, unbelieving that, after all this time, the woman could be real. "Kyril?" she managed, "Kyril—is it really you?"

The woman nodded. "Yes."

"From the bar—two years ago?"

Kyril nodded again, a smile playing on the dark red mouth.

"How? Where—?" Kathryn sputtered, completely perplexed.

Kyril laughed softly, a warm sound in the night. Light glinted off a gold chain around her neck, on which was suspended a pendant shaped like an elongated circle, with a line through the elliptical axis. "May I come closer?" she asked, indicating Mindi, who stood watchfully at Kathryn's side.

Further remembrance: the faint hint of foreign sibilance to her words. After a moment, Kathryn bent to re-attach the leash. "It's okay, girl," she assured, patting the dog's shoulder lovingly. "Good dog, Mindi." Although she wagged her tail at Kathryn's touch, Mindi did not relax her alert stance. Kathryn found that rather peculiar, but set it aside for the moment.

"Could we sit?" Kyril requested, motioning towards a bench down the path a way. When they were seated, Kyril attempted to make friends with Mindi, but Mindi eyed her askance and would not allow herself to be touched.

"I don't understand why she's being so standoffish," Kathryn said. "She's usually more friendly with people." She stroked the dog's head and neck, trying again to reassure her.

"What breed is she?" Kyril asked, making small talk.

"She's mixed—golden lab and beagle."

"She's very pretty," Kyril replied. Then, realizing the dog was not going to come closer, Kyril sat back. "It's okay," she said, the colloquialism sounding odd on her tongue. "After all, I am not what she is used to."

Their eyes met in the silence. Kathryn shivered and pulled her summer-weight jacket closer around her. "So—what are you doing here? Where have you been?"

Kyril stretched, relaxing a little. "Where have I been? Well, I shall tell you more about that, later. As to why I am here—" She paused, looking directly at Kathryn. "I came. . .back. . .to find you. I wanted to see if what I had. . .sensed. . .about you that night at the discotheque was correct."

Kathryn felt her whole body tense in suspense. "Which was?" she prompted.

Kyril sighed, let her eyes wander out over the lake. "That you were interested in me. That you were available."

Kathryn shivered again, recognizing the implicit question in the second statement. Her mind was awhirl, on edge with remembered excitement and current anticipation. After two years of fantasizing, no point in being coy, she reasoned. She fixed Kyril with a sideways look. "If you only *knew* how much I've thought of you in these past two years . . ." she trailed off, shaking her head. The wistfulness in her voice was evident, even to herself. She contemplated her hands, clasped on her lap. Sudden vulnerability brought burning tears to her throat. As she struggled for control, there was a cool touch on the back of her neck.

Months of longing and years of searching and wanting suddenly coupled with the gentle touch, and she was undone. She began to sob. Once the flood was released, she wanted nothing more than to be taken in Kyril's arms and held, comforted. Ever so smoothly, the hand on her neck became an arm around her shoulders, and she turned her face into the side of Kyril's neck, wetting the cool flesh there with the liquid pain. As Kyril embraced her more fully, she sensed Mindi tensing up and moved to reassure her, but before she could complete the act, Kyril gestured and the dog quieted and lay down beside them.

Kathryn lost herself in Kyril's embrace, giving way to the hurt and hunger until she felt purged of them.

In the end there was a silence, a quietness over them, and, at length, the two drew apart. Kathryn moved away from Kyril, looking at her out of unguarded eyes that saw in a new way. No longer a phantom, the subject of her erotic fantasies had become more than flesh: She was a person, who, Kathryn sensed intuitively, had a self to share. More than ever, Kathryn wanted Kyril in her life.

"Walk with me?" she said.

Kyril smiled assent, waiting.

Together they arose, Kathryn with Mindi's leash, and headed out of the park. They strolled in silence, the soft breeze playing over them. Their dangling hands occasionally brushed, evoking an awareness of the new intimacy between them. At the top of the hill, Kathryn paused, unsure as to what came next.

"Have you a car?" Kyril asked.

"Well, not here. I walked over from my house," she explained.
"Let's take mine then," Kyril suggested. "It's in the parking lot."
She paused. "What about your dog?"
          Kathryn smiled fondly, rubbing the dog's head. "She'll be fine—
she goes most everywhere with me," she explained softly.
          Kyril inclined her head in acknowledgment. "Shall we?" She
gestured towards the parking lot and led off.
          Kathryn started to follow, but Mindi balked. "What is it, girl?"
she asked quietly, bending over the dog and looking into her eyes.
          Kyril paused and turned. She sensed the dog's wariness and
understood. "May I. . .speak to her?" she requested.
          Kathryn glanced at Kyril then back at Mindi who stood watching
Kyril, all four feet firmly planted. She frowned in perplexity, then
assented. "Okay, go ahead." She began to rise.
          "No, Kathryn," Kyril urged quickly. "Stay by her." She moved
forward slowly as Kathryn sank down on her heels beside Mindi. The dog
did not growl, but watched steadily as this stranger approached. When she
was but a few inches away, Kyril stopped and squatted in front of Mindi.
Very gradually, she raised her hands to Mindi's face, her eyes fixed on
Mindi's. As she touched the sides of Mindi's head, Kyril spoke softly to
the dog in a language that Kathryn could not understand, gazing steadily
into Mindi's eyes.
          Spooked by the lack of scent, the dog initially attempted to evade
the foreign touch. But as Kyril spoke to her, she grudgingly accepted the
gentle fingers against her face, first quieting, then sitting. Kathryn
observed the interchange with amazement, her hand still resting on
Mindi's flank.
          "How did you do that? What did you say to her?" she exclaimed
in astonishment. Her hazel eyes moved quizzically between Kyril and
Mindi.
          Kyril lingered a moment longer in silent communication with the
dog. When she broke contact, it was to speak to Kathryn. "I am often able
to communicate with animals in such a manner. It's something I learned
in my country."
          "What did you tell her?" Kathryn insisted, still incredulous.
          Kyril glanced back at Mindi, who was now perfectly relaxed. "I
spoke words in my native language which communicate reassurance and
calmness. But it was not that; it was the psychic message I sent which
conveyed that I mean neither of you any harm." She paused while Kathryn
regarded her speechlessly. Abruptly, she stood. "Shall we?" she invited,
motioning again towards the waiting auto.

Still disbelieving, Kathryn followed, accompanied this time by a totally willing Mindi.

As they drove, Kathryn studied Kyril. Her companion baffled her as much as did Mindi's unusual behavior. She questioned briefly whether she could be hallucinating this whole thing, whether she might awaken and discover it was yet another all-too-real dream. There was about Kyril the same presence, the same magnetism Kathryn had felt that night in the bar, and she had no doubt but what Kyril could exert considerable influence over others when she chose. Nonetheless, there was something that belied that sameness: a thinness of face discerned in the flash of passing headlights and street lamps, something in the woman's posture that suggested an experience of deep suffering.

A blaring horn in the distance broke through Kathryn's bemusement. She realized they were headed uptown. "Where are we going?" Kathryn asked.

"I am staying at the AmFac Hotel—do you know it?" Kyril responded. Kathryn nodded, in her mind an image of the building that rivalled the IDS tower for dominance of the center city skyline. "I thought we could go there."

Kathryn allowed herself the luxury of watching her surroundings as they drove. She loved downtown Minneapolis but seldom went there, except when she shopped at Dayton's for work clothing. She delighted in the bright lights and the energy of the city. Its rhythms made her feel alive in a way that nothing else did.

In deference to Mindi's presence in the car, Kyril put the car in the garage herself, and the two women walked the short distance to the elevators that would take them to the hotel lobby. In the lobby, they caught the express elevator to the suites on the top floors.

The rooms in Kyril's suite were lit indirectly, at the ceiling, and exuded a quiet elegance, reminding Kathryn somehow of the celluloid seduction scenes she had witnessed as a teenager in the 1960s. Privately, she smirked briefly, thinking that she was about to be seduced, then admitted wryly that it would be no seduction: This was her fantasy lover in the flesh and she was already heated with desire.

Kyril carelessly strewed her keys and slim purse behind her as she walked to a tiny bar and bent over a small refrigerator. "What would you like to drink? There are beer and carbonated beverages, or," she offered, straightening and turning to Kathryn, "we could order something from room service." She waited, her eyes hidden in shadow.

"Pop is fine," Kathryn said, feeling awkward, but not knowing what else to do but stand there.

Kyril regarded her blankly. "Pop?"

"Uh, yes. . .uh, something carbonated," Kathryn replied, feeling even more awkward, trying not to grin.

Kyril smiled briefly. "I guess I don't have all the idioms, yet. Please, do sit down," she directed before pulling a can and a bottle from the shelf. She popped the top on the can. "Would you like a glass?"

Kathryn shook her head and accepted the can, then took a seat on the couch.

From the glassware under the bar, Kyril chose a wine glass and emptied half the wine cooler into it. Joining Kathryn, Kyril tasted the beverage before relaxing with her arm outflung toward Kathryn.

Kathryn sipped the ginger ale she had been given, vacillating between nervous uncertainty and acceptance of the intuitive knowledge that whatever further was about to happen between them was *not* an ordinary game of seduction. This was occurring on some level of reality that Kathryn had never experienced before

She realized that there was an unanswered question in her mind. Screwing up her face in puzzlement, she asked, "Kyril, how did you find me? And how did you know that I would come with you, here? And how did you know I liked ginger ale?" she added, laughing, holding up the can.

"I just. . .knew," Kyril asserted quietly, smiling slightly at Kathryn's laughter.

"But—how?" Kathryn insisted more seriously.

Kyril studied the glass in her hand. "I knew. I could. . .feel you," she finished, looking directly at Kathryn.

Her brow furrowed. "'Feel' me?"

"Yes, I could. . .*touch* you—mentally, emotionally—" Kathryn's startled exclamation stopped her.

Kathryn gesticulated excitedly. "You *'touched'* me one night! Several weeks ago—I dreamed about you! You were in an airplane— you'd been crying—you. . .were hurting. . .a great deal. It was very real," she ended in a hushed voice filled with compassion at the now-remembered pain.

"Yes," Kyril acknowledged, setting aside the half-emptied glass, pulling off tiny gold earrings that matched the oddly-shaped pendant nestled between her breasts, against the dark fabric of her blouse. She slipped out of her shoes, tucking one leg under her, settling back to face Kathryn. Her hand remained very near Kathryn's neck, on the back of the couch. Kathryn had watched every move, mesmerized.

"That night in the bar, Kathryn, I learned far more about you than you did about me. In your language I would probably be referred to as a psychic. I have the ability to read whatever emotions and thoughts are foremost in a person's awareness—when I wish to do so." She smiled. "I spend a great deal of time keeping those thoughts and feelings out. But in the bar that night, *you touched me*—almost against my will—with the strength of your longing, and I read in you the desire to bond with someone, the need for the completion of giving." She paused for a moment.

"I was not in a position to respond to what I sensed in you that night, in any way other than to dance with you. But now—now, things are very different in my life. I came back—hoping to find you, hoping to find you still. . .unattached." Tentatively, she added, "Are you?"

"What, unattached?" Kathryn shook herself. "Yes, I'm unattached. But, I—" She broke off as Kyril's fingers brushed the side of her neck, setting her whole body deliciously atingle.

Kyril leaned forward, her hand now on Kathryn's shoulder. "Then stay with me tonight."

It was a command, an imperative, but one Kathryn had little will to resist. Once again, she experienced the vibrant sensuality of the woman as the cool fingers trailed down her sleeve to her hand. In the dim light, the full lips appeared as if painted with carmine, and the thin nose was etched against the darkness of Kyril's hair as she inclined her head in perusal of Kathryn. In the soft light, their eyes met and held, Kathryn's captured by the magnetism of the woman she had so often dreamed of, so often despaired of ever seeing again. She stared at the features which had eluded her in memory, striving for every detail, her intensity fueled by the months of fantasies and unquenched longing.

Her desire for Kyril was stronger than any she had ever felt, and as she allowed it to rise, it surged through her like a wave rushing ashore, flooding her with ardor, setting her heart thudding in her ears, filling her throat with hot, unshed tears. She closed her eyes, surrendering to whatever might happen between them, surrendering to longing, surrendering to love conceived and nurtured in secret, held at the edge of awareness, barred from her heart. With a small cry, she threw herself into Kyril's embrace, her tears scalding her cheeks, her lips burning Kyril's face where they brushed, her arms clutching Kyril awkwardly to her.

Kyril shifted, holding Kathryn in arms strong as silken cords. She swung Kathryn around so that she was cradled against Kyril's breast, with her head on Kyril's shoulder. Kyril brushed at the tears with cool fingers, her dark eyes filled with concern. "What is it, Kathryn?" she whispered.

Unable to speak, or to put into words the yearnings she had felt, Kathryn made her answer the lips she offered to Kyril as she pulled Kyril's face down to hers with both hands. Fire went through her, as on that first night, as with that first glance, and Kathryn felt herself falling into a kiss she hoped never to end. They tumbled into passion, sliding off the couch onto the thick rug, rolling together, arms and bodies entwined.

Having kept her own desire for this human woman in check for an equally long period of time, Kyril found herself now rushing to savor the body which strained so eagerly toward hers. Deftly, she opened Kathryn's jeans, loosened the tail of her t-shirt, and slid her hand under the fabric, sending chills wherever her long fingers stroked, caressed, aroused.

Under that touch, Kathryn moaned, her body aching for Kyril, her skin craving the contact.

Kyril slid Kathryn's light-weight jacket off her arms and pushed up her t-shirt, seeing that Kathryn wore no bra. She bent, teasing the erect nipples with her tongue, and ran her fingers down Kathryn's belly, into her jeans, where they circled the throbbing clitoris, playing Kathryn's body as skillfully as if it were a finely crafted instrument and she its maestra.

Kathryn lay with her head thrown back, her eyes shut, her hands clutching Kyril's shoulders, abandoning herself to the intensity of sensations she had again and again imagined finding at Kyril's hands. Kyril's fingers were a cool delight as they bathed in the hot wetness between her legs, circled her nipples, teasing, heightening, then reached deep into the well of moistness again. She panted, moaned, crooned Kyril's name in time with the rhythmn Kyril set, allowing herself to be led higher and higher, until she began to peak.

As Kathryn climaxed, Kyril thrust her fingers deep inside Kathryn's vagina and swung her hips over Kathryn's, moving with her through the heedless dance. Her cheek against Kathryn's neck, Kyril immersed herself in the sensation of the pounding of the blood that coursed through Kathryn's trembling body.

And then they lay, in dishevelment, quieting, stroking, holding one another, until the room grew very silent. Kathryn was spent, but felt she needed to offer Kyril reciprocation of what she had given.

"Kyril—" she began.

Kyril placed still moist fingers against Kathryn's lips. " 'Tis not necessary," she said softly. "But thank you."

Kathryn shivered a little. She was not used to having her intentions read. They lay together in the silence a while longer, stroking, holding. When she realized she was beginning to doze, Kathryn looked at her watch. "I have to go," she whispered.

Kyril kissed her neck. "Must you?"

Kathryn nodded. "I have to work tomorrow—and I can't leave Mindi in your car all night." She made no attempt to hide the regret she felt.

Kyril stroked her arm. A small sigh escaped her. "Then, I will drive you."

They straightened their clothing and their hair, then went down to the garage where Mindi and the rented auto awaited them. While they drove, they listened to the radio, its music a pleasant accompaniment to their mood.

As Kyril pulled up in front of her house, Kathryn suggested, "How about dinner tomorrow— I mean, tonight?" She laughed as she realized her mistake.

Kyril hesitated, then nodded. "All right," she said, smiling into Kathryn's eyes. "Where?"

"Do you like Chinese food?"

"That would be fine."

"Then how about I meet you at the Nankin? It's right down on Hennepin, behind the hotel."

"Fine."

Kathryn paused, sensing some undefined hesitancy on Kyril's part. "You sure you want to do this?"

"Yes, really. What time shall we meet?"

"I could be there anytime after six."

"Eight o'clock, then?"

"Okay." She waited for Kyril's eyes to meet hers again. "Good night," she said softly. "And thank you." She leaned across the seat and kissed Kyril lingeringly before opening the car door.

Kyril watched until Kathryn had the front door unlocked and she and Mindi were safely in, then she drove away into what was left of the night.

5

That evening found them tucked away in a booth in the colorful, multilevelled Chinese restaurant, inspecting enormous menus with far too many choices on them. Waitrons scurried about, serving water, taking orders, delivering enormous trays laden with food. The atmosphere was anything but relaxed, and Kathryn began to have second thoughts about her choice of dining establishment. She glanced around irritatedly, noting as she did that Kyril was gazing absently out into space.

Captured by the unguarded beauty of that face, Kathryn stared, aware again of the flush of sexual desire kindling inside her. As if cued, Kyril turned and their eyes met. Kathryn felt herself melting under the intensity of Kyril's regard, while the erotic energy emanating from Kathryn was as palpable as a touch on Kyril's skin. Gazes thus locked, there was a moment out of time during which no one and nothing existed but they two and their mutual attraction.

The moment was splintered by a hesitant waitron's repeating his question. "Excuse me," he said, a puzzled expression in his eyes as he glanced back and forth between the rapt women. "Are you ready to order?"

Kathryn felt herself coming back as slowly as if she had been under water. Her gaze lingered on Kyril's. It seemed to take an eternity to hear and respond to the young man. "Uh, Kyril?" She volleyed to gain time, having pegged Kyril as someone whose composure could not be ruffled. Still gazing at Kathryn, Kyril responded. "Nothing for me—just a glass of wine, please." Her expression belied the verbal denial of hunger.

The young man nodded politely and asked, "What kind would you like, Ma' am?"

With a half smile, Kyril shifted her gaze to him. "A good red— something. . .full-bodied." The smile held the slightest hint of innuendo, and she glanced briefly at Kathryn as she spoke. "I shall trust your judgement," she added before returning full attention to Kathryn.

He blushed slightly, taking refuge from the interchange he sensed but did not quite understand, and he made himself busy in writing the order down. "Thank you," he said, turning to Kathryn. "And you, Ma' am?"

Kathryn had observed the brief interaction with surprised amusement. It delighted her to think that Kyril could desire her as much as she desired Kyril, and she intuitively recognized that Kyril's flirting with the waitron was a titillation directed at her. She met Kyril's eyes again, her expression bespeaking knowledge of the game they played with the waitron as unwitting foil. "I'll have the Moo Goo Gai Pan," she pronounced softly, her gaze unwavering from Kyril's.

"Thank you," he replied, gathering the menus and escaping with relief.

"Why aren't you eating?" Kathryn asked, her voice engagingly quiet under the clatter of the room.

Kyril's eyes lingered on Kathryn's lips as she spoke. "Food does not appeal to me right now."

Kathryn's breath caught in her throat. "What does?" she rejoined, her voice thick.

Kyril's gaze wandered to Kathryn's throat, her breasts, then back to her eyes, but before she could answer, the waitron returned with her glass of wine.

He bowed briefly as he deposited it on the table in front of her. "I think you'll find this satisfactory." He waited for her to taste it.

"I'm sure I will," she said, sniffing the bouquet before sampling what proved to be an excellent Lambrusco, her eyes on Kathryn the whole time. "Yes, it's very good. Thank you," she added as he disappeared.

Kyril laid her hand across the table next to Kathryn's and ran one finger over those that cupped the water goblet. The cool touch sent a tremble up Kathryn's arm, and she closed her eyes briefly, opening them again to Kyril's. Deciding there was no need for words, Kathryn chose not to raise the unanswered question of appetite. She indulged her own hunger in silence, allowing Kyril's stroking finger to stoke the fire that fueled it. The wine remained untouched between them while Kyril drank in Kathryn's arousal with all her senses.

Kathryn's meal arrived and a silence of indeterminate length prevailed as Kyril leisurely sipped her wine, savoring the honey-gold highlights in Kathryn's hair, the hazel of her eyes, and the warm brown of her tan. Kathryn ate, the flavor of her food heightened by the excitement of anticipation. When she was done and the check was served, Kyril leaned across the table to Kathryn. "Come up to my suite," she invited.

They were scarcely in the door before Kathryn flung her arms around Kyril, kissing her hotly. With a little smile, Kyril disentangled herself gently and led them into the bedroom, undressing casually while Kathryn hastily divested herself of the blue *crêpe de chine* pantsuit she had chosen for the evening. She flung back the bedcovers and perched on the edge of the bed, waiting for Kyril.

Kyril came to her, pushed her gently onto her back, and knelt astride her. Kathryn ran her hands over the lanky body, exploring, her eyes feasting on Kyril's naked form. She raised her mouth to the firm breasts and began to caress them with her tongue. Licking and tasting, her hands and fingers continued to stroke and cup thighs, back, buttocks, and genitals.

Kyril sighed her pleasure and slipped onto her side, acquiescing to Kathryn's wish to return the joy of the gift she had received the night before. To begin to open herself to this human woman, to allow herself to be taken sexually as no one but Lanaea had, was a new experience in vulnerability. It frightened her into a tremulousness which Kathryn mistook for the trembling of innocence.

Although filled with excitement built from long-drawn anticipation, Kathryn was moved that this sophisticated woman would respond to her so. She slowed her pace and deepened her concentration, desiring so deeply to please that she felt tears spring to her eyes. Tenderly, she moved her face to Kyril's, gently brushing her lips over Kyril's eyelids, cheeks, forehead, and mouth, before trailing down the skin of her neck to the hollow at its base, where she tickled lightly with her tongue.

Kyril arched into Kathryn's caress, feeling the blood pounding in her veins as Kathryn unknowingly emulated oupirian foreplay. Desire surged through her body and she struggled to contain herself in the role of recipient. She shuddered and surrendered her will to Kathryn's.

Kathryn clasped the tautly arced body against her, feeling the crush of their breasts between them, sliding her leg between Kyril's. Following the path she had set herself, she dallied over the luscious breasts, taking the soft nipples in her mouth and tonguing them, feeling them grow hard and firm again. She placed kisses all over the flat plateau of Kyril's body as she made her way to the soft, thick forest between her legs. The musky scent drew her onward, and she lapped gratefully at the sweet, thick river that ran there.

Kyril found an intensity in their coupling she had not expected. It reminded her piercingly of sexual union with Lanaea, and the pain of the loss surged again, threatening her control. Again, with great effort, she subdued it, blended and merged it with the feelings Kathryn was creating in her body. She focused on the sensations, ignoring the unhealed pain, allowing herself to be led to whatever height of sexual passion her body could afford her. As Kathryn's tongue brought her to the edge, she cried out and reached for Kathryn, wanting to feel their bodies together, to hold her in her arms as she climaxed.

Willingly, Kathryn granted Kyril's unspoken request, her fingers finishing what her mouth had begun. Her own orgasm burst on her as their bodies rocked together. When, at last, Kathryn collapsed on Kyril, every last paroxysm had been squeezed from their pleasure.

When she was able, Kathryn rolled over and pulled Kyril against her, guiding the dark head to her shoulder. There was an extended silence between them, during which Kathryn nearly drifted asleep. Kyril's whisper brought her back.

"Did you orgasm?" Kyril asked quietly, feeling still vulnerable from her abandonment to sensation and desire, not knowing quite what to say.

Kathryn grinned sleepily at the formality of the phrasing and at the question itself. She nodded. "Oh, yes—indeed I did!" Her voice had the huskiness it often took on after good sex. She stroked the pale flesh of Kyril's cheek and throat, her fingers playing in the dark hair behind Kyril's ear. Then, feeling the depth of her own longing again, she whispered tentatively, "I've never been with anyone like you." She stared into Kyril's dark eyes.

Kyril contemplated Kathryn's expression. "Is that good?" she asked, wishing she were not feeling defenseless enough to have it hurt if Kathryn said no.

Kathryn drew back a little, as if seeing her anew. "You really are different, aren't you?" she posed softly. "You can practically read my mind, but you don't understand my words." She paused, looking hard at Kyril's face, seeing the vulnerability there. "Lady," she whispered with a touch, "you are the most beautiful woman I've ever known, and I. . . ." She paused, afraid to voice the words forming insistently in her consciousness. Instead, she said, "I want to know more and more about you, until there's hardly anything left to know." She stroked Kyril again. "Making love is better with you than with anyone I've ever been with."

"Making love?"

Kathryn laughed. "Making love: sex, intercourse—Americans have lots of words for it!" She laughed again. "Where are you from, Kyril?"

Kyril considered; she was not ready to tell all. "I came here from Hungary." She paused, not wishing to seem reticent, yet not wanting to volunteer too much too soon. "I am a physician. I have specialized in. . ." she thought how to word it, "diseases of the blood and their relationship to the body's immune system."

Kathryn pushed up on her elbow, suddenly more awake. "Are you working with the AIDS problem?" she asked expectantly.

Reluctantly, hesitantly, Kyril shook her head. She hated to disappoint so soon. "No, I am not. What is that?"

Kathryn frowned, puzzled at Kyril's ignorance. "Acquired immune deficiency syndrome—a disease complex that was recognized in this country a little over two years ago, linked initially with gay—homosexual—men, now with intravenous drug users and Haitians. It's also begun to show up in heterosexual women. Some authorities are afraid that there may be hemophiliacs who have already received transfusions from donors with infected blood. Kyril, are you su—"

"Infected blood?" As Kathryn was speaking, Kyril had felt something begin to come alert in the back of her mind. "Can't your medical people screen for the disease organism? How does one make a positive diagnosis?"

"Up 'til now, no. There's been no reliable screening because we weren't even sure exactly what was causing the syndrome. We now know there's a virus which is believed to come from Africa and which is thought to be the original source of infection. But we as yet have no idea of how it replicates—in fact, it was only this past January that the virus was clearly identified as such. After someone has been infected, it seems that it's months, even a couple of years, afterwards that the immune system seems to break down and the debilitating diseases emerge, such as lymphadenopathy, Kaposi's sarcoma, and pneumocystis. Apparently without exception, it is these opportunistic infections—or other complications arising from impairment of the immune function—that bring about the death of the AIDS victim. The virus itself doesn't kill—it somehow sets the body up for falling prey to some other condition which, ultimately, results in death. By the time we know someone is ill, it's too late—the virus is gone. At the present time, more than half of all the cases diagnosed as AIDS have died, and that within two to three years of initial diagnosis. Kyril—how could you *not* have heard of this?"

Kyril shook her head, trying to clear her mind as Kathryn's words, "the virus is gone," echoed over and over behind Lanaea's wasted image. She stammered, seeking a plausible explanation. "I—I've been on sabbatical. I—I haven't been working."

After a hard, disbelieving look, Kathryn sighed, then went on, a bitter set to her mouth. "The part that I get so *angry* about is that, until this thing began to threaten *heterosexual* people, there was almost nothing done on a national level in the way of research into causes, prevention, or cure. People in this country have labelled it the 'gay plague' and viewed it as retribution for gay men's life style. It was even referred to as GRID—Gay-Related Immune Disease—at first. Now, here it is some five or six years after the first *known* cases appeared, hundreds of people have already died, and the current administration in Washington isn't even thinking about apportioning money for research that should have already begun."

Kathryn broke off, musing. "The part that *scares* me the most," she said in a wholly different tone, "is that the lesbian women in this country have sat back, sympathizing with our gay brothers, smugly assuring ourselves that there's no threat to us, when, in reality, I believe, it's just a matter of time until it makes the circle back to us."

"Why do you say that?" Kyril posed, as Kathryn paused.

"It's logical! There are bisexual men—and women—out there in that so-called 'straight' society who have already picked it up from gay men, *will* pass it around amongst themselves, and *will* bring it back around to lesbian women. The researchers who've worked with this think its transmitted much like hepatitis B. I can't help but believe that, if it's as contagious as hepatitis, then it's just a matter of time before it starts to show up in the lesbian population." She flopped back down on her side, heaving a shivery sigh. "God, it frightens me."

Kyril regarded Kathryn in silence, her mind churning at all she had just been told. It suggested a horrifying answer to the riddle of Lanaea's death. "Kathryn, how do you know all this?"

"I'm on the board of advisors to Project AIDS here in the Twin Cities." Seeing Kyril's questioning look, she went on. "It's a voluntary organization which has been lobbying for funding to support research into AIDS."

"How successful have you been?"

She sighed again. "Not very. Most of our donors have been private ones—individuals or groups—not governmental sources. There has been a growing amount of political activity generated at state levels, but the impetus has needed to come from the federal level: I think there's too much to do to expect more than marginal success from localized endeavors. Besides, the Centers for Disease Control in Atlanta, Georgia, has already been established as a clearing house for information—I see it as unaffordable waste to duplicate efforts state by state.

"Last month, the Project had a substantial grant from a private donor, but the board has been unable to arrive at a consensus about how to handle the money. I have mixed feelings myself.

"On the one hand, Minneapolis, because of our fairly large and relatively open gay and lesbian community, seems a logical place to set up a clinical research facility. On the other hand, that work is already being done on both East and West Coasts, in varying degrees; why not send the money to those already established facilities, which are desperate for more funds?"

She sighed again. "It's such a dilemma. People want to serve this particular community and, at the same time, contribute something of value to the good of the whole. I don't know if we can do both—or do both and do both well."

"Kathryn, what did you mean when you said the virus is 'gone'. . . after someone has become ill?"

"Mmm—that it can't be detected in the bloodstream. It's. . .disappeared, gone from the body." She shrugged tiredly, unable to find any better words to explain something that was not, itself, completely understood.

By this time, the intimacy of their sexual interchange had faded, leaving in its place a slight chill and a growing awareness of fatigue. With a groan, Kathryn grabbed at her watch. "Geez! It's after midnight! I don't know about you, woman, but I've got to get up for work in the morning." She rubbed Kyril's arm, briskly, affectionately, noting again how cool her skin was.

Willing for now to allow the subject to drop, Kyril asked, "Where do you work?" As she spoke, she rolled back, stretching the whole of her lithe body.

Her eyes greedy, Kathryn watched the ripple of lean muscles under the bone-white skin. "At the U—the University of Minnesota. I'm a biochemist. I mainly do research and teach an occasional class—a rather dull and boring job, actually, but it pays well and I like the benefits of being associated with the U. One of these days, I'm going to get out of there and do something else with my life." She leaned forward and kissed Kyril, feeling the stirrings of desire blossom again as her lips met Kyril's.

Kyril's hand came up behind her neck, holding her in the kiss for a long moment. "May I stay with you tonight?" Kyril asked, her voice a husky whisper.

Kathryn's surprised gaze lingered on the dark eyes. "In my place? I wish you would," she replied, a pleased smile on her face.

A few short hours later, from where she lay in Kathryn's bed, Kyril watched the dawn begin to pale the windows. The slumbering Kathryn lay tucked warmly against her. Kyril's custom in this dimension had been to keep a nocturnal schedule, so she was not far behind her usual bedtime. That, however, was not what had kept her wakeful. Rather, it was the jumble of thoughts and feelings that had come as her scientist's mind linked what Kathryn had told her about AIDS with Lanaea's illness and death. She felt herself reeling mentally with the shock of that connection, wondering how it was that such vital information could have escaped oupirian notice. Of *course, if the virus is "gone" by the time the illness manifests itself. . . . By the Blood!* she swore silently. *A plague could be loose among us already!* As she slid finally towards sleep, she released a prayer to the Goddess for her part in what now seemed a fortuitous chain of events that had brought her to someone so informed on the topic. With it was a request for support in her resolve to delve to the bottom of this matter as quickly as possible. When the alarm jarred Kathryn awake a scant hour later, Kyril scarcely stirred, so deep was the repose she had finally attained.

Kathryn arose, bathed, breakfasted, and took care of Mindi. Then, before leaving for the bus stop, she left Kyril a note telling her to let herself out of the house. Kathryn carried with her a mental picture of Kyril asleep in the bed, one arm thrown back, her face peaceful, seeming totally vulnerable. It was a picture that touched Kathryn deeply.

6

Kathryn's phone rang, drawing her out of her reverie, back into the lab. She turned from her window on the drizzly, overcast day and lifted the receiver from its cradle. "Biochemistry, Kathryn Hartell speaking."

"Kathryn?" The softly accented voice was unmistakably Kyril's.

Kathryn's heart leapt at the sound. "Kyril! What a wonderful surprise!"

"I hope it is permissible for me to call you there."

"Of course. What is it?" she encouraged, wondering simultaneously how Kyril had obtained her office number. The University information system was not noted for its efficiency.

"I have been thinking over what you told me last night about AIDS. I wonder if you could introduce me to another physician with whom I could discuss the medical details."

Kathryn was puzzled. She could not fathom Kyril's sudden interest in AIDS when she purported never to have heard of it prior to their conversation of the previous evening. "Well, I don't see why not. Do you want me to call and set up an appointment, or did you want to do that yourself?"

"Whatever seems best to you. But I should like to do it as soon as possible—today, if we could."

Kathryn glanced at her watch and sighed. "I think today is out— it's nearly four o'clock. The best I could do is try for tomorrow or the next day." She paused, then decided to give voice to her confusion. "Kyril— What's this all about?"

There was a moment's hesitation. "I would rather not talk with you about it on the telephone. Perhaps we could meet again later this evening?"

Kathryn contemplated that prospect with relish, but remembered plans already made. "How late?"

"Around nine-thirty? At your place?"

"All right," she agreed. Her dinner date with her friend Megan Kastner would be ended long before that. Mentally, however, she groaned over another late weeknight. She had thought to make it an early evening.

"Good, I'll see you then," Kyril was saying.

Kathryn hung up the phone and returned to her work, but the question of why Kyril wished to consult with another physician about AIDS nagged at the back of her consciousness the rest of the afternoon and into the evening.

Promptly at nine-thirty, Kathryn's doorbell sounded and she opened her door to find Kyril on the stoop. Rain glistened wetly on the fashionable, shiny slicker Kyril wore, which hung open to reveal a charcoal grey jumpsuit with black blouse underneath. Gold jewelry glinted on her breast. The white of her face stood out against the dark of her clothing and the rainy evening.

They exchanged amenities while Kathryn shook out Kyril's coat and hung it to dry. "You have a very nice home," Kyril complimented, taking in her surroundings in a leisurely glance. She seated herself on the low sofa. "I didn't really get a look at things last night." They laughed, enjoying their newfound intimacy. "I like the natural wood," she went on, gesturing at the oak woodwork and floors in the front rooms.

Kathryn, who had lingered in the arched entryway, was gratified at the praise. She had put a lot of time and money into redoing the interior of her home and it gave her pleasure when others responded positively to the results. She allowed herself to see again the warm earthtones she had used in decorating, the framed prints on the walls, the green of her plants, and the other colorful details of her belongings. She smiled at Kyril, thanking her and noticing that, in the lamplight, Kyril's complexion had a slightly rosy hue she had not seen before. Her gaze measured Kyril appreciatively as she commented, "You look very nice tonight, and. . .different, somehow."

Kyril's eyebrow went up and a smile twinkled in her eyes. "Oh? How so?" she led.

Kathryn joined her on the sofa. "There's some color in your face tonight—you've seemed so pale before." There was no response. "It's very becoming," she finished, feeling herself beginning to be drawn by whatever charm it was that Kyril exuded. She delved into the now sparkling dark eyes, losing awareness of the room.

The smile crept over Kyril's lips, joining the sparkle in her eyes. "Thank you," she replied. "I had a very good sleep, and a good day."

It seemed to Kathryn that Kyril's eyes danced and teased with a hint of something unspoken. She blushed a little at the recollection of their lovemaking, taking that for Kyril's reference. She saw that Kyril's gaze was now on her throat, where the blood surged with remembered passion. Kathryn's blush spread, suffusing her body with warmth. Then, recalling what Kyril had come for, Kathryn breathed, shaking herself free of the seductive atmosphere that had gathered about them like a charge. "Could I offer you. . .a glass of wine?" she veered, her own eyes on the full red lips opposite her, her awareness brushed by lingering tendrils of desire.

Kyril's eyes flashed at her, followed by the quick smile. "Yes, thank you."

When Kathryn returned, she noticed that Kyril had slipped out of her low-heeled black boots and had her legs tucked under her. She raised a long arm to accept the wine, then settled herself again in the thick cushions.

After a few moments of desultory conversation, Kathryn's need to know gained ascendance: She broached the question she had been harboring since Kyril's call that afternoon. "So, why do you want to meet with someone to talk more about AIDS?"

Kyril twirled the glass of red fluid between her fingers, watching the light refract as the liquid swirled and shifted. It reminded her of the ritual of commitment she and Lanaea had performed, during which they had drunk the cup of their mingled bloodlines and made their vows of honor and respect to one another. She felt sudden, hot tears flooding her eyes. As she turned her head to set down the goblet, they spilled onto her cheeks and coursed down her face. She wiped at them brusquely, begrudging her vulnerability in front of Kathryn. She set her jaw rigidly. "Because—I think someone very close to me died of AIDS." A small whimper of uncontrolled anguish escaped her at the last.

Kathryn was stunned by Kyril's tears as much as by her words: She had appeared so invulnerable. With second sight, she recalled her "dream" of Kyril on the airplane, and instinctively laid a hand over Kyril's clenched fist.

Kyril's instinctive response was to jerk away from the human touch, but she sensed Kathryn's intense concern and compassion for her and left her hand where it lay. She forced her gaze back to Kathryn's. "You remember your 'dream.'"

Kathryn nodded, aware of the stinging of her own tears in response to the misery manifested in those dark eyes.

Kyril turned her fist over and grasped Kathryn's hand, stroking the veins on the back of it with the fingers of her other hand. "Will you hold me?" she asked, the tears thickening her voice. She went with Kathryn's gentle pull, feeling, in spite of their sexual intimacies, awkward and unused to needing anything from anyone but Lanaea—or Guardian Tyrell. As the warm arms enfolded her and her face came to rest against the softness of Kathryn's breast, she sank down into grief, clutching the other woman until she made a small noise of pain, sobbing wordlessly out of a well full to overflowing with unexpressed sorrow. Her tears soaked the front of Kathryn's blouse and her cries seemed to fill the room, until she had emptied herself of both.

Stiff and drained, Kyril at last sat away from Kathryn, holding Kathryn's hands in hers, seeking to read in Kathryn's face her reaction to her mourning: The eyes were very sad and the cheeks were streaked with tear-traces, which tugged at Kyril's heart and brought the warmth of gratitude rising within her.

"I would like to tell you what happened to Lanaea," she requested tentatively, the words rough and whispery.

Kathryn nodded. "Yes, of course," she replied, her own voice quiet in the still room. *AIDS: Lanaea: a woman.* The *click!* sent a chill over Kathryn and set questions colliding with one another in her mind. Who was Lanaea? Kyril's lover? Did Kyril think she herself might have AIDS? Was that why she wanted to see a physician? Were Kathryn's worst fears about to be confirmed?

Apparently oblivious to Kathryn's inner turmoil, Kyril sighed and sat back, letting go of Kathryn's hands. She had visibly paled again and her hair was wet around her ear where she had lain against Kathryn.

"Lanaea and I had known each other since we were. . .very young. We had been together for many. . .years," she began, hearing herself faltering. She always found the transition from her native tongue to those languages necessary in this dimension difficult. Equivalents did not come easily to her. "We were separated a great deal of the time, due to our travels and our work. She was an archaeologist," she interjected. "Her last visit to this. . .country was followed by a period of illness; then she seemed to recover.

"But only for a while. She soon developed symptoms for which we could find no cause. She wasted away before my eyes, while I, with my medical training, could do nothing." Kyril broke off her narrative, lost in a bleak inner tableau. "There was so little time. We shared what we could together, but the certainty of her death lay over us like a pall." Fighting for control, she paused again. "Life without her has been very lonely." She swallowed pain. "Agonizing." Tears threatened to break through once more.

"That's where you were, when you weren't working—taking care of. . .Lanaea?" Kathryn struggled with the pronunciation.

Kyril stared at her blankly for a moment before realizing Kathryn was referring to her earlier statement that she had been on sabbatical. It was close enough to the truth. She nodded.

"You were very happy together," Kathryn posed; it was not really a question,

"Yes. Oh, yes," Kyril responded fervently. "Even with the separations, our life together was rich and full. Mentally, emotionally, we were never apart. Only physically." She glanced at Kathryn, remaining on guard even in this. "We had an empathic link that was developed very early in our relationship and which sustained us over all the divisions." Noting Kathryn's puzzled expression, she went on. "I couldn't always know just where she was, or what she was doing, but I always knew when she was safe or endangered, experiencing joy or pain, or," she smiled wanly, "thinking of me."

When Kyril did not continue, Kathryn reached out to her again, offering solace for the painful memories, seeking easement of her own pain for Kyril. For now, she pushed all her questions aside. Something about the woman affected her keenly, and she acknowledged briefly that their emotional lives were rapidly becoming entwined. As she stroked Kyril's slender back and arms, she mused that the kind of bond Kyril had described herself as having with Lanaea was exactly what she yearned for with a lover or partner, but had found only with her animal companion, Mindi.

As if called, the dog arose from her place on the rug and came over to them. Kathryn looked at her inquiringly, then patted the couch beside her. Mindi jumped onto the cushion and curled next to them in one nimble movement, obviously content to share their closeness.

Much later, Kathryn awoke with a start. Kyril was dreaming, moaning and fretting in her arms. Gently, Kathryn kissed her forehead and soothed her face with cool fingers, crooning Kyril's name in a soft whisper. After a few moments, Kyril lay quiescent. With a passing thought for how stiff both would be come morning, Kathryn soon rejoined Kyril in slumber.

7

The following Thursday, having received directions from Kathryn, Kyril drove to her meeting with the Minneapolis Project AIDS director, Dr. Mark Hamyl. Rain came down in a steady drizzle as she sloshed through puddles in the parking lot to the meticulously groomed lawn in front of an older, but well-cared-for building. On the edge of the downtown area, the structure had retained its trees and shrubs, along with its early 1900s character. She briefly studied the wet brown brick facade, thinking as she did how clean and attractive this city was in comparison with the large cities she had visited in the East. The interior of the building had obviously been refurbished, but in a tasteful and unostentatious manner. The aesthete in Kyril approved.

Shedding her rain slicker, she awaited Dr. Hamyl. As she sat staring out of a second floor window at the pattering gloom, her mood matched the pervasive grey. She now felt driven to learn as much about AIDS-related disease as she could: If she were correct in her new conviction that Lanaea had died as a result of an AIDS-related condition, it did not seem unreasonable to her that the fate of the entire population of Kornägy might well be decided by how quickly and accurately she could diagnose, determine etiology, and develop prevention and/or cure for the disease complex. Her musings were interrupted by a voice behind her.

"Doctor Vértök? I'm Mark Hamyl." He held out his hand as he came toward her.

Grasping his thick fingers in her cool ones, she inclined her head in acknowledgment. "Doctor Hamyl." She was aware of his gaze on her, taking in the elegant ensemble of wine-dark, flowing skirt draped over slim hips and topped with a champagne colored blouse of similar softness. About her neck was the gold chain and pendant she had worn the night she met Kathryn in the park. Drops of water lay like tiny gems in the dark, thick waves of her hair,

"Please, come in," he invited, motioning the way into his small office. Kyril noted that the anteroom was larger than this space and concluded that the picture Kathryn had painted regarding funding was an accurate one. "Have a seat, Doctor Vértök." They seated themselves together, facing one another from comfortable overstuffed love seat and chair.

"Kathryn tells me that you want to discuss acquired immune deficiency syndrome with me," he continued warmly.

Kyril decided she might be able to like this sandy-colored, direct man. If so, it would be a first for her in this dimension. In response to his statement, she nodded.

"Please, tell me what you'd like to know."

Kyril sat back, loosening herself. "Actually, I have a proposal for you. I am a specialist in blood disorders and diseases of the immune system. When I could not see you right away, Kathryn made it possible for me to have access to the university medical library and I took the opportunity to review what literature there is."

This was not exactly true. In reality, Kyril had drawn on her extensive contacts in the oupirian network, gaining rapid access to otherwise inaccessible data from the National Institutes of Health, and the Centers for Disease Control, having it directed to Kathryn at the University. To her growing horror, she had learned that everything Kathryn had told her was true. She had also reviewed the scanty medical literature on the subject—most of which, through inattention or bad timing, or both, had escaped the notice of those of her kind who currently Visited in this dimension. Privately, she was appalled at the gross failure of the government and medical community to grasp the nature and implications of this threat. She suspected that Kathryn's hypothesis that homophobia was behind the negligent attitude had a great deal to do with it. However, she saw no need to allude to any of this in replying to Hamyl.

"I believe that I possess knowledge and skills which could be useful to your project, Doctor. What I propose is that you open a clinic for the treatment of, and research into, AIDS and AIDS-related disease, with me as the chief medical officer."

Hamyl raised his eyebrows in mild surprise. Clearly, she could be as direct as he. "I assume Doctor Hartell told you that funds for such an undertaking are not presently. . .available?"

"Yes, she did," Kyril rejoined. "However, if you appoint me as medical director, with complete responsibility and authority for clinical research and its applications to treatment, I will guarantee you both initial and ongoing funding."

Hamyl studied her. "How will you manage this?" he prompted.

"I am a member of an international organization which has—and will make available at my request—the assets required," she replied matter-of-factly.

Hamyl changed direction. "If I may ask, Doctor, why are you so
. . .eager to be involved in the establishment of such a clinic? And why
here, in Minneapolis?"
        Kyril measured him with her eyes. "Have I your confidentiality
in that?"
        In turn, his grey eyes were candidly appraising of her. "I think I
could guarantee that," he agreed.
        Still, she hesitated. Speaking of something so personal to her was
not easy in this human stranger's office. They shared no blood. She also
wanted no hint of what was between her and Kathryn—yet. "I have reason
to believe that the AIDS-causing virus has spread to my country." She
paused again, lowering her gaze momentarily. "I also believe that my
lover died of AIDS-related disease."
        The coolness in the grey eyes softened, matching Hamyl's voice.
"I'm sorry," he offered. Then, after a brief silence, during which he
wondered if her lover were male or female, he said, "Doctor Vértök, if we
were to take you up on such an offer, we—the board and I—would need
to know that you truly were the best qualified person for such a position.
That is, that we weren't hiring you just because you could provide the
money we want, and need."
        *Maybe he's someone who **can't** be bought,* Kyril reflected to
herself, a grudging respect for this particular human male beginning to
take shape within her. Aloud, she responded, "I assure you that I am well
qualified, Doctor Hamyl. If you check my credentials, you will find that
they show that I attended Semmelweis Medical University in Budapest,
where I am now also an adjunct professor, and that I have worked at the
Postgraduate Medical School in Budapest in hematology. I am listed with
the Hungarian Academy of Sciences as a fellow at the Institute of
Experimental Medicine. I have, in fact, done research with the Institute,
the Medical School, and the University of Veterinary Science in the areas
of blood disease and disorders of the immune response." She paused,
knowing it was an impressive recitation.
        He acceded graciously. "You have been very busy in your
professional career, Doctor." His smile crinkled his tanned face. "It is
difficult to comprehend how one so young as yourself could have
accomplished so much."
        With her own smile of private knowledge, she returned, "I am a
great deal older than you might think, Doctor Hamyl. But, thank you for
the compliment."
        Slipping forward on the edge of his chair, he voiced his pressing
question. "Doctor Vértök. . .please, forgive me, but. . .was your lover a woman?"

Kyril regarded him uncomprehendingly. "I don't see the significance. . . ."

"Well, if your lover were a woman, she would be the first woman I've known of to have died from AIDS."

Realizing that he was politely awaiting her reply, she merely nodded, hoping to stave off any further questions with an obvious unwillingness to talk.

After a further pause, he arose, accepting her refusal, bringing the interview to a close. "I must discuss your proposal with the full board of advisors. I assure you I will *not* discuss your personal interest in this." He extended his hand. "It has been an enjoyable meeting, Doctor Vértök."

Kyril grasped his hand, relieved at his apparent willingness to let the matter of her lover's gender go. "Thank you for your time, Doctor Hamyl. I shall look forward to the board's decision." She turned to leave.

"Oh, Doctor—I wonder if I could ask you to leave a copy of your *vita* with me for reference when I meet with the board?"

Kyril acknowledged the courteous phrasing of his request for her credentials with a warm smile. "Certainly, Doctor." She unzipped her slim briefcase and pulled from it a single sheet with a great deal of printing on it. Handing the *vita* to him, she nodded and exited his office, grateful again for the oupirian network which could provide her with the flawlessly forged medical credentials. Of course, some of the paper history was true, for she had indeed served a two-year residency at the Institute for Experimental Medicine during her previous Visit, some years ago. It had been her first experience with the medical community in this dimension, arranged for her by a high-ranking Academy member who was an oupir.

As she drove back to her hotel, she reflected that she had already used nearly three months of this Visit, much of it in ambivalent dallying before she had set about locating Kathryn. She had best get busy! She would have to work more efficiently. As soon as she reached her suite, she called a travel agency and put them to work booking flights to Washington, D.C., New York City, Philadelphia, and Baltimore. In each city, she had determined to visit existing clinics treating AIDS patients to acquaint herself first hand with the work they were doing, and to ascertain if there were staff members in those agencies who could be lured to Minneapolis to work with her. She also put in calls to oupirs who were contacts in the governmental organization of the United States, alerting them of her intended journey to Washington and soliciting their assistance in setting up the clinic interviews. Last, she called Kathryn, briefly summarizing her interview with Mark Hamyl, and informing her of her newly impending trip East. It was not without a twinge of regret that she heard Kathryn's voice explaining that she could not see her that evening.

"I've made plans to go to a movie with a friend," Kathryn said apologetically. "When is your plane leaving?"

"I don't know—I must call the travel agency back."

"When you find out, let me know." Kathryn paused, and Kyril heard the hesitancy in her voice. "I'd like to come to the airport to say good-bye."

Kyril smiled, gratified that she was not alone in her regret. "I'd like it if you could come," she agreed. It was her turn to pause. Words warred within her, but, "I'll miss you, Kathryn," was all she allowed. "Good-bye."

The travel agent had done his work very efficiently. When she called again, he was ready with all the information she required. They negotiated details and she arranged to walk the few blocks to his office and complete payment. As she came out into the early evening, the sky was still dreary and heavily overcast. The wet-darkened buildings of the city's center lent an air of premature night to the landscape of glass, stone, and steel. Everything glittered wetly in light from street lamps, buildings and stores, and in the headlights of myriad automobiles sloshing through the rush hour traffic. Kyril gathered her slicker around her and stepped out into the scurrying crowds, finding the thought distasteful that she would have to hunt in this drizzle tonight. She was tired, having had less than her accustomed amount of sleep today, and looked forward to that evening's repose.

As she wove her way through the milling throng, she contemplated the risk she faced each time she hunted in the downtown area. Minneapolitans were somewhat friendlier than their eastern counterparts, and less likely to ignore the unusual event on the street. The difficulty of finding the privacy and anonymity she needed for the kill was equal to the difficulty of disposing of the drained body afterwards. There were no convenient waterfront dives in this well-lit city, and she had not yet taken the time to familiarize herself with any of the areas that bordered on the downtown, let alone the suburbs. So far, she had fed only in the center city areas of Minneapolis and St. Paul. She vowed that she would remedy that when she returned from her trip East.

8

FIFTH IN A SERIES OF BLOODLESS BODIES FOUND

By Neal Vaughn, Staff Writer

Sometime during this past Sunday night, someone drained the blood
from the body of yet a fifth frequenter of the Twin Cities' nighttime
haunts. The body was abandoned in a dumpster.

The body of 26-year-old Minneapolis resident, Carl Rikjavik, was
uncovered Thursday in an alleyway off Hennepin Avenue by the
early morning arrival of a construction crew. This is the fifth in a
series of apparently related killings over the past several weeks.
Although the victims have been discovered in widely varying
locales, in each case the body had been nearly drained of blood.

Both Minneapolis and St. Paul police departments are involved in
the investigation of the murders, and have alerted other forces in the
metro area. There are no suspects, and no apparent motives for any
of the murders.

Kathryn dropped the paper on the table and clunked her coffee
cup down disgustedly. *Bloodless bodies—yuck! This reporter must be a
Kolchak-type.* She grimaced, glancing at her watch. She had met Kyril at
the airport very early that morning and seen her to her flight. After
returning home, she had prepared breakfast and was reading the paper, a
luxury she seldom could indulge in on weekday mornings.

She put Mindi out one last time, then bade her good-bye, gathered
her things, and hurried through the still-dripping morning to the bus stop.

Once seated, she glanced again at the story she had been reading
and shivered. Abruptly, she folded the paper tightly, decisively, and
rammed it into her backpack, deliberately turning her thoughts to Kyril.

The suddenness of Kyril's decision to leave had really brought
home to Kathryn how little she knew the woman—and the proposal she
had made to the Project was clear evidence of how little Kathryn knew *of*
her. She was a riddle: A stunning, irresistible enigma. As Kathryn stared

out the window, she wondered for the first time what attraction she could possibly hold for Kyril. However well-read Kathryn might be, she had none of the things Kyril had in the way of worldly sophistication and apparent wealth. Further, there was about Kyril an aura of secrecy, of some hidden thing in her life, which made Kathryn feel on edge. It drew her but it also frightened her. She knew there were questions she ought probably to ask, but did not know how to frame them. She wondered briefly if another session with her therapist was in order.

Mentally, Kathryn replayed their leave-taking in the airport: Kyril had turned to her at the gate and smiled the shy-bold smile—the one tentative on her lips but strong in the depths of her eyes. "Good-bye, Kathryn," she had said simply, the sibilance of her words almost a caress. Kathryn had responded by boldly stepping forward and embracing her, planting an illicit kiss hotly against the side of that cool neck. "Good-bye, Kyril," she had whispered as they parted. Her eyes caught Kyril's, and, ever so briefly, there were again only the two of them. Then, Kyril was absorbed by the crowd, lost around the corner of the boarding tube.

Kathryn jerked back to reality as the bus slowed at her stop. As she threaded her way out, she realized that there had been tears behind that whisper, and they now stood afresh at the back of her throat and eyes, burning for release. She slowly walked towards her building in the humid morning air, unwilling to admit fully how very much she wanted this sphinx of a woman in her life. She sensed that somehow she and Kyril might become partners. And yet, she was afraid—afraid to let herself love the woman of her dreams, to care more than Kyril might, to give herself completely and risk the pain of disappointment and loss. It was too soon to know how Kyril felt—suddenly here, in her life, then, gone again, as suddenly.

Kathryn's uncertainty was heightened when, several hours later, a florist delivered to her office eight blood red roses clustered around a single yellow bud. The card said, simply, "Kyril." Eight was precisely the number of times they had made love over the days since Kyril's reappearance in her life. *Was the yellow bud a promise of more to come—or a good-bye?*

Kathryn realized she no more knew the answer to that than to how Kyril could propose to fund a clinic for the treatment of, and research into, AIDS. Mentally, she steeled herself for the separation, and against the reluctantly admitted possibility that Kyril might not return.

9

K yril's flight East was uneventful. She was met at Baltimore-Washington International by Däg, an old friend of *fér*Vlad, Kyril's paternal parent. In his human identity, Däg had chosen to remain in this Other dimension and was now firmly ensconced in the government bureaucracy of the United States. As a result, he had a variety of resources from which to draw for classified information in many fields. Posing as Däg Svensen, Ph.D., he had lived several decades in America, a naturalized citizen whose expertise in nuclear physics had made him a valuable commodity in an international market. He introduced Kyril to his human colleagues as his niece and gave her a semi-classified tour of the facility in which his offices were housed.

The second evening Kyril was in Washington, Däg arranged a private meeting of some of his oupirian compatriots at his home in Arlington. Several, enticed by the prospect of hearing from someone so newly arrived from Kornägy, were to drive down from Baltimore and Philadelphia to meet her. Kyril arrived early and toured the elegant estate, noting its separateness from other estates, the thoroughness of its security system, and how successful its designers had been in causing it to blend into its surroundings. Customarily, oupirs provided themselves with comfortable, secure places of residence when travelling in this dimension.

As she surveyed the growing crowd while waiting for Däg to appear, she estimated that there were at least fifty of her kind present. She wondered how they managed to avoid suspicion when so many were concentrated in the relatively small area that the Washington, Baltimore, and Philadelphia metropolises were. While puzzling over the logistics of feeding fifty oupirs at least twice every eight to ten days without attracting notice, she was startled by the touch of a hand on her elbow. She turned to find a woman, somewhat shorter than she with greying hair and a rich, chocolaty complexion, standing behind her. Instantly, she felt a pang, missing Guardian Tyrell.

The other woman observed the swift play of emotion across Kyril's face, and wondered at the sudden wistfulness which so quickly replaced surprise in the dark eyes. "I'm sorry," she said in a voice as rich and full as her coloring, "I didn't mean to startle you. I wanted to introduce myself to you. I am known here as Dumare Warenga. Däg tells me that you have some news for us tonight that may be of grave import for our native world."

Kyril inclined her head in the customary attitude of respect for an elder, but said nothing.

Dumare continued. "It is my hope that we who are gathered here tonight can be of service to you, Kyril. You probably do not know; I was Kolayna's spiritual Guardian when she was very young, and before I came to this dimension to stay."

Kyril's eyes widened in surprise and she felt sudden tears behind her lids. She could scarcely recall her maternal parent, she had died when Kyril was so young. "Mother," she stammered, using the honorific, lapsing into her native speech, "I am without words. Please, forgive me."

"It is nothing, Child," Dumare responded in kind. Both spoke in Oupirian Standard. "My intent was not to unsettle you. Rather, it was to try to welcome you to our community here with some personal touch. I see I have chosen badly," she apologized, noting the tears threatening to spill out onto Kyril's flushed cheeks. Dumare touched Kyril's shoulder reassuringly.

"It is that I do not remember much about méhKolayna," Kyril said. "Guardian Tyrell has served me as you served méhKolayna," she explained further, feeling that she had regained her composure. "Seeing your serene face has reminded me of her." Kyril inclined her head again. The oupirian tradition was one of reverence for one's elders, and their many languages were replete with formalities that reflected thousands of Cycles of Seasons of social custom and ritual. It was a far richer and more stable culture than that of the country in which they stood in this Other dimension. While Kyril sometimes found it difficult to transit between the two worlds, it grounded her to talk with Dumare in a familiar language, and call forth the weight of the associated customs that went with their words.

Before Dumare could speak further, Däg entered the room and raised his voice for attention from the crowd. A tall man with white hair, he, too, spoke in Oupirian Standard. "My compatriots, I wish to express my gratitude to each of you for being present with us tonight. As you all know, we have with us a Visitor recently transited, Kyril no Kolayna, who would speak with us on a matter concerning the well-being of our kind here and in Kornägy. I ask that everyone attend," he ended, moving to Kyril's side and guiding her to a position in front of the assembly. Bowing slightly, he bade her begin. "Kyril."

She acknowledged his introduction with a lowering of her gaze, as was proper, and awaited silence. When all the rustling and shuffling was done, she raised her eyes and began to speak of her partner's last Visit and subsequent death, of her own return to this dimension with the intent to solve the mystery of Lanaea's illness. She then sought to explain to her listeners what she had thus far learned from Kathryn Hartell and her own rapid study of AIDS-which the French had dubbed the lymphadenopathy-associated virus—and its deadly sequelae.

"I have used our contacts inside the medical establishment both here and in Europe to attempt to assess the risk from AIDS to our species." She paused, drawing a deep breath. Her eyes met those of her audience squarely. "I have concluded that the situation is far worse than it could possibly have appeared at first sight. In this country, there has been an active *cover-up* of data and other information relevant to this disease complex." Her voice became heated with anger. "There is so much abhorrence in American culture of homosexuality that no one of power outside the Centers for Disease Control has wanted to deal with the reality of AIDS, or the potential consequences to the American public if the disease is allowed to run its course unchecked." Seeing the expressions of benign amusement on the faces of her listeners as they contemplated human foibles, Kyril pressed onward.

"The virus has only been recently identified—and it is clearly separate from anything previously encountered by human or oupirian medical sciences. In my opinion, the demographics indicate an origin in Equatorial Africa, probably in Zaire. The length of incubation seems uncertain—possibly years. The mode of transmission among humans appears to be through sexual contact—same- or opposite-sex—or via contaminated blood." There was an uncomfortable stir in the room. "I have become convinced that the first Westerner's death attributable to this virus was in 1977, human reference—a Danish doctor, Grethe Rask, who was, it appears, a lesbian woman, and who had practiced surgery under very primitive conditions in the jungles of Zaire for several years during the 1970s. More recently, intravenous drug users in this country, who share injection apparatus, and Haitian practitioners of religious rites involving the exchange of blood, have contracted the disease." She paused again to allow the import of her words to be absorbed. The quiet deepened. "As of the beginning of May of this year, one thousand, three-hundred and sixty-six cases of AIDS had been documented by the Centers for Disease Control in the United States alone, of which five-hundred and twenty have died. Two-thirds of the states in the United States have reported AIDS cases, as have fifteen other nations.

"At present, the mortality rate for human beings reaches one-hundred percent within five years of onset of the disease." She swallowed hard. "Lanaea died within less than *two* years, human reference, of her return to Kornägy from this dimension." Alarm shot through the crowd.

"I would not presume to suggest that I have all the answers needed to fully assess the dangers to ourselves and our world, nor do I wish to provoke a panic. I *do* believe that the matter is grave—that it requires our immediate attention. There is, as yet, no way of detecting the virus in human blood—it was only definitively established as a new virus in January of this year. What seems clear is that oupirs *can* contract it—I believe Lanaea's death is proof of that." Her throat constricted in pain, and her voice, when she spoke again, was barely above a whisper. "I do not believe any of us here would willingly see another of our species undergo the horrors of such a death. We must put a stop to its spread and find a cure—before more of us fall victim." She could not bring herself to say the words she herself did not wish to hear, that some of them might already be infected with this unseen and so-far unconquerable enemy. Instead, she added shakily, "And we *must* be cautious in our feeding, here in this dimension." Clutching herself tightly, she strove to suppress a shudder.

Däg stepped forward, his face somber, and addressed the group again. "I would solicit your prompt cooperation in mobilizing our funds for the support of Kyril's efforts at solving this problem. She has discussed her plans with me and I find them well-made, and thus, recommend them to you. I *implore* you all to take extraordinary precautions in feeding from here onward. I will be in communication with the Congress of Health in Kornägy and will notify each of you of any directives they may issue relative to this matter. Meanwhile, I urge anyone who has specific questions to talk with Kyril individually. She has prepared a written document with the details of her findings and her current conclusions. It is available on the table at the back of the room." He gestured there. "She will be visiting Baltimore later this week and Philadelphia the middle of next week. From there, she goes to meet with our community in New York City before returning to Minneapolis, where she proposes to locate her research site."

There was a loud hum of voices as the crowd broke into smaller groups for discussion, leaving Kyril and Däg in the center of a miniature maelstrom of activity. It was several hours before he deemed it appropriate to take Kyril's elbow and steer her onto the patio, where Dumare soon joined them.

Kyril stretched tiredly, breathing deeply of the fresh night air. "I'm hungry;" she complained gently, returning to speaking in English.

"How does one go about feeding safely here?" she asked of her companions.

As Däg opened his mouth to speak, one of the Philadelphia contingent beckoned to him from the sliding doorway. He excused himself and deferred to Dumare for the response to Kyril's question.

Dumare sighed. "It is difficult out here, in Arlington," she admitted. "If you would like, I'll drive you into the city—at this hour you can have your pick of the derelicts."

"Dumare, how do all of you manage to feed without drawing notice to yourselves? There are so many of you here."

She smiled. "We are not as many, relatively speaking, as it may seem, my dear. Metropolitan Washington is a city of three-quarters of a million, Baltimore of more than two million, Philadelphia of four million, and the population density in the outlying areas is high. Even so," she conceded, "we have established methods for choosing the terminally ill and the terminally outcast to avoid detection. We also find that we can feed from several *different* human beings, so that none is drained—or even severely taxed—avoiding, in these cases, death and the notice of the authorities altogether."

Kyril pondered that information and saw that it was not unlike their practice in Kornägy, where mammals were raised for the explicit purpose of feeding the peoples of Kornägy. They were herded on large preserves—managed such that a fair semblance of life in the wild could be attained—where they were hunted for a portion of their blood. None was ever drained completely, and, other than being asked to regularly give a portion of their blood, their life cycles were not interfered with. The larger animals—on the order of moose, elk, or bear in this Other dimension—could provide half an adult feeding with minimal effect on their bodies. For the oupir, the excitement of the chase was retained, and the animals, when captured, were mentally pacified immediately following the feeding, so that no permanent trauma was inflicted on their psyches. The differences here, in this dimension, were that it took the contents of an entire human vascular system to satiate hunger and that the excitement of pursuit, in most instances, had to be replaced with the excitement of seduction. Adrenaline was the elixir of life for the oupir. Kyril wondered aloud what compensation was made when the feeding was taken from the aged, the ill, or the stuporous.

"Oh, an occasional out and out chase, a seduction, or—" the mischievous light in Dumare's eyes darkened into seriousness—"through inducing fear which is subsequently hypnotically erased from consciousness." She paused. "Life in this dimension, in this society, has become less pleasant over the decades, what with the difficulties in finding human beings who cannot be traced, and with the spiritual malaise of Westerners, in particular. I sometimes think that our species will eventually decide to leave this world, never to return." Almost to herself, she added, "Perhaps this disease will be the final stimulus." Then, sighing heavily, she went on. "However, the human species struggles—almost in spite of itself—on the edge of true spiritual awakening. Many of the people of this world have begun a call for cessation of their 'nuclear madness,' and the battle between altruism and selfishness is intensifying in a climate of awareness that one round of fire loosed by their leaders could annihilate life as they have known it on this planet."

Dumare shook her head and came to stand in front of Kyril. "Child," she whispered sadly, "I have seen too much slaughter in my time among these peoples to *believe* that spirit will win out over baseness—and yet, the history of our own peoples tells me that it *is possible*. So, I have stayed, watching, contributing in my own small way toward the establishment of a lasting international peace in this world. And—because I have grown fond of these foolish races—I hope." Her eyes locked with Kyril's.

Kyril stared at Dumare in surprise, then dropped her eyes. "Fondness? Hope? You speak as Guardian of Child," she commented in Standard, straining to keep the derision she felt from her tone.

Dumare laughed softly in her dark voice. "That is how it is," she affirmed.

Kyril laughed as well, a short, harsh sound. "I cannot feel the compassion for them you feel—in my mind, they have condemned themselves by their millennia of violence." She shuddered. "Especially the males. I pick only the males for feeding—they, far more than the females, have perpetuated the heinous acts of their species.

"Is that not why our kind have always chosen to avoid emotional entanglements with their kind?" Even as she uttered the bitter words, Kyril was aware of her own internal conflict over the human woman who drew her so.

Dumare had listened to Kyril's words without judgement, knowing something of Kyril's passion and background. But her response reflected her own experience. "As I have said, my dear, there are those who would change the course of their species' actions." She chose not to disclose her own "emotional entanglement" with an internationally known African leader.

"Then," Kyril inquired, reverting to English again, "have you found some human beings who are more. . .morally, spiritually evolved— more worthy of your service?" *Your commitment?* she added silently.

Dumare regarded the other directly, reading her emotions and thoughts before answering. "Kyril, there are always, in any race, in any species, some who stand out as more ready, more able to achieve spiritual growth than their compatriots." She waited.

"How am I to know—how could I recognize those?"

Dumare grasped Kyril's shoulder. "Trust your own lélek," she advised, using an Oupirian word for the spiritual aspect of self which apprehends reality at all levels of consciousness. "You have known those worthy of your commitment—you can recognize them again, Daughter, whether here or among your own kind."

Grateful for the wisdom distilled from Dumare's centi-Cycles of experience, Kyril lowered her eyes, then raised them for permission to act. It was given, and she embraced the shorter woman. "Thank you, Mother."

They stood arm in arm, gazing out over the wooded hills and sleeping homes, until Däg wandered onto the patio.

He stopped behind them, put an arm around each. "It is lovely here at night, isn't it?"

His question was acknowledged with nodded heads and a fond smile from Dumare. The silence was broken only by the cries of night birds and the whirrings of insects and tree frogs croaking. It was a rare moment of peace that Kyril would find herself remembering with longing over the next few months.

10

The jangling telephone dredged Kathryn from a deep sleep. As she lunged for the object of her sudden hostility, she glanced at the clock: 9 a.m..

"Hello," she grumped.

"Kathryn, this is Megan."

Kathryn's groggy brain managed to comprehend that her friend was crying. "Megan— What's the matter?" she croaked, dragging herself into an upright position. Mindi, thinking it was time to get up, jumped onto the bed for her usual weekend tussle in the sheets. Kathryn absently laid a hand on her neck as she listened for her friend's response.

"I need to talk to you," she replied. Her voice was muffled and she sounded distraught.

"Well, okay," Kathryn agreed. "Can't you say any more?"

"I'd rather wait until I see you," she replied with more snuffling.

Kathryn sighed, striving for mental clarity. "Okay—why don't you come over. I'll try to be more awake when you get here."

"Okay." Then, as if an afterthought, "Thanks."

"Bye." Kathryn hung up and stared in perplexity at the phone. Her friend Megan was never reticent; therefore, something must be dreadfully wrong. She responded to Mindi's pawing her with a groan, and flopped over on her side, pulling the auburn-haired dog against her. "Oh, Mindi," she moaned, "my Saturday morning!"

By the time Megan was outside her door, Kathryn had dragged herself in and out of the shower, and consumed enough coffee so that she could begin to think of herself as alive and functioning. She even had bacon frying and bread in the toaster.

Megan, a smaller woman with thin, strawberry-blonde hair, followed her into the kitchen. Behind her glasses, her eyes were swollen and red. She dropped her backpack on the floor and stood watching Kathryn, who was hurriedly tending the bacon which was beginning to burn. "Kathryn," she demanded.

Kathryn turned, caught by the pleading in Megan's voice. She saw need written on the thin face. Turning off the gas burner, Kathryn came quickly to her, wrapping her in a firm embrace. They stood thus a few moments, as Megan sobbed wordlessly against Kathryn's shoulder. When her tears had subsided, Kathryn handed her a paper towel on which to wipe her face and blow her nose, then guided her to a chair. "So tell me what's *wrong*," she urged gently, as she worked rapidly to finish preparing their BLT's. When they were completed, she seated herself opposite Megan, who had remained silent. When she still did not speak, Kathryn began to eat.

Megan stared listlessly at the food. After a few moments, she addressed the salt and pepper shakers in the middle of the table. "Joel has AIDS."

The quietly uttered words sank into Kathryn's consciousness like a stone in water. *Oh my God!* she exclaimed silently, unable to mouth the words out loud.

"He just found out yesterday and he—he went crazy! He went out and got drunk and didn't tell me where he was and when I called his office, they said he hadn't come back after lunch and nobody knew where he was and I was really worried and I thought maybe I should call the police but I thought if I called the police and he was just out at the bars he'd be really pissed—" Megan broke off her frantic recital, gasping for breath.

Kathryn remained frozen in position, her sandwich suspended halfway to her plate, her mouth full of food. She was supremely grateful that Megan had not disclosed this devastating information over the telephone those very short forty-five minutes ago.

"And so—" She was sobbing again, gulping for air. "So I waited until he finally came home and he was so drunk he could hardly stand up and one of his bar buddies had driven him and he told me and— Oh, Kathryn, I'm so scared!" she wailed, dissolving in a flood of tears.

Kathryn felt something icy tighten around her innards as Megan's tears began, and was released from her frozen position to put her sandwich down. She swallowed, her mouth suddenly dry and appetite equally suddenly vanished. *Here it comes!* announced the voice of doom that lurked in the back of her head, always ready and waiting to broadcast pronouncements of a cataclysmic nature. Megan and Joel Kastner were a bisexual couple whom Kathryn had known for nearly four years. She and Megan had had sex together a few times early on in their relationship, but each had agreed that they made better friends than lovers and they had continued to see each other occasionally for a movie, a walk, or a shared meal. Most recently they had had dinner together just a few weeks ago.

She reached across the table and took Megan's clenched fist in her own cold hand, wanting, needing the contact. *What to say?* she asked herself. *Nothing,* came the reply. And so they sat, Kathryn clutching Megan's hand as she poured out the details more fully, cycling back over and over again to her shock and horror. Kathryn listened, suppressing her own fear. Although she had not been sexual with Megan for nearly three years, she knew only too well the delay in symptom development that followed infection with the AIDS virus.

When Megan had exhausted herself, Kathryn took her hand and led her into the bedroom, pulling her onto the bed with her. They lay holding, rocking, soothing one another in their closeness for a long time.

℩ ℩ ℩

Once the initial shock was past, the crisis blew Megan and Joel's relationship wide open. Megan was terrified, full of rage that Joel might have infected her, even as she knew with her intellect that he would not have chosen such a course had he known of the infection. He was diagnosed with Kaposi's sarcoma and was told he probably had two years to live. No one knew for certain if he could transmit the newly identified virus to Megan, or, if so, for how long a period of time he might be contagious; no one knew whether or not, if she became infected, she would ultimately develop symptoms of AIDS.

The uncertainty of their futures was debilitating. In the days that followed, Megan withdrew from her classes at the College of St. Catherine, where she was enrolled in the Weekend College program, and Joel took a leave of absence from his computer programmer job at Control Data until he could formulate a longer term plan. They argued violently, repetitively; finally, Joel stormed out of their home, screaming about suicide.

Megan promptly called Kathryn, who called the AIDS hotline, who put out an informal a.p.b. One of Joel's previous sexual partners saw Joel outside a bar on Hennepin Avenue two nights later and talked him into coming to his apartment with him. At that point, he called Megan to tell her that Joel was okay and that he would keep him there that night, and asked what she wanted done with him the next day. She took the address and they agreed that she would pick him up that following morning, Sunday. Then she called Kathryn and asked if she could stay the night with her.

As they lay on the floor at Kathryn's, a record playing softly in the background, soft drinks and popcorn at hand, Megan spoke tentatively of new awarenesses. "You know, I love him, I've *always* loved him, even as I've known I need women in my life, too." She paused. "It's not right that it should be this way, that we should be estranged like this. I mean, even our marriage vows said for better and for worse.

"Kathryn." She rolled over, raising herself on her elbows. "I guess I'm not mad at him anymore. I mean, when I really thought he was gonna *kill* himself, I realized how much I want him around—for however long—and that seems more important than blaming him for something he didn't even know about.

"Besides," she fell on her side, grabbing her can of Sprite, "I'm pregnant—and I don't want to do this alone." Her voice cracked.

Kathryn turned to her, stunned. "Megan! How long have you known?"

She busied herself drinking pop and eating popcorn to quell tears. "Well, I thought I might be a couple of months ago, but I didn't go for the test until after I had talked with you last weekend. Judith's office called yesterday afternoon with the results." The tears leaked through the mask, and she came into Kathryn's arms, needing the physical comfort.

"Megan. . .what about. . .an abortion?" Kathryn queried gently.

Megan shook her head vigorously. "I couldn't do it—I just couldn't do it."

"But, Megan—the baby could be born with AIDS—"

"I know, but I just couldn't do it." She tucked her head. "Kathryn, I—Will you—"

Kathryn took Megan's chin and raised her face. "Will I what, Megan?" she prodded gently.

"Will you help me with this? I mean, what if Joel can't. . .what if he isn't. . . ?" She swallowed hard, then forged on. "I feel like no one else will understand." Her eyes pleaded desperately.

Kathryn stroked her hair and cheek. "You know I'll be there for you as much as I can. We'll get you through it one way or another, I promise." She smiled at her as encouragingly as she could, ignoring her private reluctance to commit to such a task.

Megan gazed at her, clear-eyed for the first time in nearly two weeks. That "we" meant to her that she was not alone, either in her fear that she might now be a carrier and/or succumb to AIDS, or in her fear of death. If Joel did not return to her, emotionally, she felt she could count on Kathryn for support. "Thank-you," she whispered hoarsely, her eyes shining with tears. She snuggled against Kathryn's shoulder.

As Kathryn held Megan, her thoughts turned to Kyril and she wondered where she was and what success she was having. Kathryn had not heard from her since they had parted at the airport three weeks ago yesterday. She longed for someone with whom she could share her burdens—she had ultimately disregarded the impulse to schedule a session with Eileen—and ached for the healing of sex.

Aloud, she mused, "Maybe it's best that there *be* a research facility here, in the Cities:" Just in the past week she had told Megan that she was seeing Kyril, and that Kyril had gone East with the certainty of raising the funds needed for such a facility and with the conviction that the Project AIDS board of advisors would agree to her proposal. In fact, they had; but not before a long battle during which Kathryn had vacillated between her prior concerns that they not duplicate facilities already in existence, and her personal desire to have Kyril around. When it seemed clear that the other seven members of the board would vote in favor of the clinic, she had abstained, pleading, to everyone's surprise, personal involvement. As she now contemplated Megan and Joel's plight, it seemed providential that things had evolved as they had.

Oh, Kyril! she implored, *hurry back! I need you.*

She awoke to an echoing silence, and realized the telephone had been ringing. As rapidly as possible without jarring Megan, she slipped from their embrace and dashed into the bedroom. *Let it be Kyril,* she beseeched the universe.

"Kathryn?"

"Oh, Kyril, it *is* you!" she exclaimed, her voice suddenly unsteady. "Oh, God, I've missed you!" She clutched at the receiver as if it were Kyril herself.

"Kathryn," the voice was quiet, insistent, concerned. "Kathryn, what's wrong?"

She breathed deeply, trying to calm herself. "It's a long story. Just tell me you're coming back soon." The tears began to drizzle down her face.

"That is why I've called: I shall be there—tomorrow."

Kathryn nodded, wiping at her face. "That's wonderful."

"Kathryn—" There was a long pause. "I've missed you, too."

"Oh, Kyril." She felt herself on the verge of dissolving into a sobbing heap. *What is **wrong** with me?* she admonished herself.

"Will you meet me at the airport?" Kyril was asking.

"Yes, yes! When?" Relief threatened her coherence.

"At 7:20 tomorrow evening, your time. Delta flight seven-one-three."

She hastily scribbled the figures on her notepad. "Okay, I'll be there. Kyril—" She breathed deeply. "Why did you call—just now?"

"Because I 'got your message,' " she said, attempting by the use of the colloquialism to inject a bit of lightness into the conversation.

It failed.

"I see," Kathryn stated, not quite wanting to believe that her mental entreaty could have been "heard" so clearly over a thousand miles away.

"Kathryn, you *did* reach me—it just took a while for me to get free to telephone you." In fact, she had been in the middle of an important conversation with the informal head of the oupirian community in New York City when she had apprehended Kathryn's silent cry. Now she found herself slightly annoyed at Kathryn's difficulty in acknowledging the truth. "Listen, we can talk about this when I get there. I must go now."

"Right, right," Kathryn nodded, then brought herself up sharp. "Kyril—" She projected something akin to love and waited. In a moment, she felt it returned. Then, quietly, "Tomorrow," she promised.

"Yes, tomorrow. Good-bye, Kathryn."

There was a click followed by a hum on the line as Kathryn stood holding the receiver, unwilling to complete the disconnection, until she realized that they were *not* disconnected, that, rather, their connection had been made more complete with the exchange of their sentiments.

Her relief at hearing from Kyril unsettled her, but she passed it off as emotional exhaustion and strain arising from recent events with Megan and Joel. She allowed anticipation at seeing Kyril again to overcome her nagging doubts, and returned to the sleeping Megan.

11

athryn struggled into her stiff, newly pressed Levi's, glancing anxiously at the clock. As usual, her day had not gone the way she had envisioned it, and she was running late. She grabbed her watch, strapping it on her wrist, snatched a light gold chain off the dresser and dropped it over her head as she stepped into her sandals. Mindi preceded her excitedly into the front of the house, scampering out the door as it was opened.

Twining in and out of the traffic on the freeway, Kathryn experienced momentary resentment that it was crowded even on a Sunday evening. Muttering and occasionally cursing under her breath at other motorists innocently returning home from their weekends up north, she made her way to the airport, finding, upon her arrival, that she had time to spare. She parked and cut the motor, then relaxed against the seat back, letting out a long sigh, and, with it, her tension. She knew she was whirling in a mixture of emotions about Kyril's return.

It had been a long three weeks, seeming longer, and Kathryn felt as if she had gone through hell. She now allowed herself to admit that she was angry that Kyril had been unavailable to her even by telephone during this time. She sighed again, disgustedly. *So what did I expect?* she asked herself, feeling bitter that there were no commitments between them and unreasonable that she wanted something more substantial than their present relationship seemed to provide. She did not like the fact that Kyril had gone off to New York—or wherever—without so much as offering to call her while she was to be gone. The apparent ease with which Kyril could leave made her feel that this mysterious woman had more power in their relationship, because she knew that she could not so easily have separated herself from Kyril. With that, she recognized how much she wanted Kyril, how her body already was afire with anticipation of their reunion. Shaking her head, she gripped the steering wheel, blinking back a scant gathering of tears. None of this was helped by the fact that she was premenstrual at the moment. "Dammit," she muttered. "God damn it!" Resolutely, she put her hand on the door handle and took a deep breath.

Catching Mindi's reflection in the rearview mirror, she turned, briefly stroking her before getting out of the car.

As she weaved through the crowded terminal, looking for the red concourse, she allowed memories of her lovemaking with Kyril to surface. By the time she had reached the gate where Kyril's plane was to dock, she found that anger had receded and desire was dominant. Waiting, she felt an inner trembling composed of equal parts of eagerness to see Kyril and anxiety that her emotion would not be returned. She was reminded of Holly Near's song, *Coming Home:* "What if I love you more than before, but it's not me that you adore?"

Then, her breath caught as she glimpsed the tall, dark-haired woman, clad in a well cut, two-piece grey suit, coming up the ramp towards her. Her heart pounding in her ears, she followed Kyril with her gaze, loving the sheen of the burnished silk fabric on the long thighs, anticipating the moment when Kyril's eyes would find hers in the crowd and they would lock with that same jolt she had experienced the first time she had ever seen Kyril. As their gazes at last crossed, the bustle dimmed. She closed the distance between them as if there were no one but they two in the teeming airport. Joyously, she flung her arms around Kyril, and clung to her until, feeling suddenly vulnerable, she looked up into Kyril's dark eyes. She saw there an expression which made her know that Kyril had, indeed, missed her too. In that moment before their lips met, Kathryn realized that Kyril had not left her as easily as she had thought. She put her gratitude at that into a lingering kiss.

When it began to penetrate that people were staring, Kathryn relinquished their embrace and slipped an arm through Kyril's, hugging it to her as they moved from the concourse toward the baggage claim area. Neither seemed to require words, finding their nonverbal exchanges sufficient until they had captured Kyril's suitcases from the baggage carousel and departed the terminal.

"Would you like me to drop you at your hotel?" Kathryn asked, hoping Kyril would say no. She opened the trunk of her car and put the luggage in, then turned to Kyril, one hand on the trunk lid.

Kyril regarded her with an expression that reflected an inner struggle. She had in mind Kathryn's emotional plea of the night before and sought some sense of what it might have meant. She could, however, apprehend nothing more than Kathryn's barely contained joy at seeing her again. Thus, with unease nagging at the back of her consciousness, she was uncertain of how to proceed. Seeing Kathryn's puzzled expression at her hesitancy, she hedged. "I—I hadn't decided yet. . . ."

Kathryn's face fell in disappointment, causing Kyril to hurriedly append, "But we could go to your place first, if you like." Kyril saw gratefulness in Kathryn's sudden smile.

"Yes, yes, I *would* like," Kathryn affirmed, shutting the trunk with a solid *thunk!*

Kyril admitted fleetingly to herself that it was what *she* would like, as well.

Mindi greeted them excitedly as they climbed into the car, seeming as glad to see Kyril as Kathryn was. Laughing with the sheer relief of being at the end of a tiring time, Kathryn drove off into the still light evening. Having no desire to talk yet about her three weeks, she asked Kyril about her trip.

"It was. . .busy," she replied enigmatically, momentarily enjoying the cerulean blue of the late-evening summer sky. Then, "It was also very profitable. I have a check for Doctor Hamyl, and several clinicians with whom I spoke have indicated an interest in negotiating with us to come here and work with the clinic—if the funding is accepted," she added. She took Kathryn's hand in hers briefly, squeezing it lightly. "But, let us not speak of business now," she urged gently.

Kathryn glanced at her quickly, feeling her throat flush with the touch, knowing that she had her own business to bring up. Not really wanting to talk about it made it easy to let it go, and so both rode in noncommittal silence while Kyril stroked Mindi's head over the seatback.

At Kathryn's home, they left Kyril's luggage in the car and entered the darkening dwelling. Kathryn dropped her keys on the bookshelf next to the entryway and turned to Kyril, who had paused a few feet over the threshold. There was a taut silence as they stared at one another in the falling gloom.

"Kyril." Kathryn squeezed the word from a throat aching with longing.

Kyril took her hands, pulling Kathryn towards her, into her embrace, forestalling any further words from Kathryn. "Oh, Goddess," she murmured against Kathryn's ear, "I missed you *so* much." She bit the words out, crushing Kathryn against her, feeling her own yearning rising with the tide of sexual desire. They kissed deeply and long. Then, without a thought for Kathryn's surprise, Kyril lifted Kathryn in her arms, carrying her into the bedroom where she deposited her tenderly on the bed. Her oupirian eyes required no light to see the woman she had begun to love. Proceeding to undress her, slowly, lingeringly, with many kisses and caresses, she finally discarded her own travel-wilted garments to lie naked with Kathryn on the coverlet. The twilit room received their wordless cries, cradling them in gathering darkness as each further lowered her barriers and came closer to the intimacy which both needed, desired, and feared.

After lovemaking, they shared a bottle of wine and lay, half-dozing, in the dark. As Kathryn, sedated by the wine, and having eaten little that day, slid into sleep, Kyril's thoughts turned to the position she now found herself in. She accepted that she could not continue indefinitely to deceive Kathryn about her real identity and origins. But neither did she know how she could tell her the truth. No matter what was said, she ran the risk that Kathryn would think her either insane or a monster personifying the countless legends that had grown up around her kind over the centuries of their Visitations in this dimension.

Whatever she decided to do about that, there was the larger matter of her mission here and the urgency that had prompted her return across the Boundary. And finally, even more grave for her personally, was the fact of her own make-up: that she could not indefinitely continue to open herself to this human woman without finally approaching the point at which she must make a mate-bond with her, as she had made with Lanaea. She sighed, moving restlessly, rousing Kathryn.

Impulsively seizing the opportunity of Kathryn's vulnerability fresh from sleep, Kyril pressed quietly, "Kathryn, what was it that made you reach out to me last night?"

Half awake, still intoxicated, Kathryn propped herself on her elbow, dredging up memories of the evening before. "Kyril...what if you have AIDS?" she murmured groggily.

Taken aback, Kyril stared at her for a moment before replying. Even though she was certain that Grethe Rask had died of AIDS, Kyril had never really believed that Kathryn's fear for lesbian women in general was grounded. Rask had been celibate for several years before her death. Most certainly, in Kyril's mind, the doctor had been infected through her surgical work in non-sterile conditions. "Why do you ask?" she evaded quietly.

Kathryn dragged herself upright. She shook her head, trying to clear it. "I wondered if you had been exposed. You said Lanaea died of AIDS—I assumed you were lovers." She shrugged, struggling to become more alert. "I thought that, being lovers, you might have been exposed." She looked at Kyril for confirmation or denial.

There was a bare flicker of Kyril's eyelid in response. Then, she said softly, "No, I was not exposed. You needn't worry, Kathryn. Go back to sleep."

"No, wait—Megan—my friend Megan—Joel has AIDS. I—I was gonna tell you—but you didn't call."

Call when? she wondered silently, thinking that she had indeed called when she had apprehended Kathryn's silent plea. "Who is Joel? Her husband?"

Exasperated with Kathryn's disjointedness, Kyril asked, "Kathryn, how did he get AIDS?" Then she wished she had not initiated this conversation. She felt a knot of anxiety gathering again. Was Kathryn trying to tell her that *she* had been exposed to AIDS?

Kathryn tried again to shake her fuzziness "Joel is bisexual—so is Megan. I haven't been—I mean, I don't *think* I've been exposed—Megan and I were sexual together a few times when I first knew them—but not for a long time—years—we've just been friends. Joel undoubtedly got it from some other guy."

Kyril eyed her silently for a moment, fear streaking through her. *Goddess,* she implored, *strengthen me, guide me to the choices I must make, and— protect me from folly in seeking to meet my needs.* Giving up thoughts of going to her hotel tonight, knowing the calls she had intended to make would wait, she sighed, moving to hold Kathryn again.

Kathryn, her worry eased by Kyril's assurances, drifted back into drugged slumber. *It is I who must worry,* Kyril told herself. Thinking of the work before her in trying to unravel the mystery of a cure or preventive for the deadly disease, she wondered if now she must add worry about Kathryn's health to her list of concerns. Then, sighing wearily, she gave that worry to the Universe, recognizing that, at this point, there was absolutely nothing she could do that would effect any change whatsoever.

FALL 1983

12

The soft glare of the desk lamp illuminated the stacks of newspaper and magazine clippings, computer printouts, journals, and folders crammed with papers full of figures and reports—all of which were piled in every degree of order from neat to complete disarray on the large desk. The remainder of the room was shadowy with the indeterminate gloom of an office whose sole occupant has worked late into the evening. Somewhere, an electric clock whirred, the only audible sound.

Behind the desk, Kyril sat, her arms folded under her lowered head. The nearly three months since her return to Minneapolis had been filled with the endless activities of setting up the clinic offices, bringing staff aboard, and beginning work with patients. What she had learned on the East coast—that there *were* no other research facilities presently in existence there, only poorly organized treatment programs—had reinforced her conviction that the clinic was desperately needed. She had been constantly in attendance, overseeing every detail with meticulous and unfailing patience. Often the last to leave at night and the first to arrive in the morning, she had seemed indefatigable.

Tonight, she had thought she would rest for a few moments before returning to the larger suite she had moved into at the AmFac Hotel. She knew that the steady diet of bottled bovine blood on which she had existed since her return to Minneapolis was as insufficient to her needs as a steady fare of canned foods would have been to a human being. However, she felt that continued hunting would have compromised her personal security, so she had arranged with an out-of-state medical supply company to have liters of the whole blood delivered to a warehouse space she rented under the name of a fictitious business. It was taken from there by a private delivery service and brought to her at the clinic in the evenings, where she signed for it as though it were a routine delivery of medical supplies. With it inconspicuously tucked away in a locked cooler unit, she felt fairly sure none of her human colleagues knew of her cache. She also felt it was safer than taking the chance that some poorly chosen human prey might be harboring the AIDS virus.

Suddenly, Kyril jerked and lifted her head. In a moment, the sound—perceptible only because of her oupirian hearing—came again. *Where is the security guard?* she wondered worriedly. There was no delivery scheduled for this evening.

Raising her tired body from the heavy chair, she straightened her rumpled lab coat over her skirt and blouse and headed determinedly for the front door as the night-entry buzzer sounded for at least the third time. The buzzer continued impatiently as she quickly covered the long hallway from her office in the back of the building to the stairs leading to the first floor.

As she rapidly descended the stairs, her spiked heels echoing on the terrazzo steps, she saw the security guard hurrying to the entry. He slid his key into the dead bolt and grasped the handle, pulling the heavy inner door back to reveal a woman in a raincoat standing behind the glass of the outer door. Kyril caught sight of her: It was Kathryn. She released a tightly held breath.

"Evening ma'am," the guard drawled as he pushed open the outer door.

"Hello. I'm Kathryn Hartell. Is Doctor Vértök still here?" Kathryn's voice held concern.

Kyril glanced at her watch: 9 p.m. She shook her head ruefully, realizing she had fallen asleep over her desk. "Yes, I'm here," she responded, interrupting the guard's hesitant reply.

Kathryn glanced behind him into the darkened foyer and saw Kyril's white-coated form. "Hi. I was worried about you—you missed our dinner date. " Her voice seemed carefully neutral.

Kyril sighed. Once again, she had forgotten completely. "Yes, I see. I'm sorry. Please—come in. " She reached for Kathryn's arm, guiding her past the young guard. Kyril did not recognize the sandy-haired fellow. "What was the delay, officer?" she inquired.

He was closing the inner door behind Kathryn. "I'm sorry, ma'am. I was in the restroom," he replied, flushing with embarrassment. "I figur'd soon's I went, somethin' would happen." He grinned apologetically.

Satisfied, Kyril smiled at him. "Yes, that is usually the way, isn't it?" Touching Kathryn's elbow, she gestured towards the stairs. "Let's go to my office."

Neither spoke as they traversed the unlit corridor, and Kyril found herself unable to read Kathryn's mood. As they entered her office, Kyril caught sight of the flask which had held her previous day's feeding sitting on the floor beside her waste basket. She had been negligent by not disposing of the emptied container and now hoped Kathryn would not notice it. The heavy odor of blood was quite discernible to her sensitive nostrils. "Ugh, it's stuffy in here," she declared, moving directly to the window and opening it to the night air.

Kathryn remained inside the doorway, glancing around the dimly lit room. It was the first time she had been there since the clinic had opened to patients, four weeks ago. Her gaze travelled over the crowded desk and overfilled waste basket, lingering only momentarily on the empty bottle beside it before passing on to Kyril's wrinkled lab coat. Kyril's face was hidden in the shadows created by the glare of the desk lamp. Kathryn's mix of thoughts and emotions now came clearly to Kyril: relief that Kyril was all right; anger because she had been stood-up; curiosity about Kyril's work; concern at how tired Kyril had appeared in the light of the entryway; and an unfamiliar weariness.

"I was worried about you," Kathryn repeated.

"I'm sorry," Kyril apologized again. "I—I must have fallen asleep." Feeling somehow weakened by that admission, she leaned against the window, her arms folded at her waist. She realized she looked defensive, but was unable to change how she felt at the moment.

Kathryn moved to a chair in front of Kyril's desk and reluctantly lowered herself into it. "I've seen you so little since you got started with this project," she said sadly. "I miss you, lady."

Having prepared for anger, Kyril was touched by the sadness. She came to Kathryn and squatted beside her, her hand on Kathryn's arm where it lay on the chair. They regarded one another in silence for a moment before Kyril conceded quietly, "We need to talk. . .soon." She squeezed Kathryn's arm.

Then, with a tired sigh, she stood and stretched. "Let's get out of here."

As Kathryn pushed herself to her feet, Kyril glance around the room, her eyes lighting again on the empty flask. She decided she had better dispose of it now. "Will you wait downstairs for me while I throw out my trash?" she asked.

Kathryn nodded and left without a word, feeling her own tiredness. There had been many late night telephone conversations and brief meetings stolen from sleep during the past several weeks. The strain of her early risings and the lack of quality time between them was taking its toll. She clumped slowly down the stairs to where the security guard slouched in his chair, reading an *Amazing Stories* magazine.

As soon as Kathryn disappeared down the hallway, Kyril scooped up the flask and tucked it under her arm, then gathered the trash bag from her waste basket, stuffing crumpled computer print-out sheets down into the plastic sack. She traversed the hall in the opposite direction, tossing the sack of garbage into the trash chute. Continuing to another door, she fished her keys from the pocket of her lab coat and unlocked the portal marked *Hematology*. As she entered, a wave of chemical odors washed at her, some welcome, others unpleasant, all familiar. She crossed the dark room and deposited the flask in a box with other empties.

Returning to her office, she removed the limp lab coat and hung it on a coat tree. Slipping into her navy blue suit jacket, she realized she felt as wilted as her lab coat and wanted little more than a bath and a comfortable bed tonight. At least it was Friday and she and Kathryn could have some time together tomorrow. Perhaps then they could talk. Sooner or later, Kyril knew she must deal with what she had easily avoided in the crush of getting the clinic functioning. She shut off the desk light and left, locking her office door behind her.

When she reached the lobby area, Kathryn was nowhere to be seen. "Did Miss Hartell leave?" she inquired of the guard,

Smiling amiably, he put down his magazine. "Yes, ma'am—said to tell you she'd be waitin' at her car."

She nodded. "Thank you." The guard's warm blood-smell assaulted her defenses as he neared her.

"You're welcome. G' night, ma'am." He followed her to the door and locked it behind her.

Glad to be in the fresh evening air, Kyril inhaled deeply, then looked ahead of her, trying to see outside the glare of the lights on the front of the building. After a moment, she spotted Kathryn leaning against her car, her arms crossed, gazing across the top of the clinic building to the downtown skyline.

Kyril approached but said nothing, sensing a change in Kathryn's mood.

Kathryn slowly brought her gaze to Kyril's and looked hard at her for a long moment. "Kyril—" she began.

"Kathryn—" Kyril said simultaneously.

Kyril paused. "Go ahead."

Kathryn began again. "I know you have been very busy—and are very tired. But I need more from you than what we've had these past few weeks—" She faltered, fighting tears. "We've hardly even had time for lovemaking—you always manage to get out of our dinner engagements— I'm *worried* about you," she repeated. "You aren't taking very good care of yourself."

Kyril sighed heavily. "We need to talk," she reiterated. "I don't suppose it could wait until tomorrow?"

Kathryn looked away.

Without deliberation, she grasped Kathryn's arm gently. "All right then, let's go."

They got in Kathryn's car and began the short drive to Kyril's hotel in silence.

Meanwhile, Kathryn was aching with longing and confusion. She thought how they had never discussed the subject of their living apart or together. How the initial closeness after Kyril's return from her trip East had been replaced by distance—distance that resulted from their lack of time together, and something else she could not quite name. She wanted something substantial with Kyril—and had felt sure upon Kyril's return that Kyril did, too. Consequently, she did not understand, and was hurt by, the emotional reserve that Kyril had so carefully maintained, and the string of broken engagements. Struggling to retain her composure, she swallowed a lump in her throat as she turned the car onto the AmFac ramp.

When they entered Kyril's suite, Kathryn noted again how it never appeared that anyone lived there: The meticulously kept rooms had a sterility that was due to the absence of any of the most trivial of personal belongings. Had Kyril no private life, no life outside her work and her relationship with Kathryn?

Kyril dropped her purse and keys and stepped out of her shoes as she advanced across the sitting room. She pulled off her earrings and discarded them on the coffee table, slipped out of the linen jacket and folded it across a chair back, then proceeded to the broad picture window, which was uncovered to the night. She looked out, sighing heavily again, then turned to Kathryn where she stood, waiting, not even out of her raincoat, in the middle of the room.

Tired and frustrated as she was, Kathryn's breath caught in her throat as the dark eyes sought hers across the distance between them. Yet again, she recognized Kyril as the most alluring woman she had ever met. At this moment, she longed to come together with her and feel that lithe body next to her own in the cool heat she had learned to savor.

Kathryn's wanting washed at Kyril like a wave breaking on a shore. Desire tugged at her from within, trying to suck her under. Should she give in? Should she make love with Kathryn, then tell her? Or tell her now, allowing the distance both would probably need. She opted for the latter, and stepped away from the undertow. Moving to the couch, she invited Kathryn with a gesture to join her.

The blood pounding in her throat, Kathryn complied, sitting close to, but not touching, the long arm that lay across the sofa back. Having already indicated her choice of subject, she waited determinedly for Kyril to initiate.

Across the space between them, Kyril reached for Kathryn's hand, looking directly into her eyes. "I have to tell you some things that

may be hard for you to hear," she began gently. "But, you *must* know."
She let go of Kathryn's hand, clasping hers in her own lap.

Kathryn's heart missed a beat. This was not exactly the tack she
had had in mind.

"Kathryn, I am not what I have presented myself to be," Kyril began.
"I am not Hungarian." She paused and watched surprise replace
the apprehension on Kathryn's face. This was difficult, but she knew she
must give Kathryn the truth. "What would you think if I told you that I am
not from your world at all?"

Kathryn's eyes widened. She shook her head, making a sound of
disbelief. "What? What do you mean?"

Kyril forced herself onward. "There is—parallel to this world in
space and time—another world, another dimension, populated by another
humanoid species. I am from that parallel dimension. I crossed through a
dimensional boundary to get here, to your world." She paused again, to let
her words sink in.

Kathryn gaped. Was Kyril playing some bizarre prank? She said
harshly, "Of all the things I wondered about you— An alien? Oh come on!"

Kyril looked down at her hands, then back at Kathryn, ignoring
the jeer. "Well, I am *not* human, not as you understand that word. I am
oupirian. Oupirs are humanoid, but not *homo sapien.*"

There was an outward silence as that voice of doom that resided
in Kathryn's head trumpeted Kyril's insanity.

The doubt assaulted Kyril's awareness, but she forged ahead. "I
came here, as I said, because of Lanaea's death. I am, in my world also,
a physician—all those things are true." She took a deep breath, drawing
on her determination. "I am aware that you have come to care for me—"

Kathryn laughed shortly, and tightened her arms over her chest.
"That is an understatement!" She was aware of the sharpness in her words,
but could not keep it back.

"—as I have come to care for you," Kyril continued resolutely.
"But, I cannot preserve my own integrity if I continue to deceive you,
Kathryn." Kyril heard the tremor in her voice, and hated it.

In spite of her confusion, Kathryn sensed Kyril's anguish.
Hesitantly, mindful of the ravings of that inner voice, she reached out and
placed a hand on Kyril's.

Kyril felt the warmth of Kathryn's hand, and longed for that
warmth against her entire body Oh, how she had missed Kathryn next to
her these past few weeks! And without the hunt, she had not even been
warmed from within. She went on determinedly, withdrawing her hand
gently.

"I want you to know the whole truth about me, because...because I *must* either give myself to you soon in a mate-bond, or break off our relationship altogether." She eyed Kathryn sideways, waiting for her reaction. She felt exposed, speaking of her inmost secrets to someone not of-the-blood.

Stunned by Kyril's declaration of affection as much as by her revelations, Kathryn watched a tear ooze from the corner of one eye and slide slowly down the crease beside Kyril's nose, to be caught on the edge of her lip. There, it dissolved and washed over the carmine softness into her mouth. Kathryn staggered under the weight of Kyril's statements, her lips moving soundlessly. The inner voice had ceased.

Unable to bear the heavy silence, Kyril blurted, "So do you hate me for deceiving you?"

"Hate you?" She shook her head in bewilderment. "No, I don't *hate* you—on the contrary—I'm scared to believe you *want* me as much as you say. You've been so intent on preserving distance between us, I'm thoroughly confused—and now this...this declaration...I...I don't know what. . . ." She raised her hands in consternation.

"Kathryn, you *must* hear the rest," Kyril insisted quietly. "My physiology is different from yours. Oupirian metabolism is...slower. We feed less frequently than human beings do, age more slowly, live longer. Kornägy is an extremely different environment from your Earth; our sun is dimmer; we have longer days and years; our society is a global one. Oupirian technology has progressed far beyond yours in many ways—" She broke off, realizing she was drifting from the personal revelation she must make.

Listening, Kathryn realized that, *if* what Kyril were telling her were true, it could explain much about Kyril that was so strange: her seeming preference for soft illumination and the night hours; the unusual coolness of her skin; her avoidance of food; how little she slept. . . .

". . .my hearing and night vision are keener than those of your species," Kyril was saying. "And because the survival of my species often depends on the ability to physically subdue other animal species, I have more physical strength than a comparable human."

As Kathryn flashed on a memory of being carried in Kyril's arms, Kyril paused again, allowing Kathryn time for reflection, working herself up to the final disclosure.

Kathryn came to a question. "Kyril—you said you came here because of Lanaea's death—you also told me that she had AIDS—was she human or. . . ?" She searched for the alien word.

"She was oupirian. I now believe that she contracted AIDS during her last Visit to this dimension."

A perplexed frown creased Kathryn's brow. "But, how? If she were an. . .oupir. . .then wouldn't she have had to have gotten it from another oupir?" She shook her head, her fingers at her temples. "This doesn't make any sense to me, Kyril."

Kyril tried to keep her eyes on Kathryn's as she struggled within herself, shying away from revealing the prohibited truth. She worked to force the words past her lips. "Blood. She had to have gotten it from the blood of some human who was infected."

"Blood? What do you mean?"

"Oupirs consume blood—as many of your kind consume meat— for sustenance." She could go no further without Kathryn's reaction.

A look of extreme distaste came across Kathryn's face. "You mean you. . .drink blood?"

"We draw blood from a host, and feed in that way." She could see Kathryn blanch even in the dim light.

"Fresh blood? From. . . *people?*" She was aghast.

Kyril felt herself retreating again, steeling herself against the coming rejection. She raised her chin in defense. "Yes, fresh blood. Some oupirs feed from small animals, others from large animals. In this dimension, we usually feed from human beings."

Kathryn shrank back in horror. "Hu—Human beings," she repeated breathlessly. "You're. . .vampires?"

The revulsion in Kathryn's voice cut through Kyril's shield, wounding her deeply. Immediately, she began to question her judgement. Why had she allowed herself to feel anything for this human female? "Your people have called us that," she whispered, repressing her pain. She felt instead a great sadness that she had allowed herself to hope that Kathryn might be different, might respond differently out of knowing her as an individual, out of their mutual caring.

Kathryn wanted to retch. The thought that she had kissed that mouth—a mouth that had feasted off human blood. She could sense Kyril's disappointment in her, but she could not suppress her horror. Was Kyril as cold as her touch? She began to shiver uncontrollably.

"I—I'm sorry. I—I have to go." The tears flooded Kathryn's cheeks. Jumping up, she grabbed her purse from the chair where she had laid it and clutched her coat around her. Kyril made no move to stop her.

Kathryn hesitated, feeling the need to say something else. "I'll try—" No, on second thought, she could not promise that. In desperation, she fled.

13

For a long time after Kathryn had left, Kyril sat in the dimly lit room, holding herself, grieving yet again, feeling the emptiness within and her own recriminations. She had so hoped—had so feared—

At length, she contemplated going to bed. Glancing at her watch, she saw that it was just after 1 a.m. She knew the bar crowd would still be out on the street. On an impulse, she changed quickly into a dark jumpsuit and black boots. Grabbing a leather jacket from the closet, she left the apartment to hunt. The thought of warmth to palliate her inner cold was compelling. And hunting would get her away from the desolate silence of her apartment.

The wind in the street was brisk, rushing down from the tall buildings. There was an edge to it that heralded the cold weather coming. She fought the force of the wind, heading east, then doubled back around the corner, toward Hennepin Avenue. Once again, she chafed under the awareness that Minneapolis was so much cleaner and better lit than the cities of the eastern seaboard: hunting was made more difficult here.

She watched a group of people come out of one of the hetero-sexual bars and break up. One man struck off alone, northward, towards the old warehouse district. Having previously determined that area to be darker and less populated than Hennepin Avenue, and feeling secure in his presumed heterosexuality, she selected this man as her most likely candidate and set out to follow him. She concentrated on the hunt, allowing it to block the pain of Kathryn's rejection.

As her quarry moved west, over to First Avenue North, then veered north again, she narrowed the distance between them. She matched his stride step for step, all her senses working. At the clinic, she had learned well the odors of sickness. This man was not ill. He was intoxicated, but not drunk, and was sexually aroused. She sensed loneliness, and suddenly formulated her plan.

Quickening her stride, she came up beside him.

He glanced over his shoulder as she neared, unafraid but curious.

"Please, could I walk with you?" she asked, putting fear into her voice and projecting it emotionally.

He slowed and turned. He was relatively young, and smoothly shaven. The sleeves of his oversized coat were pushed up and his shirt-collar was turned up on his neck against the cool night air. He was taller than she, blonde, blue-eyed—of obvious Scandinavian stock. He smelled of stale smoke, alcohol, and sweat.

She huddled near him, not touching him, and looked around nervously. "I thought someone was following me." She smiled timidly, her eyes seeking his from under her lowered brow. "We had a fight—he was drinking too much—I left." She waved vaguely over her shoulder.

He smiled, his clean, white teeth showing brightly in the semi-dark. "Where's your car?"

Kyril shook her head. "I don't know—it was his—he parked it," she said quietly, giving a tremor to her voice.

"Hmmmh." He looked around, then at his watch. "Well, it's pretty late for the buses. Where do you live—or, are you from out of town?"

She smiled and hesitated. "Over by the lakes— Look, if I could just walk with you to a telephone—I'll call a taxi." Her eyes pleaded with him.

He grinned. "Why don't you come to my place—you can use the phone there."

She pretended reluctance. "Oh, I. . .I don't know. . . ."

He laughed, spreading his hands. "It's okay! Honest! I'm not gonna hurt you!"

After a moment, she capitulated with a nod. "All right."

Giving her his elbow, he led off. "It's just a few more blocks. I live in a loft in the warehouse district."

Kyril covertly observed their surroundings as they silently walked the blocks to his loft. They passed no one else.

When they reached the doorway to his apartment, she noted the padlock fastener. He unlocked it without comment, then tossed lock and keys on a hutch just inside the door.

Crossing to a pillar, he threw a switch on the wooden beam and the entire studio was flooded with light. "Well, here it is—the phone's over there," he said, pointing. "If you'll excuse me, I've got to make a pit stop." He grinned engagingly again and turned.

"Wait! What's the address here?" Kyril asked.

"Five-O-Five Fifth Avenue North," he supplied over his shoulder.

As soon as he disappeared, Kyril quickly surveyed the space. Everything was open, without walls—except the bath. The furniture was grouped according to function. The telephone was next to the bed, in the far corner of the studio. She hurriedly crossed to it and unplugged it at the baseboard before she pretended to call a taxi.

As she replaced the receiver in its cradle, her host returned. He had combed his hair and washed. The scent of toothpaste and fresh cologne came to her from across the room. Perry Ellis—Kathryn had said she loved it.

"Well, everything taken care of?" he asked genially.

She nodded. "Yes, but they said it would be a little while." She paused deliberately.

"Oh—well, please, have a seat." He gestured to the sectional couch. "Uh, would you like a drink while you wait?"

"I really don't want to trouble you," she began.

"Hey! No trouble," he replied quickly. "In fact," he grinned again, "it's kind of a nice surprise." His blue eyes flashed warmly in the bright light. She longed for hazel ones.

Kyril strode to where he stood at the bar. Summoning her most seductive manner, she said, "Thank you for helping me out." Her eyes lingered on his for a moment.

He offered scotch, which she accepted, then took her hand and led her to the couch. "Boy, your hands are cold!" he remarked. He took the one he held and began to chafe it gently between his. The heat reminded her painfully of Kathryn.

Eyeing him a moment, she tasted her liquor, then decisively set the glass down. Turning, she edged closer, draping her free arm across his shoulder, stroking the side of his neck with her long fingers. His skin was warm and smooth—though not as smooth as Kathryn's. She shut her eyes against the insistent memories.

Distracted, she barely caught the quickening of his breath, and then realized he had ceased stroking her hand. Leaning towards him, she inhaled his now-pleasant odors, and teasingly brushed her lips across his ear. Her fingers moved to the coarse hair on the back of his neck. Kathryn's hair was so fine. . . .

He closed his eyes in pleasure, sliding his hands around Kyril's midriff. As she moved her lips to his face, he pulled away a little. "Say, what's your name?" he questioned softly.

She gazed deep into his crystal-blue eyes. "Kyril," she replied daringly. "Kyril Vértök." She placed her mouth on his hungrily, pulling him to her.

As he became more aroused, she nuzzled into him. He stroked her gently, wanting to bring her with him into passion. His hand brushed across her breast, then toyed with the zipper of her jumpsuit before beginning to open it.

Kyril's lips glided across his smooth cheek, down his jaw, to his neck. His head lolled back and he sighed deeply. She massaged his penis through his slacks, and he gave himself completely to her ministrations. She tickled the soft skin of his neck with her tongue, finally able to commit herself to the enveloping blood fever.

Such was his arousal that he noticed nothing more than a sharp pinch at the penetration into his vein, and she drew so slowly on him that he felt a wonderful lethargy overcoming him even as he climaxed.

Kyril held him, pressing him into the sofa, until he slid into unconsciousness. Pausing as she neared satiation, she uncharacteristically contemplated sparing the young man—he had been so gentle—but remembered that she had told him her name. She could not induce hypnotic amnesia—he was already unconscious. Almost regretfully, she bent to finish him. As she completed draining him, she suddenly became aware of footsteps approaching in the hallway. Before she could react, the door was forcefully thrown open.

"Hi! Kurt—" The man stopped, his eyes on Kyril, who was still crouched over her unfortunate host. "Oh, I'm sorry, I—" As he took in the blood on her mouth, his eyes widened. "Jesus Christ! What the hell—"

Kyril launched herself at him from across the room, moving faster than he could have ever anticipated, slamming him backwards into the door frame. With a *whoosh!* of expelled air, he went down and lay still.

Her senses now alerted, Kyril could hear other voices in the building. Quickly, she pushed the dark-haired man aside, grabbed the blond man's keys and the padlock, yanked the keys from the lock and tossed them inside, then slammed the door and secured it.

Realizing she had not planned an escape route, she cursed herself for her carelessness. She could hear the others on the stairs, calling out to their friends. How many were there? She was unable to tell, but in the dimly lit hallway, she knew she had the advantage.

Wiping her mouth with the handkerchief she took from her pocket, she moved stealthily toward the exit and secreted herself in a dark niche until the three women and the other man had passed. They all reeked of smoke and alcohol, and were clumsy and boisterous. As she reached the main level, she could hear them pounding on Kurt's door, laughing and cursing.

The night air refreshed her, and she gathered herself grimly. Tonight's had not been good work. Her preoccupation with Kathryn had led her to be sloppy, her pain to take risks—something no oupir in this dimension could afford. As she rapidly covered the distance back to her hotel, in her mind, she examined the possibilities for trouble.

That the blond was dead, she was certain, As for his dark-haired friend—she feared him not fatally injured. She knew she should have verified his death before making her escape, but killing even humans other than for sustenance went against her ethics. Besides, she had been the careless one. She would have to bear the consequences of her own lack of forethought in this escapade.

As she stood—finally warmed from within—once more at the window of her suite, holding herself, looking at the night-bright city, she longed for Kathryn—longed for her touch, the sound of her matter-of-fact voice. Where was Kathryn now? What must she be feeling as she contemplated the fact that her lover was a creature of human nightmare? Kyril sensed that Kathryn was closed to her right now, preventing her even guessing at the answers to those questions.

The greatest longing of all was her longing for Lanaea—whose untimely death had set this chain of events in motion. Lanaea. Oupirs had no belief in an afterlife. *Curious,* Kyril thought. *We who are viewed as the "undead" in this world, do not even believe in life beyond this one.*

Grudgingly, she mulled over her reluctance to kill the man from whom she had fed. Unready to acknowledge the effects that Kathryn and Mark Hamyl had begun to have on her disdain for the human species, she did not linger on the subject.

Praying for guidance, she stood long at the window. As sunrise began to grey the skyline, she at last turned from her watch and went to her bed, where she slept restlessly, and dreamed.

❨ ❨ ❨

Kathryn fled Kyril's hotel suite, reeling. Images of vampires from all the B-grade movies she had ever seen assaulted her, and she clutched the steering wheel of her car, seeking some grounding in reality, trying not to vomit, as she drove blindly homeward. Halfway there, the sobs broke through her control, but she managed to make it to her curbside safely before collapsing over the wheel.

She felt horribly betrayed—and violated. She had waited so long, despairing of ever finding someone to whom she could entrust her inmost self. Now that she had risked fully, allowed herself to love—it was proven to be a sham, all a sham. She agonized aloud, beating the dashboard with her fists, bruising her fingers on the soft padding. During a momentary ebb of emotion, she realized where she was and thought she had best go inside before some concerned neighbor came out or dialed 9-1-1.

Mindi was at the door, awaiting her, her usually happy demeanor somber. Kathryn knelt to her, knowing full well the dog sensed her every emotion. Mindi licked gently at her tears, pressing against her, offering comfort.

Kathryn stroked her briefly, then rose and dragged herself to her bedroom. She kicked off her shoes, peeled out of her raincoat and suit jacket and threw them on a chair. Unfastening her skirt, she slipped out of it and added the skirt to the pile on the chair. Wearily, she collapsed onto the bed, clad in blouse and underthings. Quickly and nimbly, Mindi jumped up beside her, pressing close.

Again, Kathryn cried. When the spot where her face lay became wet and cold, she moved her face to another, then another. And when her body finally could manufacture no more tears, she lay in stillness, hugging Mindi, aching, asking herself over and over, *Why? Why?* Eventually, she rolled onto her back and contemplated the ceiling through bleary eyes She realized she was terribly thirsty. The inside of her head felt cottony, and throbbed. Slowly, she sat up, then slid off the bed and went to the kitchen. She splashed water on her face at the sink, dried it, then drew a glassful from the tap.

Padding exhaustedly into the dark living room, she flopped on the couch, Mindi at her side. Emotionally numbed now, she drank the water and began to think. What Kyril had said all fit together logically, but it seemed beyond credence. Much as Kathryn had enjoyed movies like *Star Wars* and *E.T.*, she had never really had any thought that a being from some other world—or dimension—would manifest itself to her species, in her life time. Kyril's tale required a cognitive shift. If she understood correctly, Kyril's species must have been preying on human beings for centuries. How long, she wondered, had people been talking about vampires—and in how many cultures across the world?

She sighed, laying her head back. She tried to concentrate on Kyril: what she looked like, how it felt to touch her, the sound of her voice, the things she had said to Kathryn, the little oddities. The images she conjured of Kyril simply would not fit with the celluloid images from childhood matinees.

Suddenly, she thought of her mother, who had been none too pleased to have Kathryn tell her that she was a lesbian woman. Kathryn wondered if her mother, wherever she was, knew about Kyril. *Kyril,* she repeated idly to herself, *Kyril. . ..* Kathryn shook herself and sat up.

She gazed out the uncurtained windows, then, on an impulse, went to the back door and out into the yard, feeling the grass cold against her stockinged feet. There was a cool breeze blowing and the trees rustled comfortingly in the night. In the clear sky, stars shone, penetrating the city's light-haze, twinkling indifferently. While Mindi sniffed about and urinated, Kathryn hugged herself—wishing she were in some other part of the universe, where no one had to make choices, where there was no horror, and no pain. She breathed deeply of the crisp air. It heralded fall— and its coolness reminded her of Kyril. *Odd, that. You think of warmth as the thing desired—but so often, coolness can satisfy, as well.* Memories of their lovemaking tapped gently at her consciousness. She cried out within, *Kyril! Kyril, I love you so much!* This time, there was no answering reverberation. Instead, another inner voice mocked, *Yes, but could you live with a blood-sucker, something that preys on other creatures like yourself, or like Mindi?*

Over a sudden lump in her throat, she sighed heavily. She did not have the answer to that question. Turning, she dropped her arms and went back into the house. She undressed, brushed her teeth and fell into bed.

14

An early morning chill in the house nudged Kathryn from a dreamless sleep. She tucked the covers around her and snuggled sleepily next to Mindi for warmth. She realized she had forgotten to turn up the thermostat before turning in. She had not expected the early-season chill. Neither had she pulled the shades. In the grey before-dawn, she saw her clothes strewn on the floor and across the chair. Her clock showed just before six. Her eyes were puffy and the inside of her head felt as though it were filled with sawdust. As wakefulness progressed, it brought awareness that she was stiff and sore from her emotional explosion, and from sleeping clenched on herself.

She closed her eyes in remembrance of the cause, wanting to huddle in bed all day, not thinking, not feeling, not recognizing anything but sleep. She lay waiting for sleep to return. But she was too cold. She cracked an eye: 6:15. She groaned inwardly. There was no way around it, she would have to get up and turn on the heat.

Steeling herself against the movement and the cold, she grasped the covers, then threw them back. Running tiptoe over the bare floors, she hurried to the dining room and raised the thermostat to sixty-eight, noticing as she did so that the thermometer showed barely sixty. Shivering, she hurried back to the bedroom and dived under the covers, huddling next to Mindi. Shortly, she could hear the radiators popping as they filled, and, gradually, she was able to relax as the gentle heat filled the house.

This time, when she slept, she dreamed. Kyril and she were dancing, a wild, archaic dance, in a huge ballroom with a glassy floor where only they two moved. Both were clad in flowing gowns and crinolines of a century long passed. Their hands barely touched across the spread of their gowns, and she felt herself dragged down by the weight of the ancient apparel. She longed to shed them, to free herself of their confinement.

In a heart-beat, she stood naked in front of Kyril, who was now clothed in a black cloak with a high collar. As Kyril advanced on her, Kathryn became afraid. She began to back away, but all the doors to the huge room were closed and she knew she could not escape. Kyril glided across the floor without effort and leaned towards her, grasping at her with long fingers. Finally, she succeeded in pulling Kathryn inside the cloak with her. Kathryn could feel Kyril's icy body against hers, and quickly became aroused. Feeling her knees grow weak with desire, she tried to pull away, but Kyril held her firmly, pressing her lips against Kathryn's neck. Kathryn began to swoon, a wonderful lethargy overtaking her. Then Kyril pulled back and Kathryn saw the blood on her mouth—her blood. She opened her mouth to scream, and could not.

Bolt upright in the bed, she awoke, choking, struggling for breath, shaking all over. Mindi lay next to her, eyeing her askance. She gasped for air, feeling her heart pounding in her chest, looking fearfully around the room, half-expecting to see Kyril.

The room was filled with pale daylight now—the clock showed after seven. The sun outside the windows shone greyly, through overcast. The breeze of the night before had become a wind, and it looked like rain. The room was warmer, and she could feel the dampness in the air.

As the dream-spell dissipated, Kathryn's pulse and breathing slowed. Finally, she lay back, contemplating her day. Much as she would have liked to, it seemed she would not be able to lose herself in sleep. She considered her alternatives, then formulated a plan, By nine-thirty, she had bathed and dressed, eaten, picked up the key to a friend's cabin on the St. Croix River, and was in the stacks at the University library digging out books on vampires, psychosis, and physics. Early afternoon found her holed up, with Mindi, for an uninterrupted stint of reading, while a light rainfall pattered on the roof and river, enclosing her in a soft cocoon of isolation.

☾ ☾ ☾

Kyril slept late into the morning. When she awoke, she felt physically refreshed and energized from the living blood she had consumed the night before. She opened the bedroom drapes on the dreary, overcast day, knowing already what she must do.

An hour later, she was in her office, going over records and reports, checking for loose ends, setting things in order at the clinic. While she had wanted to oversee the entire operation of the clinic, she had not wanted to control her employees. Thus, she had structured a management system which could run without her, and had worked intimately with Mark Hamyl, against the necessity that she leave. That necessity was now upon her.

A few well-placed phone calls, and everything was attended to. On the answering machines of her fellow oupirian scientists, she left messages about her sudden departure. Hamyl was the last person she contacted.

"Doctor Hamyl—this is Kyril Vértök calling. I apologize for intruding on your weekend. However, it has become necessary for me to leave Minneapolis and return to my home immediately. I would like you to take over the direction of the clinic in my absence. I have left instructions about how to reach me in case of an emergency, and will be in touch with you from time to time."

She could hear the concern in the man's voice as he responded. He had proven to be as cordial as he had presented himself at their first meeting. "I'm very sorry to hear that. If there's anything else I can do to help. . . ."

"Thank you," she replied, "but I think not."

"Would you like me to come down there before you leave?"

"No, that is not necessary. You know everything you need to know about the operation of the clinic. All the records are available to you here. I have directed our accountant to increase your salary in compensation for the extra responsibilities."

Hamyl paused, not knowing what to say. Personal finances were something he seldom gave a thought to. "That will be appreciated, but—" He paused. "I hope all goes well for you, Doctor." He said no more. He had learned not to solicit details of her private life.

"Good-bye, Doctor Hamyl."

He hesitated before replying. He genuinely liked the woman, but knew of no way to get past the shield of European formality she so carefully maintained. It seemed that only Kathryn Hartell had been allowed to penetrate that cool exterior. As usual, Hamyl was left with a feeling of sadness at Kyril's emotional isolation. He wondered if Kathryn Hartell were going to accompany her to Hungary. He hoped so. "Good-bye, Doctor Vértök."

Kyril completed her tasks in the office, including calling the delivery service and cancelling the standing orders for blood for her cache. Then, taking what few personal things had been in her office with her, she left the clinic and returned to the hotel. There, she packed her suitcases, dressed in an unremarkable grey linen suit, and summoned a porter. She checked out of the AmFac, telling the desk manager that she had been unexpectedly called home. In the drizzle, she entered the waiting taxi cab, ordering the driver to take her to the airport.

At the airport, she picked up a ticket in her name for a flight to Budapest, via JFK. She went to a cafeteria, bought coffee, and sat scanning the paper for any mention of a death on Fifth Avenue North. Shortly, she was joined by another woman who resembled Kyril very much in dress and appearance. Over cigarettes and coffee, the woman casually passed a magazine to Kyril, who inconspicuously inserted the airplane ticket in it, then returned it to the other. After her compatriot had left, Kyril disposed of her newspaper, having found nothing in it about the killing, and went to retrieve her luggage from the porter whom she had hired to watch it. Descending to the baggage claim area, she exited the terminal and hailed a taxi. She directed the driver to the airport Sheraton, where she claimed a room reservation under another name. After leaving a message on Kathryn's answering machine, she settled in to wait for Kathryn's call.

❮ ❮ ❮

Sunday was wet and chill with the late-September rain that drenched all of southern Minnesota. The view of the city, coming in on the freeway from the east, was breathtaking. *My city!* Kathryn's heart resonated in response. Never had she felt so at home, so fast, as she had in Minneapolis. The IDS Tower was wreathed in clouds and mist, and a haze hovered in the evening air. She *belonged,* here. And she knew it.

Pulling in late, and bone-weary, Kathryn hauled in her overnight bag and the box of books from the library while Mindi sniffed busily in the wet grass. She deposited her things on the living room floor and went back to fetch the sodden Sunday paper from the front step.

As she sat down to a hastily assembled supper, she peeled apart the paper and gasped at the headlines on the front page of the Metro section: GRISLY "VAMPIRE" MURDER BAFFLES POLICE. Her stomach knotted, and she read on, forgetting to eat:

GRISLY "VAMPIRE" MURDER BAFFLES POLICE
By Neal Vaughn, Staff Writer

Kurt Svensen, 26, of 505 Fifth Avenue North, Minneapolis, died late Friday night in his loft apartment. According to the coroner's report, nearly all the blood had been drained from the victim's body through a puncture on his neck. This is the latest in a series of apparently related killings which began last spring. In each case, the body of the victim had been drained of blood through a similar wound.

Svensen's body was discovered early Saturday morning by police who were called to the scene when friends were unable to rouse anyone inside the apartment. Michael Finlayson, identified as a friend of Svensen's, was found unconscious just inside the door to the apartment. Finlayson is hospitalized in Hennepin County Medical Center with a fractured

skull and other injuries. As of today, police have been unable
to question Finlayson.
There are no suspects in this or any of the other murders.
No one reports having seen or heard anyone entering or
leaving the building where Svensen lived. According to the
friends who notified the police, Svensen had left the
MinniApple night club alone and headed back to his apartment on foot. Finlayson and the other friends, who have
declined to be identified, were to have met Svensen at his
apartment at approximately 2:00 a.m.
Anyone having information about any of these killings is
urged to contact Minneapolis police.

Kathryn's originally meager appetite had been replaced by a sick
feeling in her gut. There was no question in her mind that Kyril was
responsible for Svensen's death. "Oh, God," she whispered, her forehead
in her hand, thinking of the dead man—and of Kyril. Suddenly, she needed
to vomit.

Pushing back from the table, she ran into the bathroom and flung
up the toilet seat. She bent over the bowl and retched. Having eaten
nothing, she could bring up little but bile and saliva. When the urge had
passed, she stood shakily and flushed the toilet, washed her face and
brushed her teeth, then stumbled into the bedroom. In the dark, the red
light on her answering machine flashed like a blinking eye,

She hesitated, unsure that she wanted to hear the message on the
tape if it were Kyril's. Reluctantly, she went to the machine and rewound
the tape. There were three calls. The first person had hung up without
leaving a message; the second call was from Megan, wanting to talk with
Kathryn. Then came Kyril's voice, uncharacteristically hesitant, and a
little tinny on the electronic device: "Kathryn—I have left my suite at the
AmFac and checked into a hotel near the airport, pending my departure.
I shall wait until next Friday to hear from you. If you have not been in touch
by then, I will know that it is futile to hope." She completed the message
with a phone number.

Kathryn's stomach lurched again at the word "departure." The
tears burned at the back of her eyes as she listened to Kyril's message a
second time, then wrote down the number Kyril had given. Wrapping her
arms around her middle, she began to cry, the ache an endless, dragging
need. "Kyril," she whispered again and again, beseeching the universe for
an answer to her dilemma.

When Monday morning dawned, bright, but still damp and chill,
she knew she could not face work. She re-set her alarm to call in sick.

Finally arising around nine, she ate a small breakfast, then set herself to reviewing what she had gleaned from her weekend's readings.

It seemed that vampires were the stuff of legends, myths, and superstitions in nearly every culture across the world—from ancient through modern times. The details varied—like whether or not garlic would keep them from one's door, or whether or not they could cross running water—but the essence of each was the same: A vampire was something not-human which consumed the life-force of its human victim, either literally or figuratively. The presence of vampire tales all over the world lent credence to the notion that so-called vampires were real creatures of some sort who moved among human beings and preyed upon them. Accepting that as fact—

Unless, of course, Kyril is mad, that inner doomsayer taunted her again.

Kathryn had listened to that voice over the weekend, had given serious consideration to the possibility it trumpeted, had even found case studies of people who believed themselves to be vampires in the psychology books she had checked out of the university library. But the descriptions of those unfortunates did not fit the Kyril she knew. Instinctively sure of her judgements about people, Kathryn now rejected, once and for all, that possible explanation for Kyril's story.

So, accepting the premise that there were real creatures known to human culture as vampires, the question became, where these creatures originated. If not human, then what were they?

According to Kyril, they were of a parallel dimension in space/time. The physics books Kathryn had obtained could no more than postulate the possibility of inter-dimensional travel. Perhaps only Kyril's people knew the secret of how such a phenomenon might take place. Kyril had said that their technology was more advanced than that of *homo sapiens. They. Their.* Kathryn had even found a word similar to the one Kyril had used to describe her people in one of the books she had read: *obours.* The word was from an old northern European dialect, and meant "undead." Could Kyril's people's presence in this dimension actually have affected the language, customs, and cultures of human beings? Kathryn shuddered. It seemed too much to be coincidence—and it did not seem to her that Kyril would attempt to perpetrate some sick joke.

Several times that day, Kathryn picked up the phone to call Kyril, but never managed to dial the number she had been given. Whether or not Kyril was leaving, there was a sickness inside Kathryn that needed to be purged before—if ever—she could speak with Kyril again.

15

athryn put down her fork and fixed her attention on the television as the newscaster's voice droned on.

". . .Finlayson was questioned today for the first time about the murder of Kurt Svensen last Saturday morning in his Minneapolis apartment. According to Finlayson, there was a tall woman with dark hair bending over the body of his friend when he pushed open the door to the apartment shortly before 2 a.m. Finlayson says he saw blood on the woman's mouth before she attacked him, slamming him into the doorframe so hard that he suffered a fractured skull and dislocated vertebrae in his neck.

"Police now believe the murder suspect may have been a man in women's clothing, and have issued a composite likeness of the suspect, with and without the long hair.

That's logical, Kathryn thought. With all the drag queens that frequented the gay bars on the north end of Hennepin Avenue, and with the evident strength of the suspect, it seemed perfectly reasonable to her that the police had arrived at such a hypothesis. *The thing is, I know they're wrong.* She stared at the charcoal drawing on the screen. Relieved that it did not really resemble Kyril, she let out a breath.

It was Thursday. She had stumbled through work for three days and had only one more day in which to decide if she were going to contact Kyril, or let her leave without speaking to her. As yet, she had spoken to no one about the matter. Megan had her own difficulties right now, besides which, Kathryn did not think her friend would be much help in sorting all this out. Eileen, she was sure, would have her questioning her *own* sanity. Neither alternative was attractive to her. So, she felt completely trapped in her dilemma.

On an impulse, she shut off the television and went to the telephone. Ambivalent, she stood over it, heart pounding in her chest, butterflies fluttering in her stomach. She had long ago memorized the number she was to call, but had not yet been able to dial it. She reached hesitantly for the phone just as it rang. Starting violently, she grabbed the receiver to still its jangling.

"Hello! " she demanded shakily.

"Kathryn." Kyril's voice sounded hollow, devoid of its usual command.

Kathryn swallowed. "Kyril! I—I was just—" As she began to speak, doubt engulfed her again, and she found herself unable to continue. The words stuck in her throat.

Kyril's voice came softly over the line. "Kathryn—I could not wait any longer for you to call. I've received a message—I must leave as soon as possible."

Kathryn felt her heart plunge into a swirl of emotion that was both hers and Kyril's. "Leave?" Suddenly, she was quite sure of her feeling about that. "Oh, please—you mustn't leave. Not yet—I—I want to talk to you—"

"I have a flight out tomorrow, mid-morning." She waited.

Kathryn fought madly to gather her wits. "Then—see me tonight. Come here— No, I'll come there— Oh, whatever—just—" She took a deep, steadying breath. "Just don't leave without seeing me. Please."

After a moment's deliberation, "You come here," Kyril directed.

"Fine. Where are you?" Kathryn wrote down the name of the hotel and the suite number. "I'll be there—within the hour."

"Hurry," Kyril whispered into the phone, biting back other words, words she feared might betray her.

Kathryn hung up the phone, weak with relief. Although she did not yet know just what she would say—or do—when she saw Kyril, at least she was freed from the terrible inaction of the past few days. Grabbing her keys and wallet, she called to Mindi. "Guard the house, girl," she ordered, giving the dog's ample ears a quick rub. Then she yanked her lightweight jacket off the hook in the hall and rushed out the door. As she reached the car, she realized she had never finished her supper. *At this rate, I won't have to worry about my winter things fitting,* she commented to herself.

She was surprised to discover that traffic on the freeway was heavy—then remembered it was the tail-end of rush hour. Cursing silently at the delay, she maneuvered in and out, slowly making her way to Kyril. As she finally broke free of the congestion and began to speed up, it hit her that, in her hurry to be gone, she had forgotten to check her map or phone the hotel desk to see what exit to take to get to the airport Sheraton. She kept a lookout for it, but missed it the first time around. Cursing aloud by now, she got off and turned around, heading back west. Then she saw the sign off to the north of the freeway and pulled off onto the exit ramp. Within five minutes, she was parked in the large surface lot, out of the car, and headed for the lobby.

Her heart pounded erratically as she asked the doorman for directions to the elevator banks that would carry her to Kyril's floor. She counted off the floors, realizing that her hands were perspiring. Was it from fear, or anticipation? As the doors opened onto a plushly carpeted hallway, she checked her direction, then made a right turn. Hesitantly, she moved from door to door, seeking the one behind which Kyril waited.

At the end of the corridor, a door opened to reveal Kyril standing within. "Kathryn," she said.

The sibilance rippled over Kathryn, and she wanted to run to her, to fling herself through the door and into the waiting arms. But the unresolved feelings within restrained her. She moved slowly toward Kyril, still unsure—of herself, of how to proceed. She wanted Kyril with an intensity born of having loved and lost, of years of loneliness and lack of emotional fulfillment. But another part of her had learned to be cautious, to reserve trust. And that trust had been dangerously undermined in the past few days. She was not yet able to restore it. She stopped in front of Kyril, who stood, clothed in a satin dressing gown, her hands tightly clasped, in the open door. Looking up into the dark eyes, Kathryn sought answers to her questions. She found anguish, and doubt.

"I'm so glad you've come," Kyril whispered. "I thought I might never...see you again." Her voice threatened to break and the breath heaved in her chest. "Kathryn—I have missed you so terribly—" She reached out, wavered, not quite touching Kathryn's shoulders, sensing the doubt in Kathryn.

Kathryn's gaze faltered, then returned to Kyril's. "Could we go in?" she asked quietly, nodding at the empty suite behind Kyril.

Wordlessly, Kyril led them into the sitting room. She stopped short of the couch and turned abruptly to Kathryn. Her eyes searched Kathryn's as she sought to apprehend Kathryn's feelings, and she reached out from within, wanting to convey her own. She too was confused. She had realized during her week of waiting that she had come too close to this human woman to ever feel the same about anything again. In her own way, Kathryn had changed her as much as Lanaea's death had. And Mark Hamyl, with his passionate concern for the lives of others—most of whom he would never know—had made his impact on the unremitting abhorrence for the human species that she had carried with her into this dimension. She needed for Kathryn to know she was not the heartless killer she feared Kathryn thought her. But how to tell her? She sensed Kathryn's lack of resolve and knew that they must talk, attempt to achieve a greater clarity between them.

She sat on the couch, pulling Kathryn down with her. She held the warm, unresisting hand, tracing the back of it with her fingers. Looking at their two hands, she thought of the strength that resided in the hand with the long, gracefully moving fingers—and of the tender firmness in the smaller hand that was caressed by those fingers. Ever did the differences between them emerge to remind her that they were not of the same ilk, that they shared little but the emotional and sexual bond they had made.

After what seemed a long silence, Kathryn withdrew her hand gently from Kyril's grasp. "Where are you going?" she asked softly.

Kyril took a deep breath. "Home—to Kornägy." She saw the sudden pain in Kathryn's eyes and her heart lurched. "AIDS has apparently infected others of us. I am needed there. My first commitment must now be to my own people." She paused, looking down, inward, hesitant at laying out her feelings for Kathryn again. "I did not want to go without saying good-bye." Her quick glance beseeched Kathryn to grant her a meaningful leave-taking.

"Had you planned on staying here. . .in this dimension?"

Kyril hesitated. "I had not decided. . . I had wanted to wait... would have waited, longing for your call. . . to know that you had overcome your . . . aversion. . .would have given you the time you needed. . . ." She smiled thinly, the brimming tears in her dark eyes shining with the light from an electric candelabrum.

Kathryn closed her eyes, feeling Kyril's desire for her roll over her like a wave. But, as had happened every time she shut her eyes since that night in that *other* hotel room, images of evil creatures sucking the life blood of human beings flashed across her inner vision. There was absolutely no way she could reconcile those images with the woman she knew. She sensed no evil in Kyril, even though she was absolutely certain that she had killed Kurt Svensen by draining his body of blood. She wanted to believe Kyril's words about the necessity for her to feed in order to survive, and she was realizing at that moment that she could continue to torment herself with the ghoulish pictures—or, she could accept that she still was unable to assimilate all the implications of what Kyril had told her, and go on from there. She sighed, shuddered, and opened her eyes.

"Kyril, I can *not* put all this together yet—but I want to try. I want some time to try. . .please."

Kyril shook her head gently. "Kathryn, Kathryn—"

"Please. Why must you leave so quickly? Can't it wait a few days?"

"It cannot. I must go, now." She thought of attempting to explain to Kathryn that there were only certain periods during which the parallel dimensions were in optimal interface, but gave it up as a sidetrack. The larger issue was that she no longer had any real choice. AIDS had become the nemesis of her kind, and she must face it on her own ground.

Kathryn's eyes filled with tears. "Kyril, I don't begin to understand *how* all the things you've told me are possible. . .but, you are the only person I have ever given myself to so completely. . .the only one I've ever trusted with my inner self. Even though I have sensed your reserve, I have loved you. . .*so deeply*. . . . Please, don't leave now. . .not yet. . .please." She swallowed a whimper of desperation.

Kyril reached out, softly stroking the hair at her temple. "My love—other than Lanaea, *no* one has touched me as you have—" She sighed heavily, dropping her hand. "But I *must* rejoin my own people— I have more first-hand knowledge of this disease complex than any other oupir. Can't you see that that creates a responsibility larger than my own needs—or wants?"

"Then—then—" Kathryn cast around for an argument, any argument, to forestall the premature ending of their relationship. In exasperation, without really thinking of what she was saying, she urged, "Take me with you." Surprised to find that she meant the words, she repeated, "Take me with you—I—I could help you. With my knowledge of AIDS and my research training, I could help you with your work."

Kyril gazed at her suspiciously. "Kathryn," she began again.

"Wait, listen!" she urged, ad libbing as she went. "Is there anyone there who knows as much about AIDS as I do? Anyone else who has done *any* kind of research, be it armchair or clinical?"

"Not about AIDS—you know that—"

"Then I could help you," she went on, gathering momentum with the logic of her arguments. "I've been doing my own research." Kyril appraised her, mildly surprised. "There's a growing body of clinical literature in the field of wholistic medicine which links other impairments of the immune system with AIDS. Like candidiasis, for example."

"What is that?" Kyril's brow wrinkled.

"Systemic yeast infection," A skeptical expression flittered on Kyril's face. "Yeah, well most of the traditional medical community in this country doesn't 'believe' in it either." Kathryn shook her head. "But I'm convinced. The widespread use of antibiotics in this country in the 1950s and '60s has resulted in changes in the immune systems of those in this country who took so many of them—namely, the generations born in the '40s and '50s. Now, today, twenty-odd years later, the clinical picture indicates widespread infection with candida—which, one might say, is in itself an acquired immune deficiency."

Kyril opened her mouth as if to speak but Kathryn went steadily on. "Add to the antibiotic use the invasion of chemical pollutants both within and without the home during this time, and you've got a picture of internal and external conditions which assault the immune system invisibly." She paused.

"So—what is the clinical approach to treating this candidiasis?" Kyril asked, clearly interested.

"Complete systemic cleansing—through diet, herbal, and sometimes homeopathic methods. And the administration of therapies found to be effective against the candida organism—such as nystatin."

Kyril demurred reluctantly. "I'm sorry, Kathryn, I just don't think any of this would apply to ou—"

"Kyril—if nothing else, you wouldn't have to work alone. Nor would you have to take time to train someone else. I could do both—assist you and train others." Kathryn's hands punctured the air, as if she could win her point by the force of her gestures.

Kyril hesitated, genuinely wanting to believe that Kathryn was somehow essential to her success in Kornägy. Then she shook her head. "It could never work, Kathryn. My world would be far more alien to you than yours is to me. I can feed here—how would you nourish yourself? And our customs are totally unfamiliar to you—our technology—"

"Oh, come on! Your technical equipment can't be *all* that different. Surely there are enough similarities—"

"Kathryn, *listen* to me. There are other reasons." She steeled herself, resisting the hard reality. "It is prohibited."

Kathryn was brought up short. "What?"

"It is Law: No oupir may bring a human through the dimensional boundary."

"But—but why?"

"There are many reasons why the law was established as it is. I can not take you with me."

"Kyril—please: *don't* leave me alone here."

There was a huge silence while Kyril eyed her bleakly, feeling the emptiness inside Kathryn reverberate with longing. She closed her eyes, remembering Lanaea, feeling again her own pain, the loss. She knew Kathryn implored her out of that same primordial need to bond with another creature of one's own kind, to ease for a time the existential aloneness, to soften one's passage through life, to unite diverse sexual energies. As she plumbed the depths of her own soul, she felt again that life without Lanaea would be life without passion, without purpose—a shell of what it was meant to be. She thought that she had been exceptionally gifted to have been presented a second chance at such a bond in her meeting with Kathryn. She guessed that Kathryn's life would be as barren as hers if they could not be together And yet, Kathryn was *not* of her own kind. . . . With a shudder, she opened her eyes. The prohibitions were deeply ingrained.

"Kathryn," she whispered, at a loss for the words she needed. "Give me a little more time to think about it."

Suddenly Kathryn sagged against the couch. She had been tensed all over as she struggled to an awareness of the depth of her bonding with Kyril. Now she wanted physical connection. "Hold me," she demanded hollowly, the energy gone out of her.

Kyril moved towards Kathryn, pulling her into her arms. Having grown accustomed to holding her while lying together, this sitting on the couch made Kyril feel awkward. After a moment, she picked Kathryn up and carried her into the bedroom. Tenderly, she deposited the other woman on the wide bed. Then, undoing the flimsy tie of her own negligee, she let it fall from her shoulders to the floor.

But before Kyril could climb onto the bed, Kathryn stood and reached to the shoulder ties on Kyril's gown. With trembling fingers, she loosened the soft knots. Gently, Kathryn slid the satiny fabric off Kyril's breasts, over her buttocks. Gown and robe huddled in a silken pool at their feet as Kathryn's hands brushed over the softness of Kyril's skin, raising goosebumps in their trail.

Surprised, Kyril hesitated for a moment, but Kathryn's hungry mouth on hers drove out any doubt about Kathryn's intentions. She unfastened the buttons of Kathryn's cotton blouse and peeled it off with her jacket. Her hands caressed the warm shoulders, brushing the bra straps down, She reached behind and freed the catches. The silky bra joined Kyril's robe and gown on the floor. Her cool fingers sought the fastener of Kathryn's jeans, and she pushed them down off Kathryn's hips.

In one move, Kathryn stepped out of her panties and the pile of clothing. Then, taking Kyril's hand, she returned to the bed. With the rayon coverlet underneath, and Kyril above, Kathryn felt enclosed in a cool, smooth envelope. The inner hunger drove away fear, pain, doubt— and, for the moment, even the horror she had felt when last they were together. She longed to merge with Kyril, for their flesh to become one flesh, their breath one breath—to fill the emptiness within her body with the spirit of her lover, her mate. She clutched at Kyril, willing her to stay with her, impelling her to satisfy that longing.

Kyril struggled against the depth that Kathryn demanded, want-ing to sink down into her own need to mate-bond with this woman, yet terrified of another sundering. The sexual heat seared her, scorching the last of her reserves, threatening to incinerate her remaining defenses. Anguish escaped her with a cry. "Ah, Kathryn—I cannot," she lamented, shaking her head. "I *must* return to Kornägy—and I cannot take you with me." She closed her eyes on the refusal, knifed by her grief.

Kathryn collapsed against the bed, desire suddenly extinguished. "Then I can't stay—"

"No, please," Kyril urged softly. "After tonight—" She did not finish the thought.

Kathryn eyed her tiredly, unable to decide whether it would be easier to part now, or have to say good-bye in the morning.

"Kathryn, please," Kyril whispered again.

Kathryn saw the anguish in Kyril's eyes and decided she, too, wanted every last moment together. "Then come to my place," she replied. "I can't leave Mindi alone all night."

Gratefully, Kyril nodded,

Quietly, they dressed and walked out into the cool air. The night again bordered on crisp, and Kathryn knew Minnesota winter was but a few weeks away. They climbed into the car and drove in an undefined silence to Kathryn's home. There, they made love measuredly. Afterwards, Kyril waited for Kathryn to fall asleep, then arose. In a robe borrowed from Kathryn's closet, she went into the living room and knelt on a cushion in the middle of the floor. Mindi pattered along behind her.

She centered herself for meditation as Mindi lay down beside her. Going inward, she sought guidance from an inner voice. The profound silence there disturbed her deeply. After a time, she reluctantly acceded to the silence and came out of trance. Having gained no peace of mind, she was, at least, more relaxed physically and found it possible to sleep.

Around dawn, Kyril awoke to the sound of her name.

"Kyril," Kathryn whispered sleepily, "I dreamed. . .we were together in these high mountains. . . ." She paused, searching groggily for the dream filaments.

Stunned, Kyril realized she had been having the same dream. "Yes—we were going to the Point of Interface—the dimensional crossing." As she said the words, she accepted that her unconscious had provided her with the answer she had sought unfruitfully just a few hours before. *Goddess, thank you,* she uttered silently.

Unaware of the import of the shared dream, Kathryn had already sunk back into sleep. Kyril cradled her, formulating the details of a plan for Kathryn's journey. With the sunrise, Kyril awoke her softly and told her of the dream's significance. They made love again in the thin sunlight. Their parting, now only temporary, was sweeter than either could have conceived the evening before.

16

Before she left Minneapolis, Kathryn knew she must speak with Megan, try to explain what she was doing. She knew it would not be easy. She could not tell Megan where she was really going—she only *half* believed it herself. Nevertheless, the day after she knew that she would be accompanying Kyril, she called and invited herself to Megan and Joel's home for later in the week.

The couple was living in a duplex in north Minneapolis, where they had moved when they learned that Joel was ill. Kathryn located it without too much difficulty. The neighborhood was blue-collar, with small, unadorned houses, neatly kept yards, and lots of young families. Kathryn parked on the street, then headed up the walk, pausing for a moment to look around, admiring the clear, crisp early-autumn afternoon. Fall and spring were her favorite seasons—she was going to regret missing the changing of the leaves and the first snow.

"Hi, Kathryn." Kathryn turned. Clad in oversized t-shirt and knit pants, Megan was coming down the walk toward her. Her pregnancy showed clearly now, and she seemed fairly at ease with her state. "I saw you drive up. Isn't it a beautiful day?" Megan smiled, turning her face up to bask in the warm sun.

In the unguarded moment, Kathryn could see the strain written on that face, beneath the smile. Mentally, she groaned. What she had to say could only add to it.

They walked into the house, arm in arm. "You're looking good," Kathryn complimented. Blushing gratefully, Megan left her at the door to hang up Kathryn's jacket. Kathryn gazed around curiously. The familiar furnishings were typical of her friends who were middle-income or students—well-worn furniture, throw rugs on hardwood floors in need of refinishing, lots of green plants, and the inevitable stereo and record collection. She concluded that, though not distinctive, the atmosphere was, as usual, quite homey.

"How about some tea?" Megan asked as she returned from the bedroom.

Kathryn started to decline, wanting to get on with her unpleasant task, but then thought better of it. "All right," she agreed. She accompanied Megan to the small kitchen, which was filled with the delightful fragrances of herbs and loose-leaf teas. Each chose her brew. They made small talk about the baby while the water heated, then poured their cups full and went back into the living area. They sat opposite one another, Megan on the battered couch, Kathryn in an aged armchair.

"So, why did you want to see me?" Megan began. She eyed Kathryn directly, having sensed her unease and guessed that something was up. "I haven't been able to get you over here in the three months since we moved in, and then you call up out of the blue and want to visit!"

Kathryn was disconcerted. She had wanted to be the one to broach the subject. After a moment, she set her cup down and returned Megan's gaze. Taking a deep breath, she began.

"I wanted to tell you that I'm going away for a while." She saw surprise, then pain, flit across Megan's face. "I wanted to *see* you because I know I had more or less promised to be around for you—"

Megan set her cup down, folded her arms across her chest, and looked out the window.

Kathryn watched her friend, knowing she must be feeling let down and rejected; she herself felt she was betraying a trust. "I—I'm sorry, Megan." She stopped again, hearing her voice quake.

After a moment, Megan looked back at her. "Are you going with Kyril?" The hazel eyes stabbed into hers, demanding the truth.

Kathryn nodded. "She's been called home—they need her expertise. They—they've discovered the presence of AIDS in. . . in her country. The—the government. . .you know, it's communist. . . ." Kathryn allowed her voice to trail off weakly. She hated lying, and especially to a friend. But she refused to elaborate on what she had said.

Megan's eyes questioned, *Why you? Why are you going with her?*

Kathryn faltered. *Because I can't* **bear** *to lose her, not even for a moment,* she wanted to shout. Instead she said, "I want to be with her, and I believe I can help in training some of her staff, getting them up to date with what's known about AIDS."

Megan's expression was incredulous. "You don't speak Hungarian—do you?"

"No, but I—they speak English—" She broke off in exasperation. "That isn't the issue and you know it. The issue is about a promise I made to you that I'm not going to be able to keep because I'm going with Kyril."

They eyed each other in silence again. Then Megan spoke. "She's more important to you than I am." Her voice was quiet, all the anger gone out of it.

Kathryn's fists knotted. *"Please* don't frame it in those terms." She saw that Megan's defeat was unrelenting. "Megan—you are my friend. I love you. But I am in love with Kyril—I want a chance to build something more with her, something more substantial than stolen moments from the rest of our lives." She paused, relinquishing the words reluctantly. "I care for her so *much,* Megan," she said softly. She went on, her voice gaining in strength. "She and I have been apart more than together in the time we've known each other. I—don't want to let her out of my life again. She's going to be gone for a long time, and I'm going with her." She paused again, then went on less forcefully.

"I'm truly sorry I won't be here for you—I was looking forward to sharing this experience with you. After all—I figured it's the closest *I'd* ever get to being a mother." She caught Megan's eye, saw a smile force its way to her lips. "Megan, I *am sorry."* She allowed the roughness in her voice, wanting Megan to know she felt a genuine regret about breaking her commitment.

Megan sighed, uncrossed her arms, then clasped her hands in front of her. "I know," she said in a whisper, "I know you are. And I'm angry. But, mostly, I'm hurt, and I'll *miss* sharing this all with you. You're like my sister, you know—the one I never had."

Kathryn was touched, and surprised, by Megan's declaration. "No, I didn't know," she whispered. She rose and went to sit beside her on the couch as Megan nodded, holding back tears. Slipping their arms around one another, they embraced for a long moment. When Megan pulled back, Kathryn kissed the shorter woman tenderly on top of the head. Wordlessly, they sat for a few moments longer, holding hands, drinking their lukewarm tea.

"When are you leaving?" Megan finally asked, her voice small and hushed.

"Not for a couple of days yet." Kathryn waited, hoping Megan would suggest they spend some time together before her departure.

"Could we. . . get together before you leave?"

Kathryn squeezed Megan's hand tightly. "I'd love it! In fact, I've saved tomorrow evening, hoping you'd be free." She grinned happily, relieved.

Megan smiled, the warmth reaching her eyes. "That would be great."

They worked out the details, then Kathryn collected her coat and left. Her final good-bye to Megan could wait until tomorrow. She still had a great deal to do to ready herself—and Mindi—for their trip abroad.

Once home, she had several phone calls to make. The first was to a gay couple whom she had recently met through her work with the AIDS project.

Kent Lowry and Rob Castillio were men in their fifties who had been together for nearly twenty-five years. In her astonishment at the longevity of their relationship, Kathryn had queried them about its success. They had said that it was due to mutual trust and the fact that they had had an open relationship for many of those years. However, with the advent of AIDS, that openness had proven to be double-edged—for now Rob had AIDS and had lost his job and insurance benefits, and they had already spent thousands of dollars out of their pockets on his health care.

On an impulse, Kathryn had called and offered them her house to live in while she was to be gone. Having had a couple of days to think about it, she was certain she had done the right thing, for it would mean the men could sell their expensive home in Arden Hills and live much more cheaply in Kathryn's house, stretching their financial resources further. Kent would be closer to his work, and she would have the peace of mind of knowing someone trustworthy would be looking after her home in her absence.

After finalizing the details of the transfer of keys and information about the house, Kathryn went on to other calls, one of which was to her therapist. They talked briefly on the phone, in between client appointments.

Kathryn did not try to explain why she was going, knowing she could neither disclose to Eileen Kyril's claim about who she truly was nor affirm her own complete belief in it. Instead, she informed her that she was accompanying Kyril on a research venture to Hungary, and that she would be gone for an indefinite period of time.

Eileen was clearly concerned at the suddenness of Kathryn's decision. "How much of this has to do with AIDS and how much with not wanting to let go of Kyril, Kathryn? I know it's only been a few months since she returned from out East —but are you willing to completely uproot your life to go to a foreign country, a communist country, no less, to be with someone whom you've known for so short a period?"

Kathryn winced as the questions hit home. She did not want to admit to Eileen what she had admitted to Megan—that being in love with Kyril was all that mattered right now—and hear her judgement questioned. She knew that she had seized on the idea of the expertise she could lend to Kyril's work as a lever in her argument to be allowed to accompany Kyril. She knew also that Eileen would spot the weakness in that argument, especially without real knowledge of where they were going. She herself could hardly afford to examine her choice, lest she see it as folly and decide not to go. She avoided answering Eileen's question directly, and said, with a trace of trepidation in her voice, "It has to do with both. It is a good professional opportunity for me, and an effort that I care deeply about." She forced all her sincerity into her last words. Eileen, sensing that Kathryn was keeping something from her as well as that she had no wish to discuss whatever it was, replied, reservation evident in her voice. "I hope that the choice you have made proves to be a wise one for you, Kathryn."

Kathryn heard, and chose to ignore, the doubt she knew Eileen entertained. "So do I," she said. *So do I.* She sighed. "Well—I better go. I have a few more calls to make. I just wanted to let you know where I'll be so you won't worry about me."

"I'm glad you called—and I'll be thinking of you and wishing you success. Let me hear from you when you've returned."

"I will." Kathryn struggled with the tears burning at the back of her throat. "I'll miss you," she said, her voice breaking.

"And I you. I send you a hug."

Kathryn felt the warmth in the other's voice and welcomed it. "Thanks. Good-bye."

After they hung up, she indulged briefly in her sadness at saying good-bye for an extended period. Eileen had become her surrogate mother and dear friend—and she knew she would, indeed, miss her. The conversation had reminded her that, except for Mindi, she would be totally alone in this new place to which Kyril was taking her.

She was afraid.

17

The wind moaned down off the high mountains, icing the rocky crags with its cold. There were already sparse patches of snow on the ground, and, in spite of the clear sky, Kyril knew it could not be too long before an early winter storm would drop more.

Clothed in winter mountain gear, and somewhat sheltered from the wind at the bottom of a cliff, Kyril and Kathryn were relatively comfortable in the near-zero temperature. They had camped near the dimensional boundary, and awaited the full moon, the period of optimal dimensional interface. Mindi's labrador-mix, auburn coat was thick enough to protect her as she roamed about the vicinity of the campsite, her nose leading her from one adventure to another.

The dog's presence had been debated forcefully, if briefly. Kyril knew that other non-humanoid species had wandered through the Interface from time to time without harm. So, having violated the prohibition by permitting Kathryn to come with her, her resistance to Mindi's accompanying them had been short lived.

Kyril had kept her travel plans and gone on ahead of Kathryn to Budapest. While waiting for Kathryn to join her, she had made arrangements for their journey into the Carpathians and taken care of sundry business details, such as pulling the strings that would allow Mindi to be transported without having to undergo the international quarantines. Eventually unable to conceal the fact that Kathryn was to accompany her through the Interface, Kyril had met with subsequent resistance from local members of the oupirian network. Refusing as always to explain herself, she had attempted merely to negotiate transportation to the site. When that failed, she had simply gone to the human sector and made all her arrangements there.

Now, a scant ten days after Kyril's departure from Minneapolis, she and Kathryn huddled around their campfire, taking advantage of what warmth the daylight had to offer at this altitude. Kathryn, unused to travelling transcontinentally, was still feeling disoriented. Having arrived in Hungary only two days ago, and then being transported by helicopter to their campsite just the evening before, she had scarcely had time to think. She sat on a log, cradling her cup of hot soup, trying to sort out where to begin.

She decided the best place to start was with her confusion. "Kyril, I understood that you had to return home immediately." Kyril nodded. "But now we have two more days to wait until the full moon—so why did everything have to be done in such a rush?"

"In case of delay, I wanted as much time as possible." Her accent was thicker now than when she had been living in Minneapolis. Hungarian was close to her native tongue. Speaking Hungarian the past few days had brought her back to that tongue, making English seem very foreign and very far from natural.

"So now we sit? And wait?"

Kyril nodded again, then smiled briefly, flicking her dark eyes at Kathryn. "And talk, if you like."

Kathryn sipped her soup. Fearful of losing her resolve to be direct, she plunged ahead. "And how will *you* feed, while we wait?" she inquired, her voice shaky.

"I fed yesterday, before we left Budapest," Kyril replied evenly. "Since we were flown in here, I shan't need to feed again until we cross the Boundary."

Kathryn blinked at her, trying to remember when Kyril had been gone long enough to. . . . She stopped, realizing she had no idea how long such a thing would take. "Oh," she said, eyeing the cup of soup, her appetite suddenly diminished. Kyril told her she had purchased enough food supplies to last Kathryn several weeks. It was difficult to remember that Kyril did not need to eat as often as she did.

"So, what next?" Kathryn posed, smiling woodenly.

Choosing to ignore Kathryn's obvious discomfort, Kyril poked at the fire with a stick. "I should like to tell you more about Kornägy— if you'd like to hear."

Kathryn studied her again, and with an effort of will, was able to recover the feelings that had impelled her to beg Kyril to bring her to Kornägy. "Yes," she nodded, "I'd like that."

Kyril, apprehending the genuineness of Kathryn's response, relaxed. "Where to begin?" she mused aloud. After a moment, she decided:

"Kornägian civilization is very old. During the thousands of years that it took the peoples of your world to band together and begin to create culture, the peoples of Kornägy had already begun to fight their wars of nationalism. Having previously struggled from local to national consciousness, they were struggling toward international consciousness. Over thousands of Cycles of Seasons—hundreds of your centuries—our peoples continued to fight for the domination of one another and the land. When a plague—brought from this dimension into ours—decimated huge segments of the animal populations on whom we depended for our existence, the peoples of our world were forced to recognize that only by orderly cooperation could all survive."

"You've been travelling through dimensional space. . .for centuries?" Kathryn said incredulously.

Kyril nodded, then proceeded with her narrative. "Eventually, national boundaries were dissolved—as had been the racial and ethnic boundaries long before—and we became united as one people, a global society whose energies were now free to pursue the development of the arts, the sciences, medicine, transportation, economics—all the things that people had been doing before, but as individuals or in smaller groups. Governmental systems evolved that integrated cross-cultural and trans-global populations, rather than segregating them."

Kyril paused, lifting her eyes from the fire to glance at Kathryn. "Global unity is a goal that many of my species have worked toward in your dimension. Through all the centuries of human history, we have watched your species slaughter and pillage and rape—one another, and the world in which you've lived. Now that you have the capacity to destroy your world with nuclear weapons, there is even more of an urgency to try to find a lasting global peace. There are those of us who have spent Cycles of our lives here, trying to bring that about, before it is too late."

Kathryn was amazed—and angry. "Why should your people care about what happens in this world? And how can you accuse us of pillage and slaughter? From what you've said, it sounds as if your race has been no better than ours—just been at improving things longer."

Kyril shook her head slowly, "In all the Cycles of struggle in my world, never has there been the wanton disregard for all things living that has been witnessed in this world. While there has been war, it was not to the death: Those defeated accepted the defeat and went about their lives until their governments could mount counter-strategies. Order has always been maintained, and the environment conserved. Unlike human beings, oupirs reproduce slowly and depend totally on the lives of other animals to sustain us. We could never have afforded the heedless slaughter and desecration your history has sustained.

"Our concern now is—"

"Wait, wait!" Kathryn interrupted. "What do you mean—war, but 'not to the death'?"

Kyril regarded her with quiet admiration. Kathryn was not one to let important details pass. "Battles were fought, at first, with small bands of delegates, volunteers who competed physically with one another for victory—in contests something like I gather your International Olympics to be. Victories and defeats were binding on all members of the warring group—until the next contest was staged at the demand of those who wanted to promote or defeat the *status quo*.

"The problem with this system was that these volunteer combatants began to accrue wealth and power—as well as more land—than the non-combatants they were supposed to represent. So, the non-combatants began to lobby for change. Very gradually, a system of elective representation came about wherein the elected representatives competed in the same manner as their ancestors had, with the spoils going to those who had elected them, in fair shares. This elective system eventually evolved away from physical combat to competition in economic and political realms. The representatives were bound by honor, and by law, to further the economic and political advantage of the groups they represented. In concept, our system was not unlike the one under which you Americans have lived your lives."

Kathryn was astounded. "You mean. . .there was no actual war, no killing, no deaths of multitudes of your people. . . ?"

"Not for milli-Cycles—not war as you have experienced it in your world, Kathryn." Again, she shrugged, "We could never have survived such widespread slaughter."

After a short silence, during which Kathryn grappled with Kyril's disclosures, Kyril went on. "As I was saying, the concern now is our belief that a nuclear catastrophe in this dimension would affect our world direly, especially if it should occur when the dimensional boundaries are at optimal interface." She paused, deliberating. "And, some of us have come to care about human beings as individuals—or as other beings with whom we share the universe."

Kathryn noted the softness in Kyril's eyes as she spoke of caring for individual human beings. Perversely, something in her wanted to hurt Kyril. "The predator has a soft spot for the prey?" she mumbled sarcastically.

Kyril fixed her with a cold stare. Although there was more truth in the statement than she cared to admit, it was the sudden, unprovoked attack which wounded her.

Instantly contrite, Kathryn backed down. "I—I'm sorry—that was uncalled for."

When Kyril did not relent, Kathryn put down her cup and moved closer to Kyril. She slipped her arm through Kyril's, all the while aware of the dark eyes on her. Gazing into them, she allowed regret into her voice. "I'm truly sorry, Kyril. I should never have said that. From what I know of you, I know that wasn't a fair accusation." She beseeched acceptance of her apology with her eyes.

After a long moment, the stare softened, but Kyril's eyes remained fixed on Kathryn's. "Don't hurt me again so deliberately, Kathryn," she said in a quiet voice.

Seeing the pain in Kyril's eyes, Kathryn reached up to her, cupping the side of Kyril's face with her hand.

Kyril turned into the warm palm, kissing it longingly.

Kathryn shuddered, feeling desire overtake her guilt. Her breath caught. She moved to kiss the waiting lips and allowed herself to be led into the tent. For once, Kyril seemed as eager and unwilling to wait as Kathryn. Each fumbled with the heavy winter garments, impatient to be free of them, hungry for the touch of skin on skin. They made love frenziedly, wanting the solace of sexual union.

Later, as they lay cocooned in their joined sleeping bags, Kathryn ran a finger over Kyril's nose and jawline. "Kyril—why aren't human beings allowed to cross the dimensional barrier?"

Kyril smiled in pleasure at the touch. She answered dreamily, "Because no one in this world is supposed to know that we exist."

"In other words, for protection of your species."

Kyril contemplated that thought. "Essentially, yes." She nodded and turned to Kathryn again. "During the centuries of our travel in this dimension, many of our number have been captured and cruelly put to death. It has always seemed imperative that human beings never know of our true origin." She kissed the side of Kathryn's neck, creating goosebumps on the soft skin.

"Oh, Kathryn," she whispered, "I want you so much—'tis a bittersweet longing inside me." She pushed Kathryn back gently, licking her neck, feeling the heat and sensing the pounding of the blood in the huge vessels under the delicate surface. As her tongue touched the warm skin, she felt Kathryn tense, and immediately slid her lips over Kathryn's collarbone to her breasts and began to coax her into arousal again.

Letting go of fear, Kathryn sought with her hands the sensitive places she had come to know on Kyril's body. They climbed toward another climax. This time, they peaked together, Kyril riding Kathryn's hip as Kathryn writhed in pleasure at the fingers Kyril had inserted into her vagina.

When at last they lay still again, huddled together, ardor cooling, Mindi pushed into the tent and gently nosed the back of Kathryn's neck. Shrieking, she recoiled from the cold touch, then turned, laughingly, gathering Mindi against her on the sleeping bag. Then, all three dozed, content in the moment.

The following morning was overcast, though somewhat warmer. The wind shifted, and snow began to fall from a pewter sky—small, hard crystals that stung and bounced as they struck.

Kathryn, used to Minnesota winters, but never having actually done any winter camping, was not alarmed. Kyril, acquainted with the mountains and aware of the potential for danger, was. "We are not far from the Interface, but we have another thirty-six hours to wait. This tent is not designed to withstand a serious storm. I want to look for a cave where we can take shelter if the need arises."

Observing the worry on Kyril's face, Kathryn realized she had never really seen Kyril anxious before. It took her aback, and fear prickled over her

"You wait here, with Mindi, and keep the fire going. I'll search. I shouldn't be gone long."

Kathryn offered no argument, realizing Kyril's endurance and knowledge of the area far surpassed her own. She had been a Girl Scout, but that had been in Florida, and many years ago. She hugged Kyril briefly. "Be careful," she enjoined.

Kathryn built up the fire and prepared her breakfast, which she shared with Mindi. Snow continued to fall, not heavily, but enough to limit visibility.

After what seemed like an hour or so, Kathryn became uneasy. She realized she had not looked at her watch when Kyril left, nor had she paid much attention to the direction she took.

Another hour passed, this time measured by her watch. Kathryn decided it was time for some action. She arose from the fire and cupped her hands around her mouth. "Kyril!" she called, half a dozen times.

Mindi sat and watched, her ears cocked, clearly wondering what her mistress was up to.

When there was no answer to her calls, Kathryn dropped her hands and gazed at Mindi. *Could Mindi find her?* she wondered.

"Mindi—find Kyril. Where's Kyril, Mindi?"

The dog whined softly, as if trying to understand Kathryn's urgency. She came forward and nosed Kathryn's hand.

Kathryn took the dog's face in her hands. "Find Kyril," she commanded quietly.

Mindi sat on her haunches, her eyes querying her mistress.

Fleetingly, Kathryn wished she knew how to communicate mentally with the dog, as Kyril had done. Sighing, she decided to take matters into her own hands.

She threw more wood on the fire, then bundled herself against the cold. Taking the hand axe they had used for chopping kindling, she moved off in the direction she thought Kyril had taken. Mindi followed eagerly.

Using the axe to mark a trail as she went, Kathryn began to call for Kyril again. The wind had dropped, and the snow was softer, coming down in heavy flakes that obliterated any footprints that might otherwise have been visible. Kathryn knew hers would be quickly filled if the snow continued. Even her voice was muffled by the crystalline veil.

Checking her progress on her watch, she moved forward slowly, listening for some sound other than the shushing of the snowfall. She had been searching for half an hour, while Mindi sniffed aimlessly about, when suddenly, Mindi's head came up. Then, the dog bolted up the steep embankment on their right.

"Mindi!" Kathryn exclaimed. Thinking her companion may have caught scent of Kyril, she scrambled after. The going was hard—especially for a two-footed being. She grabbed and clutched at limbs and roots and outcroppings of rock, trying to avoid sliding backwards on the slippery ground.

As Mindi attained the top of the embankment, Kathryn lost sight of her. Panicking, she hastened behind her, only to discover—as she, too, reached the top—that the embankment was more truly a ridge that gave way to another deep crevice on the other side.

She sought Mindi with her eyes, then caught sight of her scrambling and sliding near the bottom of the steep incline. There, she disappeared into the shadows, where she began to bark,

Gooseflesh rising over her again, Kathryn began a more cautious descent of the back side of the ridge. When she neared the bottom, she paused, hanging onto a scraggly sapling. From under a huge pile of rubble at the base of the wall of rock rising in front of her, a booted foot protruded.

"Kyril!" She let go and slid the remaining few feet, then bounded over to where Mindi stood eagerly wagging her tail.

"Oh God," Kathryn breathed, horrified. *What if—* She drew back from that thought, afraid of becoming immobilized. Instead, she frantically began to clear the rubble aside, seeking Kyril's form beneath. Apparently, she had been thrown half under a small overhang, and was buried from the waist down in rocks and silt.

Panting and puffing with the exertion, she finally uncovered Kyril's legs and torso and was able to get to her head. Desperately, Kathryn felt her neck for a pulse. It was there: very slow, but easily detectable under her seeking fingers. There were no obvious injuries to her head or upper torso, but Kyril's eyes remained closed and her breathing shallow. Puzzled, Kathryn examined Kyril more carefully. Her color seemed her normal paleness. Kathryn's searching fingers discovered a huge lump on the back of her head, but she could feel no cuts or abrasions on Kyril's scalp, and no bruises were apparent on the white face. She was at a loss to explain what could be responsible for Kyril's continuing unconsciousness.

Not knowing how to proceed, she sat for a moment, generating alternatives. How long had Kyril been unconscious? On a sudden hunch, she felt Kyril's forehead and cheeks with her palms, as her mother had used to do when checking her for a fever. Kyril's flesh was very cold— colder than usual. Kathryn grabbed an arm and pushed the sleeves up, feeling the wrist beneath: also very cold. Hypothermia?

Kathryn leaned back again, trying to think. She viewed herself as inadequate to the task. She felt she did not know enough about first aid or the perils of travel in a cold climate to act decisively. Instinct told her that she should get Kyril warmed, and so she decided to risk moving her. Grabbing the gloved hands, as gently as possible she dragged Kyril free of the remaining debris and up against the rock face, in the lee of the wind. Hurriedly, she gathered small pieces of deadfall, using the axe to make kindling. As she readied to light the fire, she faltered, realizing she had no matches on her. With a prayer, she scrambled to Kyril, frantically searching her pockets for the matches she had seen Kyril put there two days before. She sighed with relief as her fingers seized the small box of waterproof lucifers.

In a matter of moments, she had the blaze going and began to look for larger pieces of wood to sustain it. When she finally paused, satisfied with her efforts, she gazed upward and realized the snowfall had thickened. Alarmed, she checked her watch. She judged the daylight to be more than half gone.

Kathryn knew she could not possibly move Kyril from the ravine by herself. She also knew she could not move all the camping gear here. She measured the climb back up the ridge, trying to decide how and what gear she would need to get them through the night. She chose not to think of a storm. Nor did she wish to consider the possibility that Kyril might not respond to her ministrations.

Assuring herself that the fire was roaring and safe, she zipped her parka tight, then set off on her climb. Only once did she glance back, long enough to ascertain that Mindi had elected to stay with Kyril.

Nearly an hour had passed by the time she was back at their campsite, where the fire was burning low. She banked it and dragged a few heavy logs across it, hoping to give it enough fuel to keep it going through the night. Munching on dried rations, she quickly gathered up packets of food, what water she judged she could carry, their bedrolls, a first-aid kit, a small tarpaulin, and anything else she could imagine they might need. When it came to loading it all, however, she decided to leave behind all non-essentials. Judging the sleeping bags to be essential, she took them. She crammed everything else necessary into a backpack. Dismayed at its bulkiness and weight, she nonetheless managed to slip it onto her shoulders and set out again, retracing her trail to where she had left Kyril.

Snow continued to fall gently, steadily, the flakes larger and thicker still. By the time she reached Mindi and Kyril, the grey daylight was almost completely gone.

Exhausted as she now was, Kathryn first built up the fire again, then hauled the backpack from where she had dropped it to where Kyril lay. She examined Kyril. No apparent change. Knowing it was crucial to keep Kyril warm, she carefully maneuvered her into one of the sleeping bags, and placed the second one on top of her for additional warmth.

Before long, Kyril's eyelids began to flicker and she licked her lips weakly.

"Kyril, it's Kathryn," she whispered insistently. "Can you hear me?"

Kyril muttered unintelligibly. Searching the first-aid kit, Kathryn found what she sought: ammonia ampoules. Crushing one, she waved it under Kyril's nose.

Kyril coughed violently, and pulled away.

Kathryn's eyes widened at the reaction, but she continued to call to Kyril, shaking her gently. Finally, she was rewarded with seeing Kyril's eyes open, but they remained unfocused and unheeding. She stroked Kyril's cheek with her palm again, feeling it warmer to the touch.

Kyril muttered on, showing no signs of recognizing where she was. Kathryn became alarmed afresh. She was aware that disorientation could be a consequence of hypothermia, but she had no idea how to bring Kyril out of it. She searched her memory for a clue. *Fluids—give fluids,* she thought. She was brought up short again. What fluids? The only thing she had ever seen Kyril consume were alcoholic beverages, and they had brought none along.

She sighed heavily, tired and hungry from the exertions she had made. Should she try giving Kyril some broth, or not? Maybe in an emergency—

She dug a concentrated soup cube out of the food pack and dropped it in a cup, then added hot water from the pot on the fire. She deliberately made it thick, figuring she needed to get as much concentrated nourishment in her as she could, and knowing it was going to be hard to feed someone who was only half-conscious.

She moved to Kyril, stilled her with her touch, then spooned a few drops of the broth between her lips. Kyril swallowed reflexively. Encouraged, Kathryn gave her a few more spoonfuls. Satisfied, she put the cup down and waited, wanting to allow Kyril a few moments for the broth to set.

Suddenly, Kyril convulsed and vomited violently.

Kathryn held her shoulders, horrified, then eased her down again. Breathing raggedly, she wiped perspiration from Kyril's face. *Well,* she thought regretfully, *that wasn't the answer.* But what was? Now Kyril had emptied herself of what fluids her stomach had contained.

As she wiped up the mess, Kathryn began to feel despair. The warmth of the sleeping bags had succeeded in raising Kyril's body temperature somewhat, but not in restoring her to full consciousness. She did not know what else to do. She reached out, stroking Mindi, seeking some comfort in the touch.

Giving in at last to her weariness, she decided to bed down for the night. She toyed with the idea of erecting the tarpaulin over them, but discovered she had forgotten the stakes. Beyond self-reproach, she decided to use the tarp as a ground cover instead. Although they were in the lee of the wind, and very little snow had settled at their location, the ground was damp and cold. Every layer would help prevent further loss of body heat. She reasoned that unless the wind shifted significantly, they would be all right until morning.

She stood up tiredly, banked the fire, added more logs, and spread the tarp underneath the semi-conscious Kyril. Working as quickly as her tiredness would permit, she zipped her sleeping bag to Kyril's bag, forming a double. Too tired for food, she crawled in, calling Mindi to her. She was asleep, her body pressed against Kyril's, almost before she knew it.

18

Kathryn became aroused, feeling the sexual heat fill her belly. She unzipped her parka, then undid the buttons of her woolen shirt. Peeling out of them, she pushed them aside under the sleeping bag, then set about undoing Kyril's things. Soon, she was down to Kyril's skivvies. She pulled her own t-shirt over her head, rid herself of her bra, and proceeded to lay herself on top of Kyril. Kissing and stroking her, she tried to arouse her from the stupor in which she lay. It occurred to her that she could best accomplish that if she offered her neck to her, to drink—

Stunned at this thought, Kathryn recoiled.

And came awake.

She still lay next to Kyril, her arm around her. The fire still roared. She was disoriented, had no clear sense of how much time had elapsed since she had crawled inside their joined sleeping bags. Groggily, she sat up, looking around her. Everything seemed as it had when she had gone to sleep.

She shook her head to clear it. The dream—if that were what it had been—was very vivid. But clearly, it had not actually occurred, for she was fully clothed and so was Kyril. Shaking her head again, she slipped back down, her grogginess pulling at her, and fell quickly asleep.

She lay on the ground next to Kyril as a spirit of some sort hovered over them. The spirit spoke to her, not in words, but mentally. "Kathryn," it enunciated eerily, "Kathryn, I must drink. I must drink. . . ."

Kathryn shrank back in fear from the ephemeral form, not understanding, not wanting to understand.

It repeated itself, its hollow voice hypnotic.

She lifted herself sluggishly, leaning over Kyril, baring her neck to her to drink—

This time, she awoke screaming, *"No! No!"*

She sat trembling, trying to understand what was happening to her. It had become dark enough that she could no longer see Kyril's face clearly. She reached for her flashlight, and shone the light on her companion. Kyril appeared very pale again, and her lips moved feverishly, making unintelligible noises.

Kathryn stared at her. Could Kyril be trying to tell her something? Were the "dreams" in fact some sort of telepathy—some attempt to let Kathryn know how to help her?

Kathryn shivered, filled with revulsion. "Oh God, Kyril," she whispered. "Ask me to do anything but that." She shuddered again. What *could* she do?

She glanced at the fire. The coals still burned.

Kathryn dragged herself out of the sleeping bag and staggered to the fire. She added a few logs and waited for them to blaze to life. Realizing that it had stopped snowing, she gazed upward. There was still a dense cloud cover.

After poking and rearranging the burning logs to her satisfaction, she sat back, then realized she needed to urinate.

With a grunt, she dragged herself to her feet again. Picking her way wearily in the firelight reflecting off the stone walls of the ravine, she crossed the stony ground to her makeshift latrine. By the time she had finished, Kyril was stirring again. She hurried over to her.

"Kyril, Kyril," she urged. "Please." She shook her gently, then chafed her wrists, continuing to call her name. At last, she was rewarded with seeing Kyril's eyes flicker open.

This time there was recognition in the dark eyes. Her lips moved almost soundlessly.

Kathryn bent to her; placing her ear next to Kyril's mouth, straining to hear what she was trying to say.

"Kathryn. . .I. . .must. . .feed." The voice, though faint, was urgent with need.

Kathryn turned her face to Kyril's in dismay. She shook her head. "Please, Kyril—no, please," she begged softly.

Kyril entreated again, and yet again, while Kathryn watched the nearly silent lips in stony horror. Then, with a start, Kathryn realized that Kyril's lips had ceased to move. She pressed her fingers to Kyril's pulse. It had slowed and seemed somewhat weaker. She still breathed, but her respiration was shallower.

Kathryn began to shiver all over and her teeth to chatter uncontrollably. She felt absolutely certain that Kyril was dying. And she knew that it was within her power to save Kyril's life. All she had to do—
But she could not get past the image of Kyril's teeth buried in her neck.

She got up and walked around, clutching herself, shivering with an inner cold that nothing outside her could warm. Kathryn had never had much of a relationship with God, but suddenly she found herself praying, reaching out to the being who ruled the universe, who moved the endless sea, who had brought Mindi into her life— Could that same God have created beings who survived on the living blood of other life forms?

Kathryn collapsed on the ground next to the fire and raised her face to the clouded heavens. "Oh God," she pleaded, the tears streaming from her eyes, "please help me. *Please,* help me." She dropped her head on her chest, her confused mind struggling for clarity. She thought of the need to eat to survive. That plants grew and were eaten. That wild animals preyed on one another. That this was all part of a food chain ordained by Nature. That human beings had harnessed part of the chain, raising crops and harvesting them, raising pigs, chickens, and cattle and slaughtering them. How was any of this any different from Kyril's practice?

Human beings don't feed on their own kind, she thought.

Neither do oupirs, another "voice" replied. *We are humanoid— but not "homo sapiens."*

Struck by the truth of that, Kathryn gradually quieted. At length, a peacefulness seeped into where her tears had been. In growing wonder, she raised her head again and listened—within herself—for the doubt and revulsion she had felt. They were gone.

More at ease, she climbed stiffly to her feet and hurried to Kyril. She stumbled down beside her and felt her wrist for a pulse. It was still there—slower than before. Frantically, Kathryn grabbed Kyril's hands and rubbed them vigorously, trying to bring some warmth into them. She prayed for her return to consciousness. And as she began to think her efforts were too late, Kyril's eyelids fluttered again. "Kyril!" Kathryn leaned over her again. "I'm here—I'm ready to give you what you need—but you have to help me. . .somehow. . . ." She trailed off, realizing Kyril was too weak for any but the slightest effort.

She closed her eyes, wracking her brain for a clue— It was there! Into her mind's eye came the image of herself opening the veins in her wrist to Kyril. She scrambled to the pile of camping equipment and searched frantically for the utility knife she had packed.

When she found it, she half crawled, half ran to the fire to sterilize the blade in the flame. Returning to Kyril, Kathryn plunked down beside her and dragged up her sleeve, the handle of the knife clenched in her teeth. With a fleeting thought for the alcohol swab one always received in a doctor's office, she steeled herself to make the cut.

To her great dismay, the tender skin of her inner wrist was quite resilient. Her first attempt produced little more than a scratch, which oozed and stung, but was obviously not sufficient for her purpose. She bit her lip and grasped the blade tighter. With as deep a concentration as she could muster, she sliced, trying not to flinch. Unconsciously, she had clenched her fist, raising the veins.

Suddenly, blood welled from the wound, appearing almost black in the firelight. She sobbed shortly, releasing the air she had held, allowing the pain of the incised tissue to escape her with the breath. Discarding the knife, she grabbed her aching left forearm with her right hand and moved closer to Kyril.

Kyril was still conscious, waiting. Gently, Kathryn slid her hand under the back of Kyril's neck, lifting her head to the bleeding wrist.

Kathryn felt the touch of Kyril's lips on her skin, but could not watch as she sucked gently at the wound.

When Kathryn realized that Kyril had stopped, she laid Kyril's head back, then inspected her wrist. Blood continued to flow steadily. She decided she had better cover the incision to staunch the flow, and rummaged in the first aid kit for bandages.

Wrapping her own wrist was difficult, but she succeeded in securing a gauze pad over the cut with a strip of tape. Done, she sighed heavily and sank in on herself. She was *so* tired.

Rousing herself, she examined Kyril again. Satisfied that now she was at least holding her own, she crawled in beside her and was asleep instantly.

She had no sense of how much time had passed before she awakened again, but the stars were beginning to show through scattering clouds. She lay still, trying to figure out what had awakened her. There was the faintest trace of a dream. . . .

Turning, she raised herself on her elbow to look at Kyril. She reached to her—and winced as she flexed her left wrist. Sitting up, she noticed the dried flecks of blood on Kyril's lips. Unable to bring herself to touch Kyril's face, she lifted an inert arm. The pulse seemed stronger. As she raised her eyes to Kyril's face again, she realized Kyril was awake.

Dark eyes fastened on hazel ones, thanking, demanding, at once.

"Kyril," Kathryn said softly, "do you need more?"

"Yes," she whispered, the sound like wind over dry reeds.

Dutifully, Kathryn pulled up her sleeve again and pulled the tape and gauze pad away from the incision. "It's started to close up. . ." she began, feeling the dread of having to make another cut.

Kyril's hand seized Kathryn's wrist.

In pain and fright, Kathryn jerked her arm back, stifling a scream. "Oh, God! You startled me." Her breath came in gasps as her heart pounded furiously in her chest. Trying to calm herself, she looked at Kyril again.

"Kathryn," Kyril whispered, "it's all right." She had no strength for anything more, but her eyes pleaded with Kathryn for trust.

Slowly, her eyes closing, Kathryn gave her wrist to Kyril again, sliding down beside her in the sleeping bags.

As Kyril placed her lips to the wound, Kathryn tried to think of anything else but what was happening. The pain was minimal—a short, burning sensation, followed by a pleasant numbness, after which she knew nothing more.

☾ ☾ ☾

A creeping cold nudged Kathryn from sleep. She retreated from it, trying to snuggle in on herself. But she was stiff and sore. It hurt to move. She groaned, forcing her eyes open.

It was full daylight, and the temperature had dropped noticeably. The sun shone down from its zenith, sparkling in millions of tiny crystals wherever they lay. Blinking, her eyes protesting the brightness, Kathryn turned her head to where Kyril had lain. She was alone.

Startled, she tried to sit up. The movement set her head reeling and black patches flashed across her vision. She fell back, woozy, weak. Suddenly, Mindi's face was in hers, nosing her and licking her joyously. Kathryn raised her hands, ineffectually trying to fend the dog off. In her own time, the greeting completed, Mindi turned and collapsed next to Kathryn.

While the sun moved across the small arc of sky subtended by the gully in which they lay, Kathryn dozed fitfully, with Mindi pressed against her. The shadows had lengthened considerably before a soft touch on Kathryn's forehead awakened her again.

She opened her eyes to Kyril's face. "Kyril, where have you been?" she murmured languidly.

Kyril stroked Kathryn's face, soothing her. "Hunting," she replied softly.

Kathryn gazed at Kyril's face and saw the remnants of the ordeal she had undergone in the drawn skin and the dark circles under dark eyes. "I. . .I'm sorry. . ." she began, even as she slid again into slumber.

19

Twilight had dropped into the vale. Evening birds darted about, seeking food. The silhouettes of the barren trees and evergreens blurred softly into the settling dark. Above the crest of the ridges between which Kathryn lay, the sky was still a bright blue and the tips of the rock walls were gilded with light from the setting sun.

Kathryn sighed deeply, then turned her head from the overhead view to look for Kyril again. She discovered her sitting not far away.

"Hello," Kyril said softly, her eyes glowing equally softly in the light of the fire she had rekindled. There was a vulnerability in them that Kathryn recognized immediately, and took to heart.

"Are you okay now?" Kathryn asked, her tongue feeling stiff in her mouth.

Kyril nodded, moving to Kathryn's side. "Yes, thanks to you, Kathryn." Sudden emotion pressed at the back of her throat, making her next words difficult. "I know that what you did was very hard for you. I owe you a great deal."

"Kyril, what if I hadn't found you? What if I hadn't—" She faltered, feeling her guilt. "What if I hadn't realized—been able to— I mean, it took me so long—"

Kyril smiled forgivingly, shaking her head, touching Kathryn's shoulder gently. "I would have survived—but in a trance-like state. I was not seriously injured in the fall—"

"The fall? It looked like the embankment had caved in on you."

Kyril shook her head. "No, I was up there," she gestured with her eyes, "looking for a cave I remembered, when the ledge gave way. As I slid down, the loose soil and rock came with me. I was stunned—I think I must have hit my head. I lay there long enough to become chilled.

"Unconscious as I was, my body's automatic reaction to extreme cold was to shut down," she went on. "In such circumstances, an oupir's autonomic nervous system withdraws the vascular supply from all but essential internal organs, to maintain the core temperature. Respiration and pulse slow, and we enter what I can only describe as a trance-like state.

The only thing that can reverse that process, once begun, is the return of external warmth—or feeding.

"Otherwise, I would have lain there until my body slowed enough that I would have appeared dead. You would have thought me dead. But, in fact, it would have been a sort of trauma-induced hibernation that, barring further injury to my body, could have gone on for months—or years—until my body rejuvenated itself—cell by cell—enough to revive and feed again."

Kathryn gaped at her. "My God," she whispered, "then the stories about vampires coming back to life are really true."

Kyril studied her. "After a fashion, yes," she conceded. When Kathryn said nothing more, she glanced up. It had become fully dark in the ravine as they had talked. The sky above had deepened to indigo, and a few stars had begun to twinkle on the breast of night. In the distance, an owl now sounded its mournful cry. "Tonight is the full moon—we shall have to be moving soon. You must eat."

She rose, went to the fire where a pot of savory stew was heating, and ladled a cup for Kathryn. Returning to her, Kyril knelt beside her, then paused.

"Would you like some help with this?" she queried softly.

Kathryn pulled herself away from the inner quagmire of renewed confusion, to Kyril's words. She began to push herself to a sitting position, noticing as she did that her wrist was no longer sore. "No, thanks, I can get it," she grunted absently. She took the steaming mug from Kyril, their hands brushing as she did. Kyril's skin was cool against the hot plastic, and Kathryn shivered slightly. Surreptitiously, she inspected the cut she had made and saw that it was neatly sealed over.

She sipped at her meal, puzzling over the rapidity of her healing, while Kyril began to pack up the gear Kathryn had brought from the original camp. The hearty stew, coupled with her long sleep, restored much of Kathryn's strength. By the time the moon was nearing its zenith, they had transported all the camping gear to a site near the Interface, where Kyril stored it in a cache, against the possibility of future use. Together, they scattered the fire and began the short trek from the ravine to the Dimensional Interface.

Kathryn found herself growing more and more anxious as she contemplated their journey across the Boundary that separated her world from Kyril's. When at last they stood in front of a wall of rock which seemed to shimmer in the moonlight, she glanced down at Mindi. The dog sat perfectly still, as if waiting for the next step. Puzzled, she said, "I wonder if Mindi knows what we're going to do."

Kyril smiled. "Of course she does."

"How?" she exclaimed, surprised at the response.

"I established a mind-touch with her that first night in the park, Kathryn. Ever since then, she has known where I am—as I have known where she is—and she knows what I am thinking—when I want her to."

As Kyril paused, the implications of her statements same clear to Kathryn. "Then, that's how she knew where to find you—"

"Yes. When that part of my mind sensed her near me, it 'called' her to me, if you will. And now she knows we are going to cross the Boundary between our worlds—although," Kyril laughed, "she could not possibly understand what that means."

Seeing again the incredulous look on Kathryn's face, she took her gloved hand in hers. "I realize that much has transpired since that evening in the park, Kathryn." Her voice was quiet, comforting. "And more is yet to come. I shall try to take the time, soon, to sit down with you and explain things in more detail—I know what you've heard thus far has been fragmented and sketchy. I assure you that, in context, it will all make sense." She paused, seeking acknowledgment of her words from Kathryn.

Kathryn nodded hesitantly. "I hope so."

"It will." She squeezed Kathryn's hand. Then, "It is time."

Kathryn looked into Kyril's eyes. "Okay, let's go," she said, her voice shaky in spite of her attempt to sound casual, confident.

"Take Mindi," she directed, dropping Kathryn's hand. She hefted the huge packet of food stuffs she had prepared for Kathryn and Mindi.

Kathryn shouldered her own pack, lifted Mindi in her arms, and waited.

Kyril stepped aside, looking carefully at the shimmering rock face. "Come," she commanded, holding out her hand, not taking her eyes off the center of the glittering patch of moonlight. Together, they stepped toward the solid wall of granite.

Involuntarily, Kathryn sucked in her breath as she thought they must collide with unyielding rock. To her great surprise, the wall dissolved around her, and—for one terrifying instant—she thought herself and Mindi dissolved with it. But before she could react to the terror, she found herself emerging into a cavern lit by the wavering flames of torches, Mindi still in her arms, and Kyril beside her, still holding her elbow in a firm grip. There was a slight jolt as her feet hit the ground. At that moment, it penetrated Kathryn's consciousness that all that Kyril had claimed about her origins was indisputably true.

As Kyril loosened her grip, a figure clothed in ankle-length robes and cloak stepped from the shadows. Around her neck she wore a pendant

identical to the one Kathryn had seen on Kyril the night of their first
meeting in the park. Outrage flashed across the woman's dark face before
giving way to a stern, unyielding countenance at which Kathryn stared
with wonder. It had never occurred to her that oupirs might come in more
than one variety!

Kyril drew in on herself, and bowed to this grey-haired figure.
"Mother," she whispered reverently.

Kathryn, still holding Mindi, was surprised at the address. This
dark-skinned woman could not be Kyril's mother—could she?

Tyrell accepted the reverence as her due, even as she contemplated her spiritual Daughter's unthinkable violation of oupirian
prohibitions about bringing human beings across the Boundary. When she
spoke, her normally mellifluous voice was hard, and she spoke in their
native tongue, disregarding the fact that Kyril had used English. "Kyril—
why have you disobeyed the Laws of the Visit? What could possibly have
suaded you to such flagrant disregard?"

Kyril lowered her head further under the disapprobation, awaiting permission to reply.

"Speak," the woman commanded.

"Guardian Tyrell," she responded, also in their native tongue, "I
cannot explain myself fully until I have conveyed my news of the riddle
I sought to answer."

"Proceed," Tyrell directed.

Kyril raised her head, her eyes seeking those of her spiritual
guardian. "Mother," she began again, "there is, in that Other world, a
disease which is sure death to those who are infected—human being or
oupir. I am certain it was this which killed Lanaea—and it is this which
will kill many more of us if we do not halt its spread immediately. A few
days ago I received a communique from Däg, saying that others of our kind
have fallen ill. I returned at the earliest possible moment." She paused, the
most important message delivered.

Tyrell's expression remained unchanged. "And this human female—why have you brought her with you across the Boundary?" She
pointedly refused to look at Kathryn.

Kathryn, understanding nothing of oupirian languages, had been
unable to follow the conversation. Having put Mindi down, leash attached, she had waited quietly while Kyril and the robed woman spoke.
Now, as Kyril turned toward her slightly, she realized she had become the
subject of their dialogue.

Kyril's eyes remained on Tyrell's as she gestured toward Kathryn.

"Because I did not wish to refuse her request to come," she admitted, unwilling and unable to dissemble to this One who had meant so much to her. "And, because she has knowledge of this disease which, I believe, might be of assistance to us in defeating it."

Tyrell studied Kathryn, who stood unflinching in front of the searching umber eyes. She returned her gaze to Kyril. "The Congress of Health will want the information you bring, immediately." She turned to go.

"Tyrell—" Kyril called. The woman turned back to her spiritual ward. "I request a few hours' rest—the journey here has been arduous."

Tyrell considered, nodded. "Very well. I shall notify you of the hour at which the Congress will assemble tomorrow. Good rest to you." She nodded again, then departed in a swirl of robes. Kyril stood watching her go, before turning her attention to Kathryn and Mindi.

"Come," she said, returning to her heavily-accented English. "There are quarters here, outside the Os, where we can rest for a while—and talk." She smiled encouragingly at Kathryn.

Kathryn allowed herself to be led through long, rough-hewn halls lit with the same crude torches, until they emerged into an open area that instantly reminded Kathryn of the atria of many of the buildings she had been in, in downtown Minneapolis. Huge stone planters were scattered pleasingly about, filled with pale-green foliage, and fountains burbled and splashed, lending an illusion of naturalness. The whole of the area was enclosed by a geodesic dome made up of huge panes of a transparent substance which Kathryn assumed to be glass. Though no longer torch-light, the illumination in the atrium was equally faint.

There were few others about. "The hour is late here, too," Kyril explained. Her voice, hushed as it was, drifted over the polished stone floor, reverberating faintly in the huge grotto. They proceeded obliquely to another opening cut into the stone basewall. As they passed through, Kyril paused at a panel with a video display terminal and keyboard. She punched in a series of identifying codes. "There," she said to Kathryn. "Now Data Central knows I have returned, and we have rooms awaiting us at this very moment, down the hallway."

They proceeded along a corridor very unlike the one from which they had emerged into the atrium. This one was carpeted in a resilient, russet fabric, and the walls were a neutral beige. Lighting was dim, but even. They turned a few corners—with Kathryn becoming thoroughly lost—before Kyril stopped at the door of a room numbered with figures in Kornägian script.

She punched in another code, and an electronic lock released the door, which slid open with a soft sigh. They entered, and it sighed shut behind them.

Kathryn looked around as Kyril slung the bulky package of foodstuffs onto the floor and proceeded into the bath. Slipping out of her own pack, which contained the few personal items and clothing she had brought with her, Kathryn noted that the rooms were simply but elegantly furnished. Obviously, even in their native environ, oupirs enjoyed a certain luxury in their surroundings. Kathryn bent to Mindi, unfastening the leash, then paused. "Kyril—how will I take Mindi out from here?" she called.

Kyril reappeared from the bathroom, towel in hand, wiping her face. She smiled. "There is an exit not far from here—I can show you later." She dropped her hands, stood watching Kathryn, allowing herself for the first time to feel what it was like to have actually brought this woman she was coming to love into her own world.

Kathryn, captured by Kyril's look, remained where she stood, holding her breath, not knowing what Kyril was thinking, or what came next. She felt very alone at that moment.

Sensing her feelings, Kyril discarded the towel and came to Kathryn. She gazed deep into the hazel eyes, emotion filling her throat, preventing her from speaking. She lifted a hand, stroked Kathryn's temple with one finger. Slowly, she stepped nearer, closing the space between them; taking Kathryn into her arms, her gaze never leaving Kathryn's until their lips met and their eyes closed on their kiss.

When they parted, Kyril smiled softly down at Kathryn. She saw the tiredness in the other's face. "Would you like a bath?" she whispered.

Kathryn's eyes crinkled in an answering smile, gratified by Kyril's consideration. She nodded. "Yes."

Kyril showed her where the towels were. "I'll hang your things," she volunteered as Kathryn turned on the shower. Soon, she joined her under the warm spray. Each luxuriated in the cleansing stream, delighting in the company. They soaped one another, the act a caress, each enjoying the feel of wet skin under her fingers. Finally, emerging from the steamy enclosure, they towelled one another dry, then embraced.

Kathryn felt the warmed skin of Kyril's body against her own, and leaned into her, her breasts crushing softly against Kyril's chest. As she bent to the base of Kyril's throat, placing her lips against the throbbing vein there, she heard the rapid intake of Kyril's breath. Her lips wandered down the breastbone to the cleft between Kyril's breasts, where she licked and stroked, her hands cupping Kyril's sides and hips gently. Kyril moaned, a low noise in the silence. Kathryn continued in her meanderings down Kyril's front, enjoying the feel of the velvet of Kyril's skin under her lips. At last she knelt, turning her face into the soft flesh of Kyril's belly, her arms around her hips. Suddenly exhausted again, she sighed gently, content in the feel of her body against Kyril's.

Sensing this, Kyril caught Kathryn under the arms, raising her gently to her feet. "Let us sleep, love," Kyril said, walking with her to the bed. "We've time enough for everything, after you've rested."

20

Kathryn stood restlessly in the mezzanine, awaiting Kyril's return. Kyril was preparing herself with contemplative meditation for her meeting with the Congress of Health. The small movements that Kathryn and Mindi made disturbed the silence, echoing off the polished stone of Sziv's Great Hall. Kathryn examined her surroundings curiously. The Hall itself was indeed huge—perhaps three stories high, a great, open space surrounded by walls, with a roof supported in the center by columns of polished obsidian that reflected not at all in the glazed floor and walls, which were of the same material. Flames burning in sconces suspended on those pillars reminded her of the cavern into which they had stepped as they had crossed the dimensional boundary the night before. The mustiness in the air betrayed the age of the place, and presented Kathryn with another contradiction: that of the obviously new rooms in the lodging-place of last evening and the apparent antiquity of this and the other buildings Kathryn had observed as they had ridden through the city that morning in what Kyril had called a glidecar—a robotic vehicle for surface transportation which hovered above the ground, suspended on a magnetic field over a magnetized track.

Kathryn turned, wrested from her musings by the sound of soft footsteps approaching. In the dim illumination cast by the wavering flames, she caught sight of Kyril down the mezzanine. Earlier, both had exchanged their cold-weather garb for native garments similar to those Guardian Tyrell had worn the previous evening. On Kyril's breast lay the elliptical pendant Kathryn had first seen on her, in the park, those few months ago. It shimmered. In wine-dark robes, with her pale skin and raven hair, the gold glinting at her breast, Kyril's was a stunning figure.

Feeling small and singular among the ancient Kornägian pillars, Kathryn's isolation shafted through her consciousness. Emotion gathered in her throat, burning, and she tightened against the whimper that threatened to escape her.

Kyril apprehended the tumult of Kathryn's emotions and faltered momentarily in her step. No stranger to the loneliness she sensed in Kathryn, she wished to respond directly to that. Moving ahead, taking in at a glance the robe of deep blue that Kathryn now wore and the glint of flame in her ash-blond hair, Kyril allowed the flash of desire that shot through her. She gathered Kathryn's shoulders in her fingers, and looked directly into the hazel eyes, trying to put all the precious regard she had come to feel for this woman into her own gaze. "I am so happy you are here with me," she whispered, offering solace with her words.

Kathryn's eyes searched Kyril's hungrily, needing connection. She allowed herself to be pulled into Kyril's arms where she rested for a moment, giving herself to the sustenance of the embrace, before pulling away. She looked around her uncomfortably, by long habit wondering if others had seen, even though the Hall was deserted.

Puzzled, Kyril followed Kathryn's gaze momentarily before realizing what Kathryn was thinking. She squeezed the hand she held. "Kathryn, we have no prohibitions in our society regarding selection of sexual partners."

A strained silence followed, during which Kathryn absently studied Kyril's elliptical pendant. She suddenly realized that Tyrell had worn an identical piece the night before, and now wondered at its significance. Until now, it had never occurred to her that the pendant was anything other than a uniquely designed piece. The silence, and her musings, were broken abruptly by the grating sound of a massive door opening on its hinges. They turned in unison to see a Congressional adjutant appear in the foyer below. After catching Kyril's eye, he inclined his head respectfully and announced, "The Congress will hear you now, Doctor."

From her position above him, Kathryn gazed at the tall, thin man, thinking he bore some faint resemblance to Kyril—not a likeness, exactly—but something...a line, his carriage—not as if they were directly related, but rather of the same lineage.

This time, Kyril interrupted Kathryn's musings. "Come," she said quietly. She led her to the doors of the gallery from where she wished Kathryn to observe her audience with the Congress. She herself then descended to the waiting adjutant.

"Proceed please," she instructed, and followed him into the Congressional chamber.

The adjutant stopped just inside the doors while Kyril approached the five oupirs seated at the massive table at the far end of the room.

During Kyril's exchange of formalities with the members of the Kornägian Congress of Health, Capital Sector, Kathryn, from her vantage point, examined each of the oupirs on the dais. Although each was dressed similarly, there were obvious sub-special differences in facial features, skin color, and texture of hair. Kathryn realized that the racial groupings of Earth had their counterparts in this dimension. Something else came to her: These variations in oupirian appearance could account for the legends of vampires in all the major cultures of her world. She made a mental note to ask Kyril about that, along with a note to inquire about the pendants, she observed, that each wore.

Kyril was speaking, recounting to the Congressional members her discovery of AIDS in the Other dimension, updating them on her research thus far, acknowledging Dag's previous communications with them and informing them of his communique ordering her home. She reached into her robe and withdrew an envelope. "These," she said, gesturing with it, "are Dag's reports to the Capital Congress, along with his recommendations." She stepped forward and placed the sealed packet on the table in front of the center oupir. "I have not read his dispatch to you, but was directed in his letter to me to take the lead in developing a Kornägian research team—immediately upon my arrival here.

"Additionally, I now advise the immediate cessation of all but essential travel between dimensions, and the quarantine of all returning to Kornägy from the Other dimension. Honorable Congress—failure to implement these measures could mean an epidemic of catastrophic proportions." Her voice left no room for hesitation in the minds of her listeners, and her dark eyes moved from the eyes of first one, then another, until she was certain she had impressed upon each member the gravity of their situation.

Following a long moment of silence, the member from the state of Tét arose, her mien somber. "We thank you for this service, well-performed, Daughter." She nodded her dismissal of Kyril.

Kyril bowed briefly in return, as the other members rose. She turned and lifted her gaze, signalling Kathryn with her eyes that the proceeding was at an end.

Kathryn met her in the foyer. "Well, how'd it go?" Kathryn inquired. She had been unable to judge for herself from the solemn faces and even tones of voice.

Kyril considered briefly before replying. "They will take the recommended action." She continued walking towards the main entry.

Kathryn eyed her sideways. "But?"

"But—they are not happy with me for violating one of our oldest prohibitions." She glanced at Kathryn. "Bringing you with me today was not particularly prudent of me," she admitted, silently reproving herself for her thoughtless self-indulgence.

"What did they say?" Kathryn wondered how she could have missed such severe disapproval, even with the language barrier.

Kyril shook her head. "Nothing was said. Rather, it was what was *not* said. Our way is not always direct," she offered by way of explanation. They passed through the entryway and came out into the middle of the Kornägian day.

Involuntarily, Kathryn looked up. The sun was near its zenith, but the light it cast was so dim that she was reminded of films she had seen of the "midnight sun" of Earth's arctic circle. The incandescent body shone metallically out of a thinly colored lavender sky. "Is this as bright as it gets?" she exclaimed with a gasp.

Smiling slightly, Kyril nodded. "I think a visit to the library would be in order," she said, taking Kathryn's elbow and steering her away from the governmental center.

As they strolled along, Mindi at heel, Kyril pointed out the landmarks of the city of Sziv, which was, she had already explained, the seat of government in the state of Köros, the capital state of Kornägy. Its central location, connecting the continents of the eastern and western hemispheres, had made Köros a province long under dispute by neighboring Madaras on the west and Nagykáta on the east. Its disputed status had been settled once and for all by the logical choice of Köros as global capital.

They arrived at the huge library complex. *All the public facilities are huge,* Kathryn thought to herself, wondering why, adding yet another item to her mental list, as Kyril led them to a series of booths on one floor which she explained were "instructional" booths. "There is really no equivalent word in English," she said.

"But, how can I understand any of this," Kathryn protested, "when I don't speak. . .your language?"

"You need not speak any of the languages of Kornägy," Kyril replied, seating her in a comfortable chaise lounge and placing a small headpiece over Kathryn's temples. "This device accesses the neural centers of learning without need for language or translation—really without need for words at all. The information will seem as if it comes to you in your own language—whatever that might be. I am neither linguist nor neurologist—I cannot explain it in detail. The device stimulates the individual's language centers to process the electronic signals sent through the neural interface, so that the user understands whatever is transmitted."

Kathryn was amazed—and not a little frightened. She pulled off the headpiece. "Are you sure this will work on my brain?"

"The device calibrates itself to the neural frequencies of the individual user—whether oupirian or human should not matter. The anatomies of our central nervous systems are quite similar." She waited expectantly.

Reluctant still, Kathryn lay back in the chair and refit the headpiece. "I hope you're right," she muttered. "Where will you be while this is going on?"

"I shall remain with you for a short while. Once the process is underway, I must attend another audience. But I shall return for you before you have completed the 'instruction.'"

Kathryn closed her eyes, then opened them again quickly. "Kyril—how many languages are there in Kornägy?"

Kyril smiled, recognizing the stall tactic. "Twelve, officially, including Standard. Each has a high and low form—formal and informal. There are a few provincial dialects still extant, but everyone, via this device," she gestured, "receives instruction in Standard. When we became a global unity, a standard language was developed to simplify international affairs, which, without one language, would be very complicated.

"Now—no more stalling," she ordered good-humoredly.

"Wait! What am I learning?"

"In addition to basic Standard, first-level Kornägian sociopolitical development—which of necessity includes elementary geography, history, and cultural studies."

Kathryn gaped at her. "That sounds like a year's worth of study!"

"No, only a few hours'." She folded her arms, waiting.

"Well—if you say so," Kathryn acquiesced.

Without reply, Kyril punched in commands on the keyboard and watched Kathryn settle into a deep trance.

Patting Mindi on the head, Kyril left for her meeting with the Kornägian Security Council; Capital Sector. She expected that she would be severely reprimanded for bringing Kathryn through the Boundary with her. And she accepted that she deserved whatever consequences the council imposed on her. In her heart, however, she now felt that there was nothing they could do that would have changed her decision, had she to make it again.

⟨ ⟨ ⟨

"Do you realize what you have done?"

The thunderous voice battered at Kyril across the distance between her and the Chief of the Kornägian Security Council, Capital Sector. The absence of direct address struck Kyril more forcefully than the words themselves, confirming that she had not been wrong in anticipating the worst. She contemplated the ochre face—made sallow by rage—before replying. Her eyes met his.

"I believe that I do, Honorable Tai-gan." She kept her voice carefully neutral and avoided looking at other members of the Council.

"No!" he shouted, approaching her, his boots striking sharp retorts on the stone flooring of the Council chamber. "I do not believe that you *do* know." His hands on his hips, his black eyes bored into her, inches from her face.

Kyril struggled to maintain her emotional shields against the force of his anger. She linked her hands loosely in front of her, her arms bent at the elbows, re-establishing her space, centering herself. But she said nothing and kept her eyes fixed on his.

He in turn folded his arms across his broad chest and leaned closer. His words, when he spoke, were clipped and his voice was threateningly quiet. "This species has survived milli-Cycles of conflict and discord because and *only* because each of its members has seen fit to observe the necessity for social order imposed on us by our own biological functioning. You, in making this unilateral decision, have broken untold Cycles of tradition *and* an ethical code that was adopted when our peoples began journeying in the human world."

Tai-gan's face had moved so close she could have counted the fine wrinkles on the aged skin. His was an old life among oupirs, and his age would have been reckoned at more than three-hundred years in the Other dimension. She willed herself to give no ground and remained silent, squarely in front of him.

But neither did Tai-gan relent. His almond-shaped eyes grew narrower still. "Have you no reply to these charges, daughter?" He used the word which, in his native language, the language of the state of Dyje, made "daughter" a diminutive term and implied a familiarity which they did not share.

Kyril bristled at the tactic even as she realized it had accomplished what the Security Chief wanted by putting her on the defensive. Quelling her irritation, she sought a rational response. *Might as well deflect a question with a question,* she decided.

"And what are the charges, specifically, that I am called upon to answer, Honorable Tai-gan?" She elected not to play the game of innuendo with him, recognizing that she trod on perilous ground already.

He turned sharply and spoke to the Sarkadian Councillor. "Rania, please explain to our compatriot *our* perception of what it is that she has done." He waited, his expression grim; his black eyes on Kyril again.

Kyril shifted her gaze to the brown-skinned woman whom Taigan had addressed. Rania gave Kyril a cold stare, then began to read from a prepared document in front of her. Kyril could not suppress a slight shiver as the woman began. The formality of the proceedings was another unwelcome indication that she had failed to fully appreciate the seriousness with which others would view her actions in bringing Kathryn through the Boundary with her. She fought a growing dismay.

"The Kornägian Security Council, Capital Sector, hereby warrants that Kyril *nó*Kolayna, *fér*Vlad, *tars*Lanaea, has compromised the security of all Kornägy through her willful disobedience of the communally accepted guidelines governing transits between this and the Other dimension, and that this compromise has been effected principally by the act of bringing a humanoid from the Other dimension through the Boundary with her, as well as by any disclosures Kyril Vértök has made to said humanoid, either before of after committing this act, as to the true nature of the oupirian species and our origins.

"In recognition of the gravity of these acts, the Kornägian Security Council, Capital Sector, hereby recommends the immediate withdrawal of all privileges of transit to, or communication with anyone in, the Other dimension—"

Involuntarily, Kyril gasped. "But you cannot do that!"

"—for an indefinite period not to be less than five nor more than twenty full Cycles of seasons." Rania paused in her reading and looked hard at Kyril, her disapprobation clear. She finished by reciting the names of all the signatories.

There was a tense silence as the woman's voice died away in the stone chamber and Kyril sought for words to explain her position.

"Please—you—you cannot prohibit my communication with the Other dimension—you do not understand. My return here was motivated by the discovery of an illness in that Other dimension that has already infected members of our species and could *decimate* us if prompt action is not taken. I have already been given permission to follow Däg Svensen's directive to establish a research center and begin the efforts to find a cure or containment for this disease. It is *imperative* that I be allowed to communicate with my colleagues in the Other dimension, so as to be most fully informed of the progress of the disease among human beings."

Her eyes pleaded for understanding from the panel facing her. All but one face remained impassive.

"Is it true," Darkhan, the member from Nagykáta, began, "that the human you brought with you is a specialist in this disease?" His brown eyes focused intently on Kyril.

She nodded. "Yes, it is true."

"And is it then also true that *this* is why you brought her with you through the Boundary?"

Kyril refused the opportunity to attempt to escape the truth in front of the Council. "That was part—but *only* part—of the reason." She waited, her eyes on Darkhan's.

He clasped his hands and leaned across the table at which all but Tai-gan had remained seated. "What was the other reason?"

Kyril suddenly felt naked before these other members of her kind. Equally as suddenly, she realized that they would not understand her feelings for a human woman. Those who continued to view the human species as nothing more than prey *could* not. She swallowed hard, searching for the right words.

Tai-gan pressed her. "Well—what was the other reason?"

Kyril hesitated only a moment more. Then, "It is a matter of-the-blood. I prefer not to speak of it."

A collective inhalation could be heard in the echoing chamber. What Kyril had said was, by implication, protection of a member of her own family. Applying such to a human being was unheard of and, previously, unthinkable. The Council was, if possible, more deeply shocked by her claim of-the-blood than by the act of having brought a human to their world in the first place. The silence which followed the gasp required no definition. Kyril knew that, in making the claim, she had unequivocally and irretrievably committed herself to a course of action no oupir known to her had ever set upon.

There was a long, strained silence. Taking the absence of further response from the Council as dismissal, Kyril bowed briefly, then turned to leave.

She had reached the door when Tai-gan's voice again hammered at her.

"Doctor—"

She halted and pivoted to face him.

"If the Congress of Health determines that your communication with oupirs in the Other dimension is essential, it will be permitted *for scientific purposes only.*" His face was stony. "Is that clear?"

She nodded. "Very clear."

He glared at her but said nothing more. With one more sweeping glance at the other Council members, she turned again and exited the chamber.

Escaping the Security Building for the fresh air of the outdoors, Kyril finally allowed herself her feelings. Her heart began to pound and her breath came shallowly. *Great Helena—what have I done?* She paused on the wide staircase in front of the building. Astonishment at the changes in her that she was only beginning to recognize overtook her. She had thought out none of her responses to the Council ahead of time, preferring to trust her instincts at the moment of confrontation. At least they had said nothing about forcing Kathryn to return to her own dimension. She fervently hoped that, in the end, she would be proven not to have erred in acquiescing to Kathryn's demands to come with her. She sighed. No matter: what was done was done. *Goddess, help us to realize our goals in defeating this scourge,* she prayed. To herself she added, *Else, I will have risked all for naught.*

21

ithin a week of Kyril's return to Kornägy, she was settled in a laboratory suite at Sziv's foremost biosciences research facility, renewing her efforts to conquer the AIDS virus. She had said nothing to Kathryn of her meeting with the Security Council. Rather, she had set Kathryn to encoding all the information they had brought with them—in their brains and on microfiche—from Kathryn's dimension. Mentally prepared for the possibility of an abrupt departure, while in Minneapolis Kyril had continuously updated her hardcopy, transferring it to film, knowing that data on magnetic discs would be scrambled in transit through the dimensional barrier. Consequently, she had little to add to the microfiche she gave Kathryn. She had arranged for a continued supply of information to be sent through the Boundary to her by the oupirian scientist she had designated at the Minneapolis clinic.

Kathryn—who by now had a good command of written Standard—was charged with all future data inputting, and with delivering up-to-date information to the remainder of the staff. Kyril trusted in Kathryn's training as a researcher to organize and cross-reference all their materials. She had instructed her to include the information on candidiasis and wholistic therapies as well, in case it should prove useful to them in some way.

Meanwhile, Kyril began to design a series of experiments to gather more information about what was by now being referred to by human scientists as strain three of the Human T-lymphotrophic virus—in particular with regard to its effects on the oupirian body. To begin, she wanted to attempt to isolate the virus itself—or discover some trace of it. Four oupirs who appeared to be suffering from AIDS were housed in a nearby clinical suite, readily available for examination—or a more effective treatment than isolation and transfusion, should one be derived. As part of the preliminaries to moving into the research suite, Kyril had reviewed the *vitae* of several scientists recommended both by Däg and the Sectorial Congress of Health. From these, she had selected another physician with whom she had worked previously, Taddéos Orosziány, to head the elite team that would implement her experimental designs.

Although it went largely unspoken, Kyril was made aware quite clearly of the disapproval she had incurred amongst her peers in the scientific community. Several of its members, whom she had approached as possible colleagues, had censured her openly by refusing to work with her, even on such an important project. There was no Kornägian precedent to force someone to work on something one chose not to be associated with, no matter how it important it might be. Taddéos, knowing Kyril personally, and having nothing but respect for her professionally, had set aside any personal reservations he might have held for the opportunity to be a part of this invaluable research.

Once the team was assembled, Kathryn's days were initially divided between in-service education and entering data. When Taddéos and the twelve or so staff he and Kyril had gathered had been taught all that was presently known about AIDS and other human viruses, they went to work in their laboratories while Kathryn completed encoding their present body of information. As soon as it was computerized, the information could be made available to anyone who desired to access it, and could be acquired by future staff, in the same manner through which she had acquired Kornägian history and Standard.

Because of her interest and her familiarity with the subject, Kathryn had also been given her own patient. Kyril and Taddéos had acceded to her request to use one of the males and the two females who had been admitted to the clinic as a control group, while she subjected the other male to a regimen she developed from her knowledge of wholistic therapies gleaned while still in her own dimension. The experiment was to be supervised closely by the two oupirian physicians.

Engrossed in her work, Kathryn lost track of the passing of time. She was putting in ten to twelve hour days—by her watch —sometimes coming in early, sometimes late. By Earth reckoning, the Kornägian day was several hours longer. Whenever she came, she worked each day as long as she felt coherent, then quit and spent some time walking Mindi before falling into bed for sleep. She and Kyril had taken an apartment near the biosciences center, but Kyril—indefatigable as usual—was seldom there. Consequently, they had seen little of each other during their initial push to get the project organized and moving.

One evening, late into the third Kornägian week of their work, Kathryn finished entering the last of the data brought from Earth, then sat back in her chair and logged off. The silence encroached upon her broadening awareness, and she gradually realized she was alone. She stretched and sighed, stood and called to Mindi. Momentarily, she felt slightly woozy. Knowing she was exhausted from her long days and the unaccustomed sitting, she dismissed the sensation. She turned out the lights in her area, then, with Mindi by her side proceeded down the hallway towards the only lighted portal in the dim corridor.

Kathryn paused in the open doorway while Mindi trotted in and around the desk to where Kyril sat, reviewing printouts. Mindi raised herself and pawed at Kyril's arm Her concentration broken, Kyril looked up in surprise. "Hello!" She rubbed Mindi's head briskly.

Kathryn attempted a tired smile, but not spoken Standard. Her tongue seemed incapable of making the proper contortions to produce the language in a form recognizable to the oupirian ear. She and Kyril generally spoke English to one another. "Come back to the apartment with me," she said.

Kyril sensed Kathryn's tiredness, heard her words as demand, not request, and knew Kathryn must again be feeling as alone as she had often felt when travelling in Kathryn's dimension. "All right," she agreed quietly, and began clearing her desk. Removing the coveralls she wore in the lab, she replaced them with her own jumpsuit. The soft, wine-red fabric adhered to the contours of her body in gentle flutings and folds.

Kathryn watched, leaning against the doorway, as Kyril stripped, then climbed into the clinging garment. In spite of her fatigue, she suddenly wanted Kyril fiercely. She went to her and ran a finger over the soft fabric, caressing the shoulder beneath.

Kyril sensed the mixture of restlessness and desire in Kathryn, and felt her own pulse quicken in response. She stepped into an embrace, brushing her lips hungrily against the side of Kathryn's neck.

Kathryn's breath caught, and she felt the gooseflesh rise over her. "On the other hand," she whispered as Kyril's hands caressed her beneath her lab coat, "we could just stay here. . . ." Her words trailed off softly. She arched her head back and pushed her hips forward against Kyril's. Kyril whispered into the flesh of Kathryn's throat. "Not here—"

Kathryn groaned softly. "Then let's go home, now," she urged. Arm in arm, enjoying their arousal, the women leisurely walked the few blocks to their apartment, Mindi at Kathryn's side. Kornägy's Cycle of Seasons was not synchronous with those of Earth, and the evening was a balmy one.

There were, however, others on the streets who, by her scent, immediately recognized Kathryn for what she was and directed gazes of surprise or disapproval at them. Kathryn had learned to ignore such glances—even when they included Mindi—having been the object of them wherever in Sziv she went. Kyril had a harder time, as she was the object of the emotional emanations from the onlookers.

At the base of the steps leading up to their doorway, Kyril paused, then bent to Kathryn. Sweeping Kathryn into her arms, she carried her the few short steps across the threshold, past the lunarium, through the commonspace, and into the bedroom. She set Kathryn on her feet and bent to kiss her. Bone-weary, aware of her need, Kathryn opened herself, reaching outward, aching to be touched, yearning to be filled, longing to be taken. Without really understanding what she asked, she murmured to Kyril, entreating her to give herself and accept what Kathryn was offering.

Kathryn's murmurings, uttered in a mixture of English and broken Standard, pierced Kyril's heart. It thrilled her to hear desire expressed, however haltingly, in her own tongue. No one had spoken so to her since Lanaea's death. Her last reserves—erected to preserve the memory of Lanaea—gave way. She felt herself sliding into her own need for completion, for a mate.

With the sound of her own blood pulsing in her ears, Kyril pushed Kathryn down against the bed, gazing intently into her eyes. Slowly, she lowered her face to Kathryn's and began to kiss her again, her body moving over Kathryn's in time to the rhythm of her tongue in Kathryn's mouth. Together, they rolled on the bed, disrobing, caressing, writhing against one another.

Having been denied by time and circumstance, Kathryn's orgasm exploded within her in just moments. She moaned and clutched at Kyril as the pleasure enveloped her totally, her head lolling back. She yearned to have Kyril's belly open to hers, that they might be joined in that inmost place where pleasure and sexual union dwelt.

Kyril slid her lips over Kathryn's chin, to her exposed throat. The skin there gave off a fragrance sweet with the promise of the blood that surged in the huge veins and arteries beneath.

Kyril lifted her head and levelled her gaze at Kathryn, who languished in the aftermath of her climax. The force of will directed through Kyril's eyes and the emotional energy she put behind it accomplished unwittingly what she would never have deliberately sought: Kathryn appeared confused and lost in thought.

As the human woman willingly sank into a light hypnotic state, Kyril's heart swelled with joy. She licked the soft skin of her neck, tasting her, inhaling the sweetness. As the heat built rapidly in her belly, Kyril's tongue sheath retracted, allowing her to penetrate the skin of Kathryn's neck with her tongue's keratoid core, the *Kingró*. The *Kingró* sank into Kathryn's jugular, releasing Kathryn's life blood into Kyril's mouth. While the waves of her orgasm crested, Kyril sucked avidly at the flow, consuming several deep swallows before withdrawing. She then lapped gently at the wound, coating it with her saliva. Its chemical makeup sealed the puncture, immediately speeding healing.

Desire quenched, she slumped against the entranced Kathryn and drifted into the altered state known to oupirs as *rosu vis,* the Red Dream— a total, out-of-body high, commonly brought about by simultaneous orgasm and blood-sharing between those who were spirit-bonded. The only thing in oupirian experience known to approximate the oneness of the Red Dream was prenatal consciousness of union with one's maternal parent. That unity was a thing longed for, sought after in the eternal quest, the primal desire, to end separation—if only for moments at a time.

Ultimately, the Dream was a sacred thing, a thing to be shared only with one's *vërtar,* blood-mate, in the abiding fire of *lélek bizalmas,* mate-bond made and renewed. This—the total union—was totally apart from one's casual sexual interactions, whether in the Other dimension, or with one's own kind. Kyril had known this bonding with only one other being since her birth—Lanaea. And Lanaea had shared it equally with her, in full knowledge and expectation of the experience.

Kathryn as yet knew nothing of this sacred sharing—and yet, her spirit had risen to meet Kyril's, yearning equally for confluence.... Kyril was deeply gratified by Kathryn's longing—and, for now, content with what had passed between them. Kathryn's part in the blood-sharing—and their mutual commitment, the ritual of *lélek bizalmas—would,* she now believed, come later, after Kyril had, at long last, finalized her period of mourning for Lanaea.

❆ ❆ ❆

Oupirian culture was steeped in ritual—rituals marking the important occasions in one's journey from birth to death. Many of the step-markers were symbolically anointed with blood—the most sacred of all the physical elements in the apprehended universe.

Following a brief but very deep sleep, Kyril arose. She clothed herself in a robe of the deepest crimson, and hung the elliptical pendant about her neck. As she had earlier explained to Kathryn when queried, the ellipse was symbolic of Kornägy itself, the Great Circle; the line through it represented the Boundary between worlds. Over thousands of Cycles of Seasons, the *hasakör,* as it was properly referred to, had acquired meaning at many levels. Kyril grasped it, thinking of Lanaea, the *hasakör* a tangible reminder of the Kornägian belief in the finality of physical death. The Great Circle was firmament; beyond that was incorporeal. One's *lélek,* the ethereal self, was gifted with one physical lifetime in this Circle. Upon the death of *téstiszéria,* the physical body, the spirit returned to the Source, surrendering separation to confluence with the Oneness of the inexplicable Universe. So Kyril's people believed. So Kyril believed.

Csatlós, the Kornägian moon, had not yet set. In the eerie half-light, Kyril passed through the still quiet city, shrouded in nightmist, to the memorial park where Lanaea's ashes reposed. The small urn which contained the residue of Lanaea's corporeal self was set among many like it, with nothing but an inscription to distinguish it from any other. Kyril knelt next to it and recited to herself the words she knew by heart:

> # LANAEA
>
> *nó*Katrina
>
> *fér*Lajos
>
> *társ*Kyril
>
> 4159 — 4202 k.e.
>
> "She Has Passed Through The Dream"

"Lanaea, I have come to take my leave," Kyril whispered into the wet morning, her tears running freely now down her face. Within, she felt anew the pain of the sundering, when Lanaea had died. This time, she embraced the loss rather than denying it. This time, she allowed herself to feel the empty space where Lanaea's *lélek* had once conjoined with hers. Then, lifting her face to the setting moon, she raised her left wrist before her. With sinking Csatlós as her witness, Kyril raked the blade edge of the *hasakör* across her wrist, spilling her blood upon the ground in front of Lanaea's urn.

The new wound would heal, forming a second scar next to the one made when she and Lanaea had joined their lives together. What was begun in the blood was ended with the blood.

Finally able, Kyril's lips formed the words she had never before been able to voice. "Good-bye, my love," she whispered softly. She reached out and caressed the urn with her fingertips.

In the damp that lay on the urn, a spot of blood spread and faded against the white stone.

22

hen Kyril returned to the apartment, she discovered that Kathryn was still sleeping. She let Mindi out, fed her, then showered and dressed for the laboratory. Before leaving, she wrote Kathryn a short note and put it on the bedside table.

She bent over Kathryn, watching her sleep for a moment. Protectiveness swelled within her. She kissed her gently, stroking the thick hair from her temple. Kathryn did not stir. Kyril had taken considerably less blood from her last evening than when she had fed on the mountainside, but she knew that Kathryn had been working exhausting hours and expected she would sleep much of the day. She left Mindi with her, directing the dog to stay with her and watch over her while Kyril was gone.

Late in the afternoon, Kyril left the lab and came back to their apartment, wanting to spend time with Kathryn, to try to talk about what had transpired between them the evening before. Kyril felt a need to put into words what had happened within her, and what her hope and expectations were.

Kathryn was still sleeping heavily. The note Kyril had left was untouched. Kyril studied Mindi. The dog showed no alarm or disquiet. Nonetheless, Kyril was disquieted. She sat beside Kathryn and took her pulse, then examined her briefly. In the soft illumination from the valance lighting, she could detect the dark circles beneath Kathryn's eyes. She debated briefly, then decided to awaken her.

"Kathryn," she called, gently shaking her. She repeated herself several times before Kathryn's eyelids flickered, then opened.

"Hello," Kyril greeted softly. "How are you feeling?"

Kathryn responded slowly. "Tired. . so tired." She rubbed her hands across her face, as if wiping the fatigue away, then pushed up on one elbow.

"Could you eat?" Kyril suggested.

Kathryn collapsed. "I guess," she sighed.

Kornägian dwellings had nothing even approximating a kitchen, so a small refrigeration unit had been borrowed from the biology lab and the chemistry lab had donated a bunsen burner which Kathryn had rigged to serve as a hotplate. The stores of dried and canned foods Kyril had brought with them sufficed while a Kornägian biologist of Kyril's acquaintance continued work to formulate a suitable and complete diet from native substances for both visitors. It had already been established that several of Kornägy's mammalian species were edible, so Mindi was enjoying a mixed fare of fresh-killed raw meat and kibble brought with them through the Boundary.

Kyril knew Kathryn did not normally consume the flesh of other animals, but she felt that Kathryn's body was in need of protein nourishment. So, in the makeshift kitchen, Kyril now took a small cut from a piece of meat intended for Mindi. She threw it in a pan on the burner and seared it, as she had observed it done in restaurants in Kathryn's dimension. She had no idea how it should taste—the odor of cooking food was always faintly repulsive to her. By opening a can of vegetables and heating up something she found in the refrigeration unit that was a leftover from a previous meal, she had a meal ready for Kathryn fairly quickly. She was asleep again when Kyril brought the platter in on a tray. Although dismayed at Kathryn's lethargy, Kyril found that awakening her was easier the second time. She helped prop her up on pillows and sat with her while she began to eat.

Upon discovering that the meal included meat, Kathryn paused, but offered no verbal objection. Her first few mouthfuls seemed an effort, but as the hot food made its way into her body, Kathryn seemed to revive, When she had consumed every morsel, she set the tray aside, then declared, "I think I'll take a bath."

Kyril saw the wan smile and was relieved. "You responded to that," she declared, gesturing at the empty tray, "like an oupir to a feeding."

Kathryn's smile faltered. There was a short, uncomfortable silence, during which Kyril realized that Kathryn had not made total peace with the oupirian way of life. She was chagrined. Perhaps her expectations of the ritual of *lélek bizalmas* were premature.

"Yes—well, I think I'll shower now," Kathryn said, seeing Kyril's expression, trying to smooth things over. She slid out of bed, then staggered, saving herself from falling only by clutching at the bedside table.

"Kathryn!" Kyril grabbed her by the arms.

"Oh—I feel so light-headed!"

Kyril made a rapid decision. "I am going to ask Taddéos to come over to examine you. Meanwhile, you lie down—no shower yet." She assisted Kathryn onto the bed, then hurried into the front room where the commcenter was.

She quickly located Taddéos—still at the laboratory—and in a low voice expressed her concerns. He agreed to come at once.

Very shortly, Taddéos was closeted with Kathryn while Kyril paced nervously in the lunarium, holding herself tightly. She was trying not to give in to the panic that screamed at her from deep within: *What if she has AIDS?* She had wanted to believe Kathryn's assurances that she could not possibly have been infected; but, at the moment, she could think of no other reason for Kathryn's lethargy. Fear for her own well-being screamed at the door of her conscious mind, demanding admission. It seemed forever before Taddéos' voice beckoned her to join them.

"What do you think, Taddéos?" She heard the tightness in her voice as her gaze took in Kathryn, still appearing wan, now propped on pillows again.

Taddéos gave her a long look. "Her blood pressure seems very low—accounting for the light-headedness." He glanced at Kathryn, then back to Kyril. "The puncture—"

Kyril shook her head, interrupting him. "I took very little—less than when she brought me back from second stage trance, in the mountains."

Kathryn paled at this exchange and sat forward. She only dimly remembered the events of the night before—did not understand what they were referring to. But she said nothing. She wanted to know what was the matter with her.

Taddéos' somber expression deepened markedly. "I cannot offer a convincing reason as to why without further study, but she evidences every sign of severe exhaustion." He returned his gaze to Kathryn. "For now, I prescribe complete bedrest and. . . ." He struggled to recall the English words. "And good nutrition. Have you an adequate diet worked out?" he asked Kyril.

She hesitated. "Not yet—Josef is still testing some of the foodstuffs we gave him for compatibility with human metabolism."

"Hurry him on." He picked up his medkit. "I shall come to see you again tomorrow, Kathryn. " He nodded good-bye and Kyril escorted him out. At the door, he paused.

"I want a complete blood work-up on her. Fill this and bring it to the laboratory for testing." He handed her a small, rubber-capped tube.

The request chilled Kyril, but she nodded silent acceptance.

When she returned to the bedroom, she paused in the doorway, feeling no less concerned about Kathryn's health than she had before Taddéos had come.

"What 'puncture,' Kyril?" Kathryn's voice, though quiet, had the force of desiring to know behind it.

Kyril eyed her. "You truly don't remember?" she asked softly, disappointment swelling within.

"Remember what?" Kathryn asked suspiciously.

Kyril sighed. "Last night, we left the lab—we came here—made love—You *wanted* me to take you, Kathryn—I felt it." At Kyril's words, Kathryn's hand involuntarily went to her neck and her eyes widened. "I partook of your blood—just as you shall taste mine—" Kyril broke off as Kathryn blanched.

"Taste yours—why should I taste yours? Why did you—" She could not go on. Her mouth suddenly filled with saliva, and she knew she was going to vomit.

Kyril vaulted to the bedside, tempted to slap Kathryn across the face. Instead, she seized her by the shoulders and shook her sharply, twice. "Kathryn! Listen to me!" she barked.

Kathryn's face went blank with surprise. She stared at Kyril, her nausea gone as suddenly as it had come.

"Perhaps I judged it wrongly," Kyril admitted quietly. "But all your emotional emanations have been filled with longing—ever since I've known you—imperatives that I bond with you." Her voice held pleading justification. "I have only—finally—responded to your urgings with my own.

"Oupirs consummate their bonds with the sharing of blood. I have tried to tell you that—were you not listening?" She let go of Kathryn's shoulders.

Kathryn regarded her woodenly. "I heard—but, I guess. . .I didn't understand. . .didn't think of it in terms of me—" She averted her eyes. "I'm sorry," she whispered in a stricken voice.

Kathryn's wounded expression moved Kyril. "Oh, my love," she said softly, taking Kathryn's hands in hers. "I would never do anything knowingly to hurt you, nor would I attempt to coerce you. It has taken me a long time, but I have done with the largest part of my grieving over Lanaea. I want us to be together." She studied Kathryn. When there was no response, she went on. "Perhaps you need more time." She rose, denying frustrated hopes. "Sleep now—we'll talk tomorrow."

"Kyril—" Kathryn's voice was insistent. "I do want you. . .but you see—I never envisioned it this way." Her eyes begged for understanding.

Wearily, Kyril kissed her on the forehead, guiding her back into the pillows. "Good night, love." She patted the bed and Mindi jumped up beside Kathryn, who watched Kyril reproachfully until her eyes finally shut and her breast again rose and fell with the rhythm of sleep.

Turning from the bed, Kyril went back into the lunarium and stared out at the night. A dense fog was gathering, depositing heavy drops on the plasglass roof as the air cooled and the soil gave off its moist warmth. Kyril held herself, lifting her gaze to the dark sky. Even here, in the city, on a clear night she could have seen many of the myriad stars in a heavenly canopy over Kornägy. Her eyes sought out the positions of the constellations familiar to her since childhood. Kornägian legends and tales included the astronomical members of the universe visible from their world—and there were so many more to be observed here than in Kathryn's world. Their very profusion had made for tales of group, rather than individual, exploits. She looked where she knew her favorite, Helena, would be, low on the western horizon. Helena was an exception to the rule: Helena, Celestial Guardian of Kispest, the northernmost state in the western hemisphere, had endured much hardship and travail to bring her people a cure for a disease that had plagued the animal populations of Kispest on which the residents were dependent for food. Kyril had always pictured her in her mind's eye as a big, tall woman with thick masses of long hair—and had aspired to be like her. Her entry into medicine was emulation of the legend of Helena.

She broke off her musings as she heard Kathryn, turning, moan softly in her sleep. Kyril hunched her shoulders against the conflicts that riddled her. She realized she had had no real peace of mind since Lanaea had died—that seeking out Kathryn had added to, not ameliorated, her emotional unrest. She sighed deeply, dropped her hands, and clasped them in front of her. Admitting her need for solace, she thought of the one being she trusted most.

After leaving a note for Kathryn in case she should awaken and find her gone, Kyril summoned a glidecar and donned a hooded raincape against the damp. She keyed directions to the Os into the autopilot and gave herself to blankness while she was transported to her destination.

Her attention came to focus again as she finally stood outside Guardian Tyrell's quarters. Resolutely, she signalled for admission and stepped through the portal when it slid open. For a moment, she simply stood in the dimmed entryway, listening to the profound stillness of Tyrell's apartment.

Soft as a wind, Tyrell approached, her mental shields in place, welcoming the late night visitor. "Peace be with thee," she said quietly, bowing slightly. "How may I be of service?" She awaited whatever request her daughter might make, her chiselled features composed.

Kyril, whose face was in shadow, drew back the hood of her cape. Light fell across her face. "Mother," she greeted, bowing in return. Her mouth felt dry and the words came out hoarsely. "Mother, I have come at this late hour because—" *Because what?* she asked herself. *Because my heart aches—because I have finally let go of Lanaea, allowed her spirit to depart from me—because I want a human woman who is repelled by our customs and much that I hold dear? Because my colleagues have censured me for bringing her with me into our world? Because disease takes my brothers and sisters from me, and I cannot stop it?*

Kyril was unable to voice the words she heard in her own head— her throat locked as she struggled with them, and tears came unbidden to her eyes as her psychic barriers dropped.

Inundated with waves of emotion washing at her from Kyril, the older woman's quietude was threatened. She strengthened her empathic barriers in defense even as she reached out for Kyril's arm. Advisor she might be, but she was also Comforter—and Spiritual Mother to this One. "Come," she urged softly, "come, sit with me." She led them into her private study, to the comfortable couch for two.

As Kyril sank beside her, Tyrell said, "Give me thy thoughts, Child. Give me thine heart." The aged voice broke.

Kyril pleaded mutely with her—for what, she neither knew nor cared to know—as she struggled with the desire to be strong and without need. Tyrell's silent, steady gaze reminded Kyril of their relationship— and their bond. At last, she relented and gave herself permission to need from this One who had nurtured her so many times before. She bowed her head and sought Tyrell's strong, dark hands with her own pale ones.

Tyrell clasped Kyril's hands firmly and closed her eyes, slowly opening herself to the emotional turmoil within her Daughter. As in a waking dream, she experienced the tumult of Kyril's quandaries and saw the images that went with them. She reached out, mentally, emotionally, and accepted the burden of Kyril's pain—giving in return the solace of her spiritual embrace.

Kyril felt the pain drain from her, to be replaced by a calm stillness that she recognized as Tyrell's love and compassion for her. With the stillness came the tears she needed release from as well. Tyrell held her shoulders gently while Kyril sank to her knees in front of her. Her arms clutching Tyrell's waist, Kyril buried her face in the lap of the woman who had raised her.

Neither knew how long they sat thus, nor Kyril when her tears ended and she drifted into the respite of emotional nothingness. At length, Kyril loosed her arms from Tyrell's robed legs and raised her head from her mentor's knee, looking around her idly. It had been a very long time since she had visited Tyrell in her quarters, but nothing seemed to have changed. Her books and sculptures were in their customary places, her desk neat as always, the video display blinking with some interrupted task. On the low table in the middle of the room sat a vase with fresh cut blooms in them—Tyrell's one personal indulgence. The elegant sameness was steadying.

When Tyrell sensed that Kyril was ready, she rose silently, beckoning to her. They went into Tyrell's bedroom, where she turned on the light in the bath and laid out a fresh robe for Kyril. "I shall await you in the study," she said, departing.

Kyril indulged in a long, hot bath, allowing the heat to soothe away the remains of her physical tension. She rejoined Tyrell, feeling, at long last, deeply and completely relaxed.

Tyrell had prepared a mellow beverage, distilled from a fruit of her native Tét. Kyril stood while Tyrell measured out their portions and seated herself opposite Kyril.

After a few moments of enjoying the taste and bouquet of the *cognak*, Tyrell asked, "What is it about this human woman that draws you so, Child?" Her eyes seemed fixed on a point far away. But Kyril knew well that Tyrell listened intently when possessed by that faraway look.

Kyril considered her reply. "It is. . .difficult to articulate, Mother." She paused. "In some ways, I am not at all sure—" She unconsciously duplicated Tyrell's faraway demeanor. "I suppose that part of it is that she reminds me—a bit—of Lanaea: her laughter, the way she looks at me. . .as if she wanted to see all the way to the center of my soul." She smiled slightly. "And, of course, there is the physical passion. . . ." Kyril paused again, as if listening within. "But I cannot find the words to express the way her spirit touches mine. . .as if she were. . .certain. . .that we were destined to be together." She shook her head. "I cannot say more." She shrugged helplessly.

The older woman's gaze had centered on Kyril, gathering Kyril's attention again, as Kyril spoke of Kathryn's certainty. "Do you allow yourself to be suaded by her determination, her desire for you? What of her inability to accept the being that you are—and all that that means?"

Kyril shook her head, smiling again. "No, my dear Mother Tyrell. I, too—if truth be told—feel some of that same. . .certainty." Her brow wrinkled as she grew serious again. "I do not understand it, but I feel as if I have been given a second chance at a life partnership.

"The *pain* of it, the conflict," she went on, "has to do with our being from two such different worlds. *Can* we understand and accept one another on the level of our physical, day-to-day realities? *Where* will we live our life together? And—" Kyril's hands grasped at the air as she struggled with the idea of it: "What will I do when she has lived out her natural life and I. . .once again. . .am left alone?"

Tyrell saw her Spiritual Daughter begin to relive the pain of Lanaea's death yet again, and sought to stay her from it. *"Nothing,"* she said, "can be foreknown. And if we lived our lives awaiting knowledge of the future, the present would be no more than a wasted dream. If you have *any* certainty about what is *now,* honor it, Kyril—else it, too, may pass with the changing Cycles."

Kyril listened, rapt, to Tyrell's words, realizing she was being given tacit permission to pursue her relationship with Kathryn, wherever it might lead her. Joy breathed deep within, and a smile arose from it to overtake her face. "Yes, Mother," she whispered, grateful tears caught behind the smile.

23

Kathryn struggled upward, through layers of sleep that seemed as heavy as the woolen blankets her mother used to pile on her bed during the winters of her Florida childhood. The weight of it was oppressive and she surfaced, at last, feeling as if she had been suffocating.

Her eyes searched the room and she noted that grey dawnlight entered through the windows that occupied most of the eastern wall. Although Mindi lay beside her on the bed, Kyril was nowhere to be seen. She glanced at the pillow next to hers. It appeared unused. She listened intently for some sound of Kyril's presence. A sudden, small panic edged its way into her awareness at the unoccupied silence of the apartment.

In response, Mindi raised her head and eyed Kathryn closely, then looked around the room, seeking the source of Kathryn's fear.

Kathryn laid a hand on the back of Mindi's neck, intending to reassure the dog, but drawing, instead, calmness from her steady companion. They lay together for a few moments, Mindi's head in the crook of Kathryn's arm, while Kathryn tried to orient herself.

She knew she had slept deeply—but not for how long. She vaguely remembered leaving the lab with Kyril and coming here to make love. . . .She also recalled faintly that Taddéos had visited them. . .and that she and Kyril had had a disagreement. She struggled with the why of it, unsuccessfully.

Glancing at the windows again, she affirmed that it was indeed early morning. Gradually, she raised herself to a sitting position, stretching, as Mindi often did on first awakening. She was beginning to realize how hungry she was. That, and her feeling of being completely rested, added up to having had a *long* sleep.

She threw off the covers and set about her morning tasks. The note Kyril had left next to the bed went completely unnoticed until Kathryn returned to straighten the bed after her shower.

Kathryn read it over, but gained little in the way of answer to her questions about why Kyril was absent. She knew next to nothing about her lover's relationship with Tyrell. There had been little time for personal talk in the past weeks, and Tyrell had not been among their topics of exchange when they had managed to steal a few moments to themselves. Sighing, frowning, Kathryn laid the note on the bedside table and drifted into the kitchen area.

She prepared a meal for herself and fed Mindi, who seemed hungry too. While she ate, she sat in the commonspace and tried to decide what to do in Kyril's absence. Not knowing how long she had slept made her feel particularly disjointed. She was also restless, and ready to be up and out. In minimal time, she had finished her vegetarian fare, donned her working clothes—a serviceable set of coveralls in a soft synthetic—and was ready to go. She called Mindi and they stepped out into the clear, moist morning of what promised to be a relatively warm Kornägian day. Kathryn inhaled deeply and actually felt invigorated. She decided to walk Mindi before going to the lab, and set off for a nearby park.

Like the city thoroughfares, the park was deserted this early in the day. Empty paths meandered along the banks of a winding stream where waterfowl swam and fed in the spring warmth. Kathryn still wrestled with the apparent incongruities of Kyril's universe: The huge, dimly lit planet with its longer solar days and years, and its cooler climate, had nevertheless spawned an incredible variety of flora and fauna—much of which resembled, at least outwardly, those that populated the Earth that Kathryn had been born to. She wondered, not for the first time, if the principles that governed the physical universe could be—were—different in this different dimension.

She sighed. There was so much she did not know about Kyril's world—so much she longed for the time to know. She felt like a babe among these people, and wondered if Kyril had ever felt the same when in her world. She supposed not. From what Kyril had said, oupirs had been studying human beings for thousands of years. She had been in the oupirian world for— How *long is it, anyway?* she wondered, brought back to her missing hours—or days. She glanced at her watch and realized it had stopped running. *Hmm. I wonder if one can get a new battery around here?*

Vexed at her confused sense of time, she remembered her intent to go to the lab. She called to Mindi and they now joined the few others who were about their business this early in the day. Later, the city would be teeming with pedestrians like herself, with the robotic glidecars filled with passengers, and, overhead, with the raised branch of Sziv's public transit system—all of it seeming still more orderly than in any major city she had visited in her own world. For now, what little foot traffic there was parted around her and her canine companion, allowing them an unimpeded, brisk walk towards the medical building. As she neared the laboratory, she put off her self-consciousness at being an alien in this world, and encouraged herself to slip into her accustomed work-mode.

She wanted first to check on her patient, for whom she had derived a cleansing regime similar to those she had learned of for human beings. While she had been occupied with entering data, her oupirian colleagues had been searching for Kornägian herbs with properties analogous to those used by the wholistic practitioners on Earth. Fortunately, there had been no "age of reason" in Kornägian history. Consequently, the ancient herbal lore had not only been preserved by Kyril's ancestors, it had actively been incorporated into their sciences, accounting, in part, for the progression of Kornägian medicine far beyond that of western medicine on Earth. Kathryn shook her head to herself, marvelling that the oupirian species had somehow avoided some of the most disastrous of human mistakes.

As she and Mindi entered the biosciences building, Kathryn glanced at the clock in the foyer, cognizant again of the early hour. The shifts had just changed. She greeted the front desk attendant and proceeded into the wing that housed the offices and research facilities. It was, as yet, completely dark. With a sinking feeling, she realized she had hoped to find Kyril here. She turned on the lights in her office and glanced around. It was as she remembered leaving it. She was disappointed: She had hoped that her work was important enough—and that she herself had been accepted enough—that, in her absence, a colleague might have come to her office in search of some piece of information she might have that was of use to others.

Turning, she decided to walk down to the clinical wing and check on her patient. At the medstation, she stopped. "Is anyone up and about yet, Federic?" she asked the dark-haired medtech. He was a tall oupir, lean, and remarkably handsome. He reminded her of one of her favorite up-and-coming actors, Mel Gibson,

In answer to her query, he shook his head, then said, "I understand that you have been ill." He spoke awkwardly in English,

Kathryn nodded half-heartedly and shrugged, appreciating the cultural gesture. "Sort of."

"I do hope that you are better now?" He seemed shy about expressing himself to her, but his Mel-Gibson-eyes were warm.

She smiled, touched by his concern. "Yes, I am—thank you, Federic!" She paused a moment, then asked, "How is Orlov doing?"

A frown furrowed his brow. His dark eyes became serious. "I—I have not looked at his chart yet this morning. . . ." He moved to retrieve it from the rack in which it hung.

Kathryn stilled him with a gesture. "No need—I'll just walk down there." She started off down the hallway.

"Doctor Hartell—I believe he was moved." Federic glanced at his room assignment board. Six of the twenty-two blips were lit. "We had two more admissions while I was off-duty—the others were moved further down the wing to allow the two newer patients a period of quarantine." He gave her the new room number of her patient and she turned and went down the still night-lit corridor.

As she passed the rooms where the newest of the clinic's patients had been assigned, she heard a slight moaning sound from the room on the left. Hesitating, she motioned Mindi to stay and went to the door, which was slightly ajar. She pushed it gently. As she stepped into the darkened room, she was seized by her left arm and yanked inside. The sudden violence startled her and she cried out involuntarily.

Her assailant whirled her around and slammed her into the wall, knocking the breath from her. Stunned, she felt herself sliding helplessly toward the floor. She gasped for breath as hands with the strength of a vice fastened themselves on her upper arms, lifting her towards a face she could only dimly see. The rank odor of disease washed at her. She fought to regain control of her voice against a rising tide of panic and nausea.

As if in slow motion, the face came clear: a face with demonic eyes, contorted in a killing frenzy, teeth bared. The insanity in those eyes paralyzed Kathryn and she stopped struggling. Then the eyes dropped to her throat. The intent of the mind behind the face was obvious. Immediately Kathryn screamed—a weak, airless sound at first—then again and again, the scream gaining strength with each attempt. As the distorted mouth stretched, opened, reaching for her throat, a rage exploded from her. *"No!"*

She felt the dry lips against the skin of her throat. *"No! No!"* She fought frantically to break the iron grasp, kicking and squirming, unwilling to acknowledge the futility of her struggle.

Growling and snarling, Mindi leapt from behind Kathryn's captor, sinking her fangs into an unprotected arm. The dog held on, slinging her weight against the creature who threatened her beloved Kathryn.

With a shriek of pain and rage, the oupir let go of Kathryn with his wounded arm. Whirling, he attempted to shake off the furred creature whose teeth tore at the tissues of his body.

Mindi clung, her jaws locked, until the demon finally released her mistress completely. As Kathryn lurched away, Mindi loosened her grip and dropped to the floor. Her feet slipped and slid as she attempted to gain footing on the slick tiling. The demon lunged. An iron fist dealt her a glancing blow on the side of the head, slamming her against the bedframe. She yelped in pain, shaking her head to clear her vision. Before she was able, the hands that had held her mistress had her in their grip. She snarled and bit down, bringing blood. The hands recoiled, then struck again. This time, she was flung against the wall. Stunned by the sharp pain that knifed through her ribs, she paused momentarily, gathering breath to attack again.

Suddenly there was a commotion behind the demon. Mindi saw others of Kyril's kind fling themselves through the doorway just as Kathryn swung a chair at the demon's back. The demon lurched and fell to his knees in front of Mindi, who bared her teeth and lunged at him again, catching him off balance. Her fangs ripped through the soft skin of the demon's face and she tasted blood again.

And then there were familiar hands pulling her off the demon, touching the pain in her side. Unable to control the reflex, Mindi yelped and turned on the hands that tugged at her, trying desperately to damp the force of her bite. Instantly the hands let go, and Mindi fell to a crouch, whimpering, begging forgiveness.

Sobbing with fright and relief, Kathryn held the dog's head gently but firmly, murmuring soft words of comfort. Again time seemed to slow—or stop—and Kathryn gently gathered Mindi to her, knowing that, had the dog not been injured, she would never have turned on her mistress. Behind them, the medtechs finished subduing the wounded oupir. After what seemed an eternity, the lights in the room came on and Kathryn turned to see her attacker. It was nearly impossible to recognize the now semi-conscious man on the floor as the frenzied assailant of only moments before.

Federic knelt beside her, his thin face pale. "Doctor Hartell—are you—is your dog—"

Kathryn stammered. "Who— What—" She desperately needed to make sense of the man's deranged assault.

Federic shook his head. "He was just admitted yesterday. . .he has been only semi-conscious. . .we had no idea. . . ." Federic trailed off in bafflement. Such behavior was totally unlike anything the young oupir had ever experienced.

Kathryn heard the click of boot heels approaching just before Kyril burst into the room. "By the blood! What has happened here?" She dropped to her knees next to Kathryn and Mindi. "Kathryn, what in Helena's name— Are you all right? Are you hurt?"

Kathryn shook her head. "I'm fine, but I don't know—" She shrugged helplessly.

"Federic?" Kyril looked at the medtech, her face as pale as his.

"I do not know, Doctor Vértök. He was admitted less than twenty-four hours ago—he's been semi-conscious the whole time, unresponsive. We had no reason to restrain him—" He broke off. "Doctor, I have *never* seen such a thing—ever." His bewildered eyes begged forgiveness.

Kyril knew her staff—she had hand-picked them. She touched his hand with her own. "I know, Federic—and I believe you. I would never have predicted this, either." She turned back to Kathryn. "Thank the Goddess you are unharmed, but Mindi is hurt—we must take care of her." She moved to where she could touch Mindi easily and laid her hand on the dog's head. Gazing into her eyes, she whispered softly, and this time Kathryn could understand the words. "Sleep, my spirit-friend. Thou hast done well. Now we shall care for thee." With a little whimper, Mindi relaxed, letting her head droop into Kathryn's hands.

"I know a woman who is a veterinary scientist. I shall request her assistance," Kyril told Kathryn. She concentrated on Mindi's sensations for a moment, grimacing in shared pain. "I think she has a broken rib—if so, Lysa can repair it." She slid her arms under Mindi's relaxed body and lifted her carefully. Federic helped Kathryn to her feet.

"Federic, if you have not, call Doctor Orosziány—"

He interrupted politely. "He has been called, Doctor."

"Good." She smiled in approval. "Would you please notify Doctor Lysa Kos that we are on our way to her laboratory with Doctor Hartell's companion? Thank you."

They exited the clinic, Kyril still holding Mindi, to await a glidecar summoned by the other medtech. To Kathryn's astonishment, it was still early. It seemed hours since she had walked down the corridor to check on the patient she never got to. She sighed exhaustedly, her adrenaline spent. She was shaking inside. "I think I just aged about a hundred years," she whispered humorlessly.

For the first time since her own arrival at the clinic, Kyril looked fully at Kathryn. She saw the pallor in Kathryn's face and the residual shock in her expression. "Are you truly unhurt?" she questioned softly.

Kathryn smiled wanly. "I imagine I'm going to have some pretty nasty bruises tomorrow." She rubbed her upper arms, feeling the imprint of the man's grip, then saw on her fingers the dried blood from Mindi's face. She froze, suddenly breathless. What if she had just been exposed to AIDS? Holding up her hand to Kyril, she stammered, "K-Kyril—look."

Kyril's expression was suddenly grim. "You had better clean your hands immediately."

Leaving Kyril and Mindi, Kathryn re-entered the clinic where she scrubbed at her hands with a disinfectant until they were in danger of abrasion from the scrub-brush. She examined her hands carefully but could detect no breaks in the skin from Mindi's reflexive bite. Satisfied that what could be done had been done for the present, she returned to Kyril and Mindi and the now waiting glidecar.

As she seated herself for the ride to the veterinary laboratory, Kathryn voiced what neither woman wanted to think about. "Kyril, if this man's behavior is some bizarre new manifestation. . . ."

Kyril's jaw hardened. "We shall begin fluid and tissue analyses immediately." Kyril tapped in directions on the control panel and they set off, joining the usual morning swell of traffic. "I want to have Mindi attended; then we'll examine you more thoroughly. After that, we'll see to our oupirian patient."

Kathryn slumped against Kyril, seeking renewal of energy through her contact with the strong shoulder. To her surprise, she dozed, awaking with a start when the car slid to a halt. They entered a facility which was not unlike the building in which their research laboratories were housed.

Kyril introduced the two women and briefly outlined to her friend what had happened. Though tired and shaken by the oupir's attack, Kathryn found herself liking Lysa Kos immediately and she had no qualms about placing Mindi in her care. While they awaited the veterinary scientist's report from her examination of Mindi, Kyril explained to her that the work of the veterinarian in Kornägy was oriented towards the care and use of experimental animals, the rehabilitation of wild animals who were brought in for treatment following some injury, and the study and management of the wild species who sustained oupirian life. "Oupirs do not keep 'pets' as you humans do. Our relationship with non-oupirian animal species does not lend itself to developing such attachments."

Kathryn nodded thoughtfully. "I've heard similar statements from any number of people since I moved to Minnesota. Farmers whose livelihood depends on their livestock apparently don't get 'attached' to their animals, either." She grinned tiredly. "Even some of my friends in Minneapolis don't understand why I take Mindi everywhere I go—they weren't raised to treat their animal companions as members of the family." The thought of losing her "family" brought tears to the back of her throat. She was grateful when Kyril touched her hand gently in sympathy.

Dr. Kos appeared a few moments later to usher them into the examining room. "I concur with Doctor Vértök's diagnosis of a broken rib, but I do not think it warrants the patient's restraint." While Kathryn watched in amazement, the auburn-haired scientist placed Mindi in a regenerative unit and initiated a treatment. "This device stimulates the bone to renew itself at a fantastically accelerated rate," Dr. Kos explained. "It is not effective for all types of tissues as yet, but is very useful in applications such as this one." As the machine emitted a soft hum, the veterinarian paused.

"Doctor Hartell— I—" She glanced at Kyril, then back to Kathryn. "It is my understanding that the nature of your research makes contact with bodily fluids very hazardous." She hesitated again, then went on. "Do you have any reason to believe that your dog may have been exposed to the disease organism with which you are working?"

Kyril and Kathryn looked at each other, then at the veterinarian. It had never occurred to either of them to worry about Mindi's being infected with the AIDS virus—she had bitten the man but received no external wounds. Kathryn said as much, and Kyril added, "Besides, it is the Human-T-Lymphotrophic virus. There is no clinical evidence to indicate that the virus infects non-primate species—at least not from Doctor Hartell's world. I do not think we need worry about Mindi."

Lysa Kos nodded in obvious relief. When the regen session was completed, Mindi was released to Kathryn with a mild sedative and instructions to return her for one or two further treatments.

As soon as they arrived at their apartment, Kyril installed Kathryn and Mindi in the bed, then put in a call to Taddéos. He came and examined Kathryn, including her hands. He also detected no breaks in the skin. And, while agreeing with her conclusion that the rough handling she had received would produce bruises, he saw no other cause for physical concern.

"But Kathryn," he said, "I am worried about the psychological effects of this attack. Would you like me to arrange for you to speak with a Healer?"

Kathryn was puzzled. She had no idea what he was referring to. "A Healer?"

Taddéos glanced at Kyril. "Why don't you talk with her about it and let me know if you require my services further."

Kyril nodded. To Kathryn she said, "I shall explain in a moment. Let me see Taddéos out."

At the doorway, Taddéos motioned Kyril outside. "Did you draw the blood I asked for?" he queried. Seeing the dismay on Kyril's face, his expression became grave. "I know you are concerned about Kathryn's understanding of our ways," he began, "but—"

"Taddéos—" Kyril's voice was steely. "I am fully aware that we *must* discover the cause of Kathryn's lethargy, for she cannot continue this way. I shall do what is necessary." The dark eyes in the face above his impaled him, but he forced himself to hold her gaze. "If you will return to the clinic, I shall join you within the hour. And I shall bring the blood sample you requested."

He bowed his head briefly. "I apologize. I shall await you."

"No," she said quietly. "Begin without me. I see no need to delay."

He eyed her again, trying to decide if she were reproving him for his lack of confidence in her professionalism, or stating her confidence in his. In a moment, he gave it up and simply nodded acquiescence, then walked away.

Kyril stood holding herself, watching him go, seeing and not seeing the colleague and would-be friend—hearing and not hearing his footsteps on the pavement. An inner horror gripped her, claiming her attention away from the outer world. She shuddered, simultaneously trying not—but unable not—to think about what this new manifestation of the disease could mean. She visualized oupirs in uncontrollable states, attacking human beings in the Other dimension, unstoppable by human authorities until they dropped from their own disease. . . . Shaking her head, she turned and re-entered the apartment, forcing her attention back to Kathryn's well-being.

Kathryn stood at the wall of windows, gazing into the garden court, her arms wrapped tightly around herself.

Kyril approached from behind and slipped her arms around her gently, feeling Kathryn give against her. They stood quietly for a few moments, then, even as Kyril drew breath to speak, Kathryn found her voice first.

"Kyril—" Her voice was quiet, yet Kyril heard as much as sensed the disturbance Kathryn was feeling. "Kyril, we have *got* to find out what happened with that man this morning." She turned in Kyril's arms, fitting her own loosely around Kyril's neck. Her hazel eyes were filled with concern. "What if this is a new strain of the disease? What if it attacks the central nervous system? What if it drives people mad?" She shivered.

"I, too, have thought of all that," she replied, her dark eyes on Kathryn's, "and must get back to the clinic and begin to see what there is to learn." She studied Kathryn's face, seeing anew the tiredness under her eyes.

"Kathryn, will you allow me to call you a Healer?"

Kathryn questioned her with a look.

Kyril sighed. How to explain something intangible to one raised in the material culture of twentieth-century America? "Someone like. . .like a psychologist in your world—only much more. Someone who can touch the spirit and. . .heal." She shrugged at the seeming redundancy. "You have suffered a severe trauma—please, do it for me, if not for yourself."

Kathryn hesitated, trying to realize that she had, indeed, suffered a trauma, and that the standard prescription in her world was a meeting with a therapist. She decided to trust Kyril's judgement. "Okay," she agreed, "if you think it's appropriate."

"I do—and so does Taddéos."

"So—when?"

"I shall call. . . ." She considered a moment. "How would you feel about my asking Guardian Tyrell?"

Kathryn looked at her. "Why not?"

Kyril considered further. Indeed, why not? She smiled and pulled Kathryn gently to her again. Holding her, she loosed a silent prayer of thanks for Mindi's actions, certain that the dog had saved Kathryn's life: She knew that an oupir in a rage was no match for a mere human. She surmised that only the weakened state of this man had made it possible for Mindi to distract him long enough for the medtechs to subdue him—and still come away with her own life.

Kathryn, unable to perceive emotions as clearly as Kyril, nonetheless felt the warmth of gratitude that Kyril emanated and guessed it had to do with her escape from death at the hands of the maniacal oupir. She sighed her own relief against the solid shoulder, and did not protest when Kyril informed her of Taddéos' request for a sample of her blood.

24

She did, however, protest Kyril's urgings that she rest further before returning to the clinic or meeting with Tyrell. "I've just slept for days!" she exclaimed.

"Yes, and we still do not know why," Kyril replied, holding up the blood sample. "That is what this is for. Please—just try to rest. If you cannot sleep, *then* join me at the clinic."

Kathryn saw the pleading in the dark eyes—and realized again that Kyril was deeply concerned for her. Grudgingly and with a sigh, she conceded defeat. "Okay—I'll lie down for a few minutes—but I'm *not* sleepy."

Kyril smiled gratefully, and watched as Kathryn kicked off her shoes and lay down beside Mindi. Within moments, her eyes had drifted shut and her breathing had settled into an even rhythm. Kyril pulled a light coverlet over her, then departed for the lab, the tube of Kathryn's blood in her pocket.

Kathryn slept and dreamed—of darkened rooms and clutching hands and screams that would not come. She awoke feeling tired and decidedly unrested. The room was in near-darkness and she realized her body had belied her words: she had lain there a long time. Mindi still slept next to her, her side rising and falling with the gentle *whuffing* sound of her breathing.

She glanced at the windows and saw that dark clouds billowed in the late-afternoon sky, carried on the wind that bent the tree limbs and flowers in the garden outside the room. Rain was imminent.

Kathryn roused herself and, after a visit to the bathroom, went to the commcenter. Shortly, she and Kyril viewed one another via the tiny video screens built into each of the units.

"You slept," Kyril greeted, sounding pleased.

"Sort of," Kathryn groused, regretting the further hours lost to her. "I'd like to come over—I never did see Orlov this morning. Are you going to be there a while?" Kyril nodded. "Then I'll be there as soon as I've eaten something." She glanced at her watch. "Say—where could I get a new battery for my watch? It's stopped."

Kyril thought for a moment. "I'll send one of the medtechs for one. Our energy cells should work in your watch. Bring it with you."

Kathryn nodded, then signed off. She awakened Mindi and fed her, and prepared a meal for herself. The dog was groggy but evidenced no sign of pain, so Kathryn exercised her briefly on her way to the clinic, enjoying the approach of the storm and the diminished activity on the streets. Although her mind was alert, Kathryn was aware that the tiredness she felt seemed to go bone-deep. Any extra effort she might have had to make—in fending off crowds and curious or hostile glances—would have been more than she could have mustered.

When she entered the building, she was greeted by Doria, one of the medtechs who replaced Federic and Zelazny for the second-shift. The diminutive woman directed Kathryn to the room where she had been attacked that morning.

Kathryn paused in the doorway, not entering, feeling a little shiver run over her as she thought back to the morning's events.

Kyril stood next to the bed of the sick oupir, flanked by Taddéos on the other side. Electronic monitors whirred and whispered and a respirator sighed and clicked. Seeing both physicians in attendance, Kathryn concluded that the man was very ill indeed.

With resolve, she went to Kyril's side and stood quietly, gazing at the pale face of the dying Petros. She knew he was dying—something in his sunken countenance conveyed that to her without the necessity for words. She felt a wrenching sorrow for him. Reaching out, she took his limp hand in hers. She stared at the gashes where Mindi had bitten him, not wanting to think what might have happened had Mindi not been with her.

After a moment, Kyril gently steered her from the room. The door closed behind them with a soft click that sounded loud in the quiet corridor.

Unwilling to be the one to break the silence—unsure of her voice if she were to try—Kathryn queried Kyril with her eyes.

Kyril sighed and spoke in a subdued tone. "He went into convulsions earlier this afternoon, after his fever peaked around midday. We have been unable to restore him to consciousness." She paused, grasping her elbows with her hands in a gesture Kathryn had come to recognize as one of tired defensiveness. She stared at a spot on the wall behind Kathryn. "The tests we have performed indicate involvement of the central nervous system—of a type that would be accompanied by delusions, hallucinations, and erratic behavior." Her eyes found Kathryn's. "I have sent a courier with this information through the Boundary to

Däg—along with an update for Mark Hamyl and a request for any information he may have obtained pertaining to similar cases."

She sagged against the wall, her eyes wandering again, still holding herself.

There was a silence as Kathryn assimilated what she had been told. "Kyril." She touched Kyril's arm, drawing her attention back to her. "Let's have a staff meeting tomorrow, after you've had a chance to rest, and assess where we are. If we scheduled it for late afternoon, there would be time for me to put in the new data and generate a summary report."

Kyril nodded. "An excellent idea. I shall notify everyone." She pushed off from the wall. "I want to review the test results again tonight."

Kathryn saw the preoccupied look and knew that Kyril was already mentally doing so. "Fine," she said. "Are there copies on my desk?" Kyril nodded again. "Okay, then I'll work on entering the information in the computer while you do that." She paused, remembering. "But first, I want to see Orlov. Has anyone monitored his progress while I've been gone?"

Kyril nodded tiredly. "Yes, and he seems to be holding his own. Empirically, I cannot point to figures that are significant as yet—but, intuitively, I would say he is faring better than the others."

Kathryn felt a rush of gratitude at Kyril's words. *Maybe, just maybe, we're on to something,* she thought, her pulse quickening excitedly. "Good!" She smiled and turned, then remembered her watch. "Oh, here's my watch." She handed it to Kyril. "Strange that it stopped—it hasn't been long since I bought a new battery."

"The transit through the dimensional Boundary probably scrambled it," Kyril replied. "I'm surprised it lasted this long."

Kathryn kissed her lightly on the cheek, then strode down the hallway toward Orlov's room.

He was resting, awaiting his first evening treatment. He sat up, genuinely pleased to see her, as Kathryn entered his room. He had been consulted about Kathryn's proposal and knew himself to be their "guinea pig."

"Doctor Hartell! How good to see you!" There was some vibrancy in his voice and a sparkle in his icy-blue eyes. He was a blond, white-skinned, Nordic-appearing oupir, tall and once muscular, a handsome representation of oupirian middle-age.

Kathryn took his hand in hers, noticing instantly the contrast between his dry, cool skin and Petros' feverish moistness. She was as glad to see him as he was to see her. "You do look well!"

He beamed. "I feel well, also," he replied in his heavily accented English. Everyone Kathryn had dealt with had accepted her inability to articulate Standard with tolerant amusement. "I was up for the third day in a row today—exercised briefly, twice, each day—and am finding myself less tired than I have felt in a very long while."

He went on about his plans for when he left the clinic as Kathryn checked over his chart, listening with half an ear. She noted to herself that *he* seemingly had more energy than *she* had had recently—and wondered idly if she should try her own "cure."

They were interrupted by Doria's bringing in the first p.m. treatment. Deriving a form for the administration of each of the components of Kathryn's regimen had actually been harder than finding the elements themselves. Oupirs could tolerate no solids and were unaccustomed to any nourishment but blood once weaned of their mothers' milk. Thus, everything used in Kathryn's treatment approach had to be either injectable or a liquid tolerable to oupirian digestion and metabolism. Orlov now consumed several decanters of fluids and received two injections while Kathryn watched. She had worked with an oupirian biochemist to formulate the liquid concoctions and knew they were not particularly palatable. Orlov's grimaces re-confirmed that fact.

He sighed as he handed back the last empty container. "Not the tastiest—but at least I am still here to complain." He laughed heartily, and his eyes twinkled.

Kathryn enjoyed his humor, and realized just then that she had come to care quite deeply for this fellow being. Sometimes, in this other world, surrounded by these people, it was hard to remember the differences between them. She gave his hand a final squeeze before departing.

Crossing to the lab/office wing, Kathryn noted that only Kyril's office was lit and surmised that others were either done for the day or were hard at work in the labs. She palmed the light switch in her space and entered. At once, she saw the reports of Petros' tests stacked neatly on her desk. She smiled, knowing that they had been placed there at Kyril's direction. She sat down, booted up the computer, and promptly immersed herself in her task.

In her work as a biochemist, Kathryn had made herself familiar enough with the normal profiles of human bio-measures that she could interpret human test results fairly accurately, and with some depth of understanding. But oupirian norms were another thing. Up to this point, she had had to depend on Kyril or Taddéos for interpretation, had barely begun to commit the battery of tests and the significance of their results to memory. Consequently, she now gained less than she would have liked from her study of the reports, but nevertheless considered studying them an essential first step in the task of correlating all the data, as she had been charged. She knew from previous research experience that the seemingly most inconsequential detail can take on sudden importance when other pieces of the "puzzle" were put into place.

Some hours later, she and Kyril sat together in the lunarium of their apartment, listening to the rain drumming on the plasglass roof and walls, Their hands were clasped loosely in the space between them. Mindi lay at their feet.

The transition between clinic and apartment had been an awkward one. Kyril, longing almost desperately for Kathryn to consummate their bonding, had not dared initiate lovemaking. Kathryn, who still neither knew how long she had slept nor what had actually transpired between them when last they had been sexual, was uneasy and unsettled.

They had wandered in here, each feeling it a neutral space where they could be together comfortably, without being forced to confront what each feared.

Finally, Kathryn broke the silence. "What happened the last time we made love, Kyril?" It was as much a demand as a question.

Kyril gave Kathryn an appraising glance before answering. "You wanted me to take you. I did—in the manner of our people." Her voice sounded even, but a nugget of fear held her breath hostage within her chest.

Kathryn sat listening, face forward. "And what does that mean?" Her voice was as devoid of emotion as her body was of movement.

Previously, when the subject of bloodsharing or feeding had arisen between them, Kyril had found herself retreating from discussing it with one not of-the-blood. To her surprise, the reluctance had diminished, and she wondered at that even as she said, "I tasted of your blood—a sacred thing among oupirs." *Perhaps the ease comes from having participated in that very act,* she thought.

Kathryn swallowed. "And just how did you do that?" Her voice was carefully non-accusatory, though a bit tremulous.

Kyril's fear relaxed its hold as she heard Kathryn's apparent willingness to discuss the subject that had lain between them, unacknowledged. The long hours of work and trauma had prevented their sitting down to discuss this delicate subject. And as Kyril realized that their time to talk had finally arrived, her breath escaped her with a tiny sigh. "Oupirs' tongues are specialized portions of our anatomy. Sheathed within the tongue muscle is a keratoid core. The *Kingró,* as it is called, is hardened and sharpened. It is designed to puncture the skin and the walls of blood vessels, when the tongue sheath retracts." Even in the dimness, Kyril could see Kathryn blanch at her words.

Kathryn took a breath, held it. "Go on." Her gaze remained fixed, straight ahead.

"There is little more to tell. The sharing of blood during sexual encounters is an ancient practice that occurs for the first time with the final bonding of the spirit-selves of two oupirs. Once they are bonded, they may choose to participate in the sharing at other times." She found herself suddenly remembering hers and Lanaea's bonding night, and for a moment was transported there—

A flash of lightning jarred Kyril, returning her to the more recent events.

"—I participated in this. . .bloodsharing?" Kathryn was asking, a tightness in her voice.

Kyril answered slowly, feeling again the ache of incompletion. "No—no, you did not, Kathryn."

Kathryn's stiffness eased with the release of her breath, and a silence fell between them.

Again it was Kathryn who interrupted the silence. "How long did I sleep then, afterwards?"

Kyril gazed at her again, curious about the direction of the other woman's thoughts, disliking the persistent lack of real emotion in her voice. "Three nights and two days. But Kathryn—" Kyril touched Kathryn's forearm lightly. "That was not from loss of blood—I took but a few swallows from you the other night. I consumed much more in the mountains before we crossed the dimensional barrier. That is why I was so worried about you—I could not account for your lethargy. " Her voice implored Kathryn to understand, to accept the truth of her words.

Kathryn glanced down, then slowly turned her face toward Kyril. The rain on the plasglass made grotesque, shadowy patterns on Kathryn's face. In her expression was a mixture of fear, anger, and bewilderment. "I feel violated," she said in a harsh whisper, unleashing the feeling she had held in check. "You *took* something from me without my permission." Her eyes flashed mounting anger at Kyril. "I had just begun to regain my trust for you, after you told me. . .who you really are. And now this. How can I—"

"Wait a moment, Kathryn," Kyril broke in. "You *wanted* me to take you—I told you before, I would never *force* you to anything." Her eyes sought and held the hazel ones in the dimness, willing Kathryn to remember the events of that night, willing her to accept her own part in what had occurred.

Kathryn wavered confused, unsure. She bit her lip, clenched her fists, then jerked her eyes away from Kyril's. After a moment, she said quietly, "I think I should talk with your Tyrell."

Kyril, who had not even realized that she had tensed, relaxed against the couch back. "I shall arrange a meeting for you as soon as possible."

Kathryn nodded, then arose.

In a few minutes, Kyril heard her get into bed. Thunder rumbled in the distance, beckoning her to sleep also. She was not long in heeding.

25

"Luc Montagnier and his staff at the Pasteur Institute in Paris first identified in January of 1983, human-reference, what they have since described as a lymphadenopathy-associated virus, or L.A.V.," Kyril began the staff meeting.

There were two members of the Congress of Health present— self-invited—so Kyril had decided to start with a fundamental review of what was known about the AIDS-causing virus. All were seated around a long table, except Kyril, who stood at the front of the room. "That virus is now being referred to as the Human T-Lymphotrophic Virus, number three, in America. HTLV-I is a human leukemia-causing virus. Related to both is the feline leukemia virus, which, in addition to causing feline leukemia, causes T-cell deficiencies in some domestic cats." Kyril paused as computer-generated images appeared on the large vidscreen at the end of the semi-darkened conference room. Representations of each of the viruses mentioned were displayed at logarithmic scales of magnification.

"HTLV-I is responsible for a rare, aggressive form of adult human leukemia usually found in Central Africa, the Caribbean, and the southern islands of Japan, in the Other dimension. I believe it worth noting that HTLV-III seems to have made its earliest appearance in Central Africa, and on the Caribbean island of Haiti. We speculate that the similarities between these two viruses, as well as to a virus found in the African Green monkey, may be due to mutations from an original, common, 'parent' virus." Again, as Kyril spoke, the vidscreen illustrated her narration with a display of the geography of Kathryn's world.

"What we have learned relative to *our* species is that once the virus is in the bloodstream, it zeroes in on the oupirian analogue of human T-cells, unfazed by the antibodies dispatched to kill it. At the T-cell-analogue, the viral invader docks with the analogue via its double-layered protein envelope—" Another graphic moved on the vidscreen, simulating the process described. "—then, having docked, the invader sheds its own outer shell and penetrates the T-analogue, where it promptly begins to take over cellular functioning."

As Kyril paused again, Kathryn watched the screen, feeling a shiver run over her as the helpless cell was penetrated and mastered. She rubbed her hands over her arms to quell the prickling, and glanced at the Congressional guests. They appeared equally disturbed.

"The viral invader, being a retro virus, next converts its single strand of RNA to DNA. The DNA molecule moves into the cell's nucleus, inserts itself into a chromosome, and then proceeds to direct the cellular machinery to begin replicating the virus.

"Eventually—" The graphic began to swell. "—the T-cell analogue dies, bursting and releasing a flood of the newly-made viruses into the blood stream to attack other T-analogues—and carry out the cycle again." There was a heavy silence in the room. "The long-term result is that, as more and more T-analogues are invaded and destroyed through the reproductive process, the immune system succumbs to the onslaught, leaving the now unprotected individual open to attack by other infectious agents."

She paused, then went on. "In human beings, such agents usually succeed in killing the host organism before the virus itself does. In human cases thus far observed, these opportunistic invaders have most commonly been a skin cancer known as Kaposi's sarcoma, and a particularly devastating form of pneumonia known as *pneumoscystis carinii*. Other, more bizarre occurrences have also been documented: cytomegaloviral infections, candidiasis—systemic yeast infection—and internal fungal infections.

"In the small sample of oupirian cases so far studied, the result of the original infection seems to be a rapidly progressing wasting similar to leukemia, except that both the white blood cells and the red blood cells are affected and die—or are killed off by the invader." Kyril halted her narration abruptly, stricken with a memory of Lanaea's illness and death.

Congressional Member Kenshasha—his voice heavy with irony—broke the silence. He gestured at the frozen graphic on the vidscreen. "So this virus lives only to replicate."

Kyril dragged herself back to the present. "It would appear so, yes—it does not 'grow,' it does not metabolize nutrients, and it cannot replicate without its host—we have now proven that." She paused, reflecting. "I suspect the same is true in the human body."

"The ultimate parasite," interjected Arpád, the other guest.

Kyril nodded. "With the ultimate cover: Once inside the cytoplasm of the host cell, it cannot be reached by any of the body's natural defenses." The Congressional visitors shifted uncomfortably as the difficulty of the undertaking was brought home to them.

"Kyril—why does this disease seem to affect oupirs so much more acutely than human beings?" Kathryn spoke from her seat at the other end of the long conference table.

Kyril considered for a moment before replying. "It would seem that our strength in milli-Cycles past has become our undoing." Kathryn met her eyes with a puzzled look. "Proportional to human beings, oupirs have more than double the number of T-cell-analogues While travelling in your dimension, this huge number of oupirian T-analogues has made it possible for us to consume most human diseases along with human blood. However, where the T-analogue itself is the target, we have more than twice as many targets, producing twice the number of invaders, and at a much faster rate than all this occurs in the human body."

She turned to the vidscreen again. "Add to this what we now believe to be happening."

"Oh my God," Kathryn whispered as, horror-stricken, she watched the image of the HTLV-III-controlled T-analogue directing a macrophage to engulf a white blood cell.

"The resultant fever, weakness, and wasting progress rapidly, as the immune system attempts unsuccessfully to cope with the invader. Death ensues—according to computer projections—within less than two full Cycles of the appearance of initial symptoms." Kyril's voice wavered and she struggled for self-control.

"I asked the Congress of Health to re-examine their statistics on oupirian deaths within the past fifteen years, Earth-reference. Of course we cannot be sure, because cremation destroys any trace of infectious agents, but the correlational data I was given suggest nearly two dozen possible deaths from AIDS during that period, most within the past three Cycles." A grim alarum moved through those gathered in the room.

"While oupirian medical science was seeking indigenous sources," Kyril continued, "thinking perhaps there was a new strain of oupirian leukemia, the real source of these illnesses completely escaped recognition." Her voice sounded bitter.

"But you've learned so much in such a short time," Kathryn reminded. "It will take human scientists *years* to figure out what you've learned in a few *weeks.*"

"Human scientists!" Kristin, the cupirian biochemist, spat in disgust. "It is tempting to blame the entire species for this crisis because of their stupidity in refusing to deal with the whole issue!" She threw up her hands.

"Blame," said Kyril, her voice hard and flat, "is useless. Neither it nor what we have learned can restore to us what we have already lost."

There was an uncomfortable silence during which Kathryn wondered about the appropriateness of her own presence in the room while others were embarrassed at Kristin's outburst. Finally, Evgeny, another medtech, voiced the question they must inevitably face. "So how can we combat it, Doctor? Given that the viral invader is protected once inside the T-analogue, and that the protein envelopes are mutating rapidly—how do we stop it? Where in the life cycle of the virus do we intervene? Do we stop all transit to the Other dimension and wait for it to expire among us?"

"That is one of the purposes of our meeting today—to develop a more coherent strategy. " Kyril stepped to the control panel on the wall and raised the illumination in the room. She began to write on the wallslate.

"These are the possibilities that have thus far been delineated: One is to use a similar virus to inoculate against it; but, as you have just stated, Evgeny, the rapid mutations on the exterior of the virus make this difficult.

"A second possibility is to block the reverse transcriptase, so that the RNA cannot convert to DNA. The problem here is to find a way of doing that without damaging the T-cell-analogue itself.

"Third would be to replace the entire volume of blood in an infected person—the obvious difficulty with this being in assuring that *all* infected cells have been removed from the body—a near impossibility. Related to that approach is marrow-cleansing—something we have already been utilizing to boost the immune system of those with immune impairments. Marrow-cleansing alone would not work if there were still any infected cells in the body. Perhaps—" She drew a line connecting possibilities three and four. "—these two could be used most effectively in combination." She paused. "But both are very drastic, invasive techniques.

"A somewhat different tack would be to apply what we have learned about genetic and cellular engineering: Perhaps we could create the chemical mirror image of the retro-virus, which might attach itself to the virus and block its docking with the T-analogues. Perhaps we could insert genes in all the immune cells which would direct them to coat themselves with a substance, such as a polymer, that would prevent the entrance of the HTLV-III virus." Kyril paused again. "As for your suggestion of a moratorium on transiting, even if we were to go so far as to withdraw all those of our species from the Other dimension, we haven't a clear enough idea of how long an incubation period the virus is capable of." She shook her head. "I fear that, in itself, voluntary quarantine is not the answer.

"Do any other ideas present themselves now?" She waited, eyeing each of her team members as they worked their creative faculties, laboring over the deadly enigma before them. At length, when no one spoke, she said, "Then, changing the focus somewhat, Taddéos has a report to make." She nodded to him and seated herself as he rose.

"The results of the tests on our violent patient—now comatose—show that his outburst was the direct result of a new manifestation of infection with HTLV-III. His delirium was produced by massive infection with cryptococcus, a fungus normally found in bird droppings in the Other dimension. In this patient, the infection has resulted in severe lesions to the central nervous system, which he is not likely to survive. We have sent a courier with an inquiry into any correlation in human cases.

"Are we taking adequate precautions against contamination, then?" queried Federic. He eyed Kyril, in whom he placed great trust.

She met his gaze and nodded firmly. "Yes—we are absolutely certain that, among oupirs, the virus can only be transmitted by direct, blood to blood contact with an infected oupir. And these opportunistic diseases will not harm us as long as our immune systems are intact."

"What about human contact, Kyril?" Kathryn posed. "Isn't that how oupirs are getting it—by ingesting the blood of infected humans? How does the virus get from the human blood stream into the oupirian blood stream?"

She and Taddéos exchanged a troubled glance. "We remain uncertain of the mechanism of transmission. One hypothesis which we early considered, then ruled out, was that the virus somehow survived the digestive enzymes of the oupirian gastro-enteric system. It seems highly unlikely that, even with the differences in oupirian and human gastric physiology, such a thing could occur." She paused and Taddéos took up the narrative.

"You see, the ingested blood is almost immediately broken down into assimilable nutrients—which are then absorbed directly through the walls of the G.I. tract. There is no organ functioning like the human stomach in oupirs. Instead, there is a digestive sac, if you will, in which pancreatic and liver enzymes are concentrated, and into which the ingested blood flows as it is swallowed. Digestion begins immediately. Continues in the first portion of the small intestine—similar to the human duodenum—and absorption follows. The oupirian digestive tract is highly effective at providing utilizable nourishment within moments after ingestion has occurred."

"The alternative," continued Kyril, "is that transmission occurs when the *Kingró* is extended, and the tongue-sheath retracted."

"Of course!" Kathryn exclaimed. "That's got to be it!" She jumped up and went to the wallslate, conscious of the eyes of the Congressional Members on her. She had worked with Kyril's staff, and knew they had, at least, become accustomed to her. She was not so sure of acceptance from the visitors. She spoke with reserve. "Look—when human males have anal sex with other males, they are exposed to infectious agents through the insertion of the penis into the rectum." She hastily sketched out her words. "If either person has AIDS, the other can contract it. If the person who is penetrated has even the most minute rectal fissure, the other partner either could contract the virus through contact with blood in the fissure, or, he could pass the virus to his partner through that same fissure.

"In the case of an oupir feeding from an infected human, the virus could enter the oupirian body when those tissues around the *Kingró* are in direct contact with the blood in the human body—just as when the penis is in contact with blood in a rectal fissure." Her eyes questioned her audience for their reactions to her reasoning.

All the faces looking at her were grave and there was complete silence in the room. Finally, Kyril spoke for all of them. "I am inclined to agree with you, Kathryn." Other heads nodded reluctantly.

Kyril sighed heavily. "If we are going to accept this as the mode of transmission, then we had best make the assumption that absolutely no blood should be shared here, in Kornägy, until we know for sure that we can cure or prevent the disease. And," she went on, hands on elbows, eyes fixed on something unseen by others, "we had also best assume that no one here should engage in anal intercourse, either."

"Kyril." Kathryn's voice was strained. "You know, some heterosexual human female cases have been reported, too. The mode of transmission is unclear, but if there is *any* doubt whatsoever. . . ." She trailed off, unsure of what to recommend.

Kyril eyed her as if she had not wanted to hear what was said, then nodded again. "Yes, you are right—we do not yet know all the ramifications of what we are dealing with." She paused again, musing. "How are we going to protect both males and females during sexual intercourse?"

"Doctor." It was Federic again. "What if Petros or some other patient *bit* me—could I be infected that way?"

Kyril shook her head. "A few moments ago, I would have said surely not—but. . .I truly do not know, Federic." She looked at Taddéos. "I think we had better get busy trying to find out."

Wearily, he nodded his head.

Kyril plunged her hands into the pockets of her lab coat, inhaling deeply. She measured her team with her eyes even as she rallied her thoughts for direction. "Let us begin with separating into teams of two or three. Each team will take one of the possibilities we have outlined here, and pursue it until you are either convinced it is a dead-end or you have found something useful from your pursuit. Taddéos, I want you to be in charge of running tests on all bodily fluids. See what you can learn about the presence or absence of the virus in these substances. Meanwhile, everyone take extraordinary precautions against infection when working with our patients and any of their excreta.

"I would like both of our biochemists to be available to all the teams for laboratory support, but I would like Kathryn to remain in charge of compiling and inputting data and Kristin to work with Taddéos on analyzing fluid samples." She paused to see if she had overlooked anything. Deciding she had not, she thanked them all for their time and dismissed them.

As the group arose, one of the Congressional Members indicated a desire to speak with Kyril. She nodded. "If you will await me in my office, I'll be with you in just a moment," she said. The two Members acknowledged her request and departed while she waited in case any of her team wanted to speak with her.

With little of the hubbub usually attending the adjournment of human meetings, however, the group members dispersed to their respective areas to begin the work Kyril had just outlined.

Kathryn watched them go from where she stood, still leaning against the wallslate. Even though she had slept long and hard last night, following her talk with Kyril, the meeting had enervated her. Seeing Kyril turn to go, she pushed tiredly away from the wall. Suddenly dizzy and lightheaded, she faltered.

Kyril, hearing the startled exclamation behind her, moved quickly to support her. "Kathryn! What is it?" She grasped her tightly by the arms, looking hard into her face.

"Oh, I—I just felt so dizzy all of a sudden." She shook her head and took a deep breath, clutching Kyril's forearms with her hands. After a moment, the black spots in front of her eyes cleared and the rushing in her ears ceased.

Kyril eased her into a chair. "Let me get Taddéos," she urged softly.

"No—I'll be all right—I am all right—really." She forced a smile, and held tightly to Kyril.

Kyril knelt beside her and spoke quietly. "Kathryn—you are not all right." Her eyes compelled Kathryn's attention. "This is the second time in less than a week that you have been dizzy and nearly fallen. Something is wrong—and I intend to find out what it is, with or without your cooperation."

Kathryn saw the set of Kyril's jaw and knew there was no arguing with her. Reluctantly, she agreed. "Okay—but I don't want him to examine me here." She had no wish to be scrutinized with the full knowledge of all the others on the clinic staff. Kyril saw that in her eyes. "I'll go back to the apartment. I'll just sit here a moment longer, and then. . .go."

Grateful that at least she did not have to argue with Kathryn over the fact of an examination, Kyril acceded to the unspoken demand and kissed her lightly on the forehead, then went to find Taddéos. Perhaps, she told herself, he could convince Kathryn to come to the clinic for a thorough medical evaluation.

When Kyril returned a few moments later, alone, Kathryn was feeling steady enough to leave and said as much.

"Do you want me to come with you?" Kyril offered.

"No, you stay here—take care of your business with the Congressional Members. I'll take Mindi with me—you send Taddéos." She, rose, took an unsteady step, then sank into blackness, never hearing Kyril's cry of concern as it burst from her.

26

More than anything else, Tyrell was a healer. While still young, she had given her Self completely to the healing arts and was, in oupirian middle-age, a vehicle for their expression in her world. An amalgam of psychotherapist, spiritual counsellor and mentor, superb diagnostician, and mistress of arcane arts, Tyrell served as Guardian to the Os at Lódz, where she was sought after by many. She had gained renown throughout the land.

At her mid-morning meditation, Tyrell was interrupted by an emotional cry from one with whom she was bonded. Returned harshly to an outer awareness, the Guardian reached for recognition: Kyril! The anguished cry reverberated in her, recalling to Tyrell another moment when the death of Kyril's mate had provoked a rare grasp for emotional support. Only something of equal agony could have been behind Tyrell's spiritual Daughter's cry; Tyrell knew well the reserve that Kyril maintained.

Letting go of her meditative state, Tyrell arose and attired herself for travel, slipping a dark cloak over the garments she normally wore. Within moments, the glidecar she had summoned sped her on the way. Having learned long ago not to attempt foreknowledge, Tyrell contented herself with waiting as she was borne through Sziv to Kyril's quarters.

Upon arrival there, Tyrell discovered Kyril's absence. Reaching outward mentally, she located Kyril at the biosciences research facility, and hastened to join her. Apprehension gnawed at her composure, knowing now that Kyril was at the clinic.

Although she had never been there before, Tyrell entered the facility with purpose and quietly demanded Kyril's whereabouts from the medstation attendant.

Federic took in the confident, decisive demeanor of the woman before him and concluded she was a person of more than ordinary importance. Still, he was reluctant to disturb Kyril and hesitated.

"Young man." Tyrell fixed her dark eyes on him. "She called for me, and I have come. You will now take me to her."

Overmatched by the force of personality that Tyrell had turned upon him, Federic could but obey. "This way, Mother," he murmured, inclining his head in submission.

He led Tyrell into the clinical wing of the research facility, to a door halfway down the corridor. "She is here," he whispered, gesturing to her to enter.

Tyrell nodded her thanks and dismissed him from her thoughts as she pushed through the wide, half-ajar portal. What she beheld dismayed her: Kyril, her back to Tyrell and the door, was half sitting on a bed in which lay the human female whom Kyril had brought with her through the Boundary. On the other side, his back to the door as well, stood a physician whom Tyrell recognized from impressions she had garnered when she had done the healing work with Kyril only a few days previously. The emotional intensity of the scene battered at her and she raised her shields automatically to avoid being overwhelmed by others' sentiments. Kyril's anguish was palpable; the physician radiated confused concern; from the human female, she detected only a deep lethargy, as if her life energy were ebbing slowly away.

All of this came to Tyrell during the brief seconds she paused in the doorway. Now she moved forward, to the foot of the bed, where she stopped. Folding her hands, she waited, a deeply silent presence, until she would be noticed.

A few moments passed as the physician continued his perusal of the readouts from the instruments measuring the human form. Kyril clutched at the hand in hers, intent upon the inert countenance before her, seeking. . .*what?* Tyrell wondered.

Kyril slid off the bed and turned, dragging her eyes from Kathryn's face, seeking to read on Taddéos' what she could not find in Kathryn's. It was then that she became aware of Tyrell.

With a swift glance back at Kathryn, she laid the limp hand on the coverlet and moved to Tyrell. Bowing her head to her spiritual Mother, she said quietly, "Thank you for coming," her voice sounding hollow.

Taddéos turned at her words and guessed immediately that the dark-skinned woman must be Kyril's mentor. He too greeted her reverently, as was customary and proper. "Guardian."

Tyrell acknowledged both with her eyes. Her face displayed concern as she spoke and her eyes returned to the human woman. "What is the matter here?"

Kyril deferred to Taddéos. "She is your patient, Doctor."

Taddéos appeared not wholly happy with the fact. He sighed. "To tell truth, Guardian, I can say only what has happened—I do not understand the cause." Turning to his patient, he elaborated. "Doctor Hartell has blacked out, for a second time, after being overtaken by dizziness. She has not complained of fatigue, but,'" he said, turning again to Tyrell, "her blood pressure is extremely low and previously she remained on the verge of unconsciousness even when sleeping. My diagnosis is extreme exhaustion...but as to the cause..." he reiterated, sighing, shaking his head sadly, "I cannot say. The bloodwork we have done turned up nothing."

"Mother," Kyril urged, taking Tyrell's hands, "will you please see if you can reach her? She— I— We had intended to contact you anyway. Kathryn was attacked by one of our patients—several days ago—and her dog was severely injured" (It was then that Tyrell noticed the animal on the floor next to the doorway...guarding?) "trying to protect her." Kyril shuddered. "Kathryn could have been killed."

Tyrell considered for a moment. "What does this trauma have to do with her blackouts?"

Kyril shook her head, but Taddéos answered. "We do not know that they have anything to do with each other. But, since you are here, I would like to see you try to reach her and bring her 'back' with you—it can only help—while I try to contact a specialist I would like to ask in for a consultation."

After a moment's deliberation, she nodded. "Very well, I will work with her." She turned and surveyed the room. "Have her mattress placed on the floor, there," she pointed. "Bring me two or three large pillows and a rug on which I may kneel." Tyrell's glance lingered on Mindi and she went to her.

Puzzled, the dog looked up as Tyrell squatted next to her. Without protest, she allowed Tyrell to place her hands against her head, and blend with her consciousness.

After a few moments, Tyrell dropped her hands and opened her eyes. She smiled and rose. "The one who is called Mindi wishes to stay and see her human companion through this."

While Taddéos and his staff took care of re-arranging the room, Tyrell spoke with Kyril in a quiet corner, raising an unseen barrier of privacy around them.

"You fear losing her to death." Tyrell looked dauntlessly into Kyril's eyes. Kyril nodded, fighting back tears.

"And what do you fear losing of yourself, Kyril?"

Taken aback, Kyril hesitated. She had given the idea no prior conscious thought. She dropped her eyes, seeking inward knowledge. After a moment, she met Tyrell's unwavering gaze again. "I fear...losing the ability to care...for anyone," she said in a near whisper, knowing it for truth as the words cut home in her own ears. Tears trembled on her lids, threatening to spill onto her cheeks.

Tyrell squeezed Kyril's arms, reaching up to the taller woman. She knew her Daughter well, had guessed rightly that more rode with Kyril's concern than the death of another mate, however trying that might be. Some gave easily of themselves, loving and losing, and, after the pain, loving anew. Not Kyril—never Kyril. Kyril had fought love since the first loss when her mother, still young by oupirian standards, had died, leaving Kyril to sorrow and be raised by Tyrell, then a stranger to her.

Initially, it had mattered not in the least to three-Cycles old Kyril that Tyrell and Kolayna, Kyril's mother, had been lovers in their adolescence and spirit-mates ever after. It was only after the child Kyril had slowly buried the pain at her mother's death—and sealed off the yawning cavern within that her mother had been meant to fill—that the young girl was able to bond with Tyrell and allow the affection and intimacy they had finally achieved to begin to grow between them. Kyril's father had been a diplomat, never at home much; Vlad was killed when the magtrain he was a passenger on derailed in southern Sarkad, during Kyril's tenth Cycle. Kyril had always suspected what Tyrell had long known: that it was the Healer in Tyrell that had enabled the older woman to bridge the gulf of emptiness in the young Kyril and make a bond that was family and more, that nothing now but death could sever.

As they now stood together, Tyrell sent love and understanding through her touch, willing Kyril to self-acceptance, as well as to acceptance of what was to come. They remained, hands linked, in silent communion until Taddéos signalled that all was ready for the Healing.

With a last grateful, imploring look, Kyril departed, leaving the two beings she loved most alone together.

Tyrell crossed to Kathryn and knelt on a pillow next to her. Mindi lay tucked against Kathryn's other side. Tyrell reached out mentally, acknowledging the dog's presence and loving support, then slipped another of the pillows under Kathryn's shoulders to raise her higher above the floor. Settling herself into trance, Tyrell circled Kathryn's wrist with the fingers of one hand and placed those of the other hand against the psi points on Kathryn's face and head. Slowly, carefully, she began to blend with Kathryn's mental Self:

> Immediately, a heavy blackness enveloped Tyrell; from her place of reserve, she passed through the vacuous fatigue to deeper levels of Kathryn's consciousness. Unexpectedly, visions of Mindi's pain and

injury came at her, and a strong fear of Mindi's death. Those Tyrell accepted and replaced with calmness and a knowledge that all was well. Immediately following was Kathryn's recoiling at violence, and a distorted visage. Tyrell recognized that the trauma inflicted was over Mindi's injury, and that was again easily relieved.

Another layer of greyness floated across their blended inner awareness like a heavy mist. They came from it to Kathryn's aversion at giving her blood to Kyril, and the panicky thought that Kyril might die. Again, Tyrell accepted all and returned serene thoughts.

Downward, inward, through other fears and hurts, Tyrell journeyed. She noted that a great healing had already taken place in Kathryn, much of it around the years of her childhood and youth. Still, there was a hollow that seemed to bespeak the same yearning for confluence, for spirit-mate, that Tyrell had recognized in Kyril. Mentally, she paused, contemplating the significance of that hollow in Kathryn's psyche. She explored it, seeking to know its origin and the need-for-completion it spawned. She concluded it was what motivated Kathryn toward Kyril, but was clearly not the source of the darkness which, even here, far from Kathryn's psychic perimeter, Tyrell sensed.

Tyrell refocused and centered, then began expanding her individual awareness, recognizing that Kathryn herself did not know from whence the blackness arose. Tapping her knowledge of the body's energy fields, Tyrell traced a black trickle down through Kathryn's psyche to the place where body joined mind. There, within the bioenergetic matrix that was Kathryn's physical Self, was the source of the malaise. Tyrell pulled back, reinforcing her separateness, as the blackness sucked at the energy she brought, threatening to leach the life force from her even as it was being drained slowly but steadily from Kathryn. Tyrell observed, from a safe distance, the ebbing of the energy from Kathryn's body, watching the luminescence give way inexorably to the encroaching darkness.

Satisfied that she had found what she sought there—even though she did not fully understand it—

Tyrell retraced her psychic steps through Kathryn's
mental Self, reinforcing the healing messages she had
already given as she passed by those aspects of the
interior landscape she travelled. When she arrived at the
outer layer where she had first encountered the blackness upon entering Kathryn's mind, she was dismayed
to find that it had grown perceptibly denser even as she
had journeyed within.

Again, Tyrell slipped through that inner dark,
to the surrounds of the room in which Kathryn lay and
she knelt, relinquishing first psychic, then physical,
contact with Kathryn.

Allowing herself a few moments of transition, Tyrell recovered
awareness of her own body, of limbs gone numb, of her own fatigue. She
opened her eyes and noted that much of the daylight was gone from the
room. Mindi still lay curled next to her mistress, but her eyes were on
Tyrell. Without thought, Tyrell reached out to the dog and stroked her
lovingly with her mind, praising Mindi's devotion to her companion,
Tyrell's spirit soared with joy as she touched the canine spirit and knew
it for its honor, loyalty, and love. Her eyes closed in bliss as she
experienced through Mindi what she had known only with her spirit-mate,
Kolayna: total devotion to the well-being of another.

When she opened her eyes again, Kyril stood in the doorway, a
question on her face. "I felt you in Mindi's mind," she said hoarsely, as
if her voice had gone unused for days. "Have you brought Kathryn back?"

Tyrell glanced down, surprised. She had forgotten that she was
to do that—why? she asked herself. She closed her eyes, touched the edge
of darkness again, knew she could not easily bring Kathryn through that.
She sighed and opened her eyes to Kyril's.

"I will need help," she began. Then, sensing Kyril's reaction,
strove to forestall her. "No—not another Healer. I believe you would be
best suited for this."

Again, Kyril questioned with her eyes, but Tyrell refrained from
answering. Instead, she directed Kyril to kneel where she had knelt and
place her hands at the psi points on Kathryn's head and wrist. She stood
behind Kyril, her hands at the psi points on Kyril's temples. Tyrell
channelled through Kyril into Kathryn's mind Self again, penetrating the
blackness at the surface, retracing the path inward to the yearning hollow
she had found in Kathryn:

Kyril, speak to her, tell her of your need, Tyrell directed. Tyrell sensed the younger woman's hesitancy, felt her reach within herself for the determination to make herself vulnerable to Kathryn in the face of her fear of losing her and her need to defend against that pain.

Kathryn—it is I, Kyril, she said, sensing Kathryn's question as she "heard" her name called. *We— I have need of you. . . .*

She faltered and Tyrell sensed it. She urged her gently on. *Tell her how you need her, call her, entreat her to return with you, past the blackness to the outer light.*

Kyril gathered herself again. *Kathryn, I want you to come back with me—I want you to stay here, with me, Kathryn. I need you—Mindi needs you—I love you, Kathryn.*

Through the link, Tyrell sensed the feebleness of Kathryn's response. *I—I want to be with you, Kyril, but I'm. . .tired. . .so tired. . .*

Tyrell "spoke." *Kathryn, your life force is weak. Join with ours and we will help you—you **must** reach out to us—we are here, awaiting you. . . .*

They waited, timelessly, until both felt Kathryn's hesitant seeking. Tyrell seized the opportunity to bond temporarily with Kathryn, simultaneously urging Kyril to strengthen the bond she had already begun. They led her quickly but carefully towards outer awareness. As they reached the barrier of blackness, Tyrell hesitated only long enough to assure herself they still had Kathryn "in tow." Then she pushed through the heavy darkness to the outer light and once again stood in the room into which she had come, long hours ago.

Opening her eyes, Tyrell dropped her hands to Kyril's shoulders and glanced down at Kathryn. Kyril too abandoned the psi points she had held to lay her hands over Kathryn's hand.

As both watched, Kathryn struggled to wakefulness, her free hand seeking Mindi as her eyes sought Kyril's in the darkened room. Her whisper came faint as a sigh to their ears. "Kyril?" Kathryn swallowed and tried again. "Kyril?"

"I am here, love," Kyril replied softly.

Mindi thumped her tail and nudged Kathryn's hand with her nose.

"Mindi?" Laughing and smiling weakly, Kathryn raised her head enough to confirm the dog's presence, then dropped back on the pillows.

"Wh-What happened?" she asked, her voice still without substance.

Tyrell stepped back as Kyril began to explain to Kathryn what had transpired since her collapse after the staff meeting earlier that day. Now fully aware of how spent she was, Tyrell wanted little more than to return to her quarters where she could bathe and sleep. She slipped out of the room, leaving Kyril and Kathryn to their reunion, seeking Taddéos.

She found him napping in his chair. As she paused in his office door, he seemed to become aware of her presence and sat up, instantly alert. It was a skill he had developed in medical college, and it had served him well. "Guardian Tyrell." He arose and offered her a seat on his couch.

Tyrell declined. "It would be but a temptation to lie down and sleep here—and I need the solitude of my own quarters, thank you. I came to request that you call me, so that I may be here when the specialist you have sent for arrives."

"Of course," he assented "I expect him sometime early tomorrow—Well, this morning." He grinned as he caught himself and looked at his wrist chronometer.

Tyrell glanced at her own. It was now after mid-night. She sighed. "Have someone signal me at seven. I shall be here." She nodded farewell and left him standing in the darkened doorway. At the entrance to the building, a glidecar thoughtfully summoned by one of the medtechs awaited her. Gratefully, she climbed in but avoided relaxing too deeply on the way to the Os. Before she slept, she must perform the rituals that would purge her of the pain she had accepted from others during her work this day. Then and only then could she safely let down her Healer's guards and give herself to sleep.

27

At the ninth hour of the next day, Tyrell returned to the clinic to meet with the colleague whom Taddéos had summoned for consultation on Kathryn's case. She was directed by Federic to join the two in Taddéos' office.

Approaching with her customary quiet, Tyrell heard a voice somehow familiar to her, and she hesitated, reaching into memory. The recognition was there, but eluded her. With curiosity, she moved through the door.

Both occupants rose. Taddéos greeted her respectfully, but she barely registered his words as astonishment overtook her.

"Riznik!" She heard the disbelief in her own voice. "I knew not that it was you whom Doctor Orosziány had summoned!"

The man whom she addressed smiled slightly, his eyes radiating warmth from a face made old and nearly expressionless with age. He inclined his head to her. "Tyrell." His voice was still clear and strong.

Taddéos glanced at each in surprise. "I—I was not aware that you knew each other

The Ancient One waited, silently permitting Tyrell to tell of their acquaintance, however she might.

Blushing darkly, Tyrell was at a loss for words as the memories tumbled through her like a mountain stream over its rocky bed. What had been between them was so private and so far back in their lives, that, in her conscious self, Tyrell had all but forgotten it—and the man. At length, she offered a few words she deemed appropriate and that she thought Taddéos would find acceptable. "Riznik was once my Teacher." She spoke reverently of the function he had served in her life, but elected not to elaborate upon it. "I had not thought you still among us," she said to Riznik, as if Taddéos had vanished with her first words.

Again the smiling eyes. "I am very much here—and very pleased to see you after so many Cycles of Seasons."

Tyrell felt herself flush again under Riznik's steady regard. They had once been lovers—after each had lost a mate—and he had taught her that giving of oneself to another can be a sacred, healing thing. Their exchange had been the foundation on which, following Kolayna's death, Tyrell had built all that she had become as a Healer. Now, looking backwards, she was suddenly aware that a great sadness was relieved with the knowledge that he still lived. That relief made her voice tremble as she spoke. "We must take this opportunity to renew our acquaintance—after our work is done."

Her eyes shone at him, and he did not miss the tremor in her voice. "So we must—after our work is done."

Taddéos had watched this interchange in curious silence, and let the silence lay a moment while the other two gazed at one another's faces in remembrance. He opened his mouth to speak just as Kyril appeared at the office door.

Sensing her arrival, Tyrell and Riznik turned to greet her. Taddéos introduced Riznik. "Professor Vläczuk has come at my request. I thought," he went on, "that he might be able to shed some light on Doctor Hartell's illness. The professor is a specialist in the study of *homo sapiens*."

Kyril's interest was piqued, as was Tyrell's. Both began to speak at once, but Kyril quickly deferred to Tyrell.

"I recall that you were unusually fascinated by that species, but I did not know you had made it your life's work." She eyed him curiously, as if to say, *Come, explain yourself, old friend.*

"Oh yes," he replied. "I have sought every scrap of recorded knowledge about human beings and have compiled it on computer. The governments have even funded my study—they have deemed it of increasing import as the world on the other side of our Door has gained the capacity for nuclear destruction. There is now even a program in Human Studies at Csongrád University where others may continue to acquire this knowledge—after I am gone." His lips pursed and his eyes smiled again at Tyrell.

"What do you know of human illness?" Kyril pressed.

"Well, in the matter of your Doctor Hartell, I believe I may have some information that will help. Doctor Orosziány has been filling me in while we awaited you." He laced his fingers together and settled himself in a chair. The others followed suit, with Tyrell unconsciously choosing the place next to him, so that they faced each other in a small semi-circle.

Riznik began. "As you all certainly know, our species has ventured travel in the Other Dimension since the first gateway opened, milli-Cycles ago. What you may *not* all know is that, not long after the dawn of human civilization, some of our ancestors tried bringing *homo sapiens* here, into our dimension, to be used as feed stock." He saw the eyes of his younger audience widen in surprise. "Kornägy was still, much of it, barren and without adequate sustenance for our expanding species.

"At that time, however, the human stock brought here succumbed to some mysterious malaise and died, all within a few weeks of transit through the Boundary. Consequently, no one attempted for a *very* long time to introduce *homo sapiens* to Kornägy. Somewhere around two thousand Cycles ago, it was tried again: A substantial number of human beings were gathered together from all parts of their world, and brought through the Boundary at a variety of points. This time they were watched closely, fed well, and generally had all their needs attended to. However, within just a few weeks, all again had died." Riznik's eyes automatically sought Kyril's as his keen ears detected the hiss of her indrawn breath.

She prodded him anxiously. "Did anyone discover the causes of their deaths?"

Riznik sighed softly. "Not immediately—but it was decided that a study of that question was in order. So, over the next few deci-Cycles, others were captured and brought here in an effort to understand what seemed, inevitably, to lead to their deaths." He paused and shook his head, his grey eyes growing grim. "Apparently, Doctor Vértök, the electromagnetic forces at work in our dimension of the universe are inimicable to human life. Our scientists discovered that the life force in the human body 'runs down,' if you will, when exposed too long to the electromagnetic radiation of our world."

"And how long is 'too long'?" Kyril interjected quickly.

Riznik leaned toward her, his hands still clasped. "Each individual seems to have had its own threshold, beyond which life could not be sustained." His words fell like a doomsayer's in the silent room.

Kyril shuddered violently. Tyrell reached across to her and placed a comforting hand on hers for a moment. To Riznik, she said, "Do you believe this to be the case with Doctor Hartell—that the electromagnetic forces here are what have induced her lethargy and weakness?"

Without hesitation, he nodded. "The symptoms Doctor Orosziäny has described are identical to those detailed in the historical works I have studied."

He leaned back and went on. "When this knowledge was undeniably validated, the final reason was provided so that the disinclination to allow beings from the Other dimension into our world, could become Law. You see, it had already been recognized that certain of the plagues that decimated our feedstock had come through the Boundary from the Other side."

Kyril was thunderstruck: Never had anyone bothered to explain to her—or Taddéos, it appeared—these particular reasons for the prohibition against bringing human beings through the Boundary. She said as much; then burst out with, "Why not? Why in Helena's name not? Did you know, Tyrell?"

Tyrell sighed raggedly. "I had. . .heard—but I did not remember."

Riznik theorized, "I suppose no one thought it of importance to explain to everyone, once the evidence was clear. Or perhaps, as we have audited the comings and goings of our kind into that Other dimension for centi-Cycles, no one who came in later lifetimes, after the law was enacted, considered that the Law might be disobeyed."

Kyril sought reproach in his words or manner, but found none. None was needed—her self-reproach was sufficient, and all present could see.

"We—I must get Kathryn out of here and back to her own dimension before—before it is too late." She stood abruptly.

"One moment, please, Doctor Vértök." Riznik fixed her with his somber gaze. "In her presently weakened state, it would probably be quite dangerous for her to transit if the interface is not at its optimal configuration."

Kyril faltered, glancing at Tyrell. "When. . . ?"

Tyrell calculated briefly. "The next full moon will not be for another week, Kornägian time."

"Taddéos, can we do anything to help strengthen her? She has been here nearly six weeks, Kornägian, already." Kyril's voice held pleading, but in the presence of these people, she no longer cared.

He looked at Riznik and Tyrell. "I don't know. Has either of you a suggestion?"

Tyrell deferred to Riznik, but he shook his head sadly. "I cannot help you there—I am not a medical man and I know of nothing the Ancient Ones tried that was efficacious in prolonging life. The only thing I can offer is that there seemed to be a great variance in the length of time an individual human might survive here—leading the researchers of old to the conclusion that the strength of the life force in that individual was a deciding factor in how long he or she survived."

"I can help," Tyrell offered. "I have been within her life space and have seen a. . .a blackness. . .that sucks at her life's energy. With assistance, I can erect a temporary barrier to any further encroachment."

"Taddéos—what about a transfusion—or an infusion of oupirian blood?"

Taddéos stared at Kyril, mouth agape. "I— don't know—has it ever been tried?"

All looked at Riznik. He shook his head. "I do not recall reading that it was."

"Then perhaps we could try mixing her blood with someone's of a similar type," Kyril suggested.

"Yes, we could try. But you are the blood specialist," Taddéos reminded her. "You will have to direct me as to the particulars—and whether or not we will want a marrow cleansing."

Kyril turned to Tyrell. "Will you come with me to see Kathryn and tell her what we propose?"

Tyrell stood. "I would rather you wait to talk with her about that until after I have had a chance to do my work." Turning, she addressed Riznik. "Would you be so good as to assist me by being my ground, old friend?"

Riznik unfolded his long frame from the chair. He towered over even Kyril, and though he was thinned with age, all could sense the strength of his personality. "I would be honored to work with you again," he replied.

Kyril led the way to Kathryn's room. Leaning over the recumbent form, she spoke softly. "My love, I have brought Tyrell for another Healing. I shall return to you later."

Kathryn reached weakly for Kyril's hand, clasping it to her breast, seeking to draw strength from it. "Where's Mindi?" she whispered airlessly.

"Here." Kyril turned to the dog and asked her to the bed. Mindi was gently helped up and placed beside Kathryn, where she snuggled against her mistress.

Content, Kathryn let go Kyril's hand and placed her other against the dog as Kyril slipped from her side.

Tyrell glided into the spot where Kyril had stood. "Kathryn, do you remember me?" The hazel eyes searched the dark face, and Kathryn nodded. "Good. I want to go inward with you again, to help you to feel stronger so you can fight this malaise. Will you allow it?"

"Yes," Kathryn whispered, nodding again. "Yes, please."

Quietly and quickly, Tyrell directed Riznik to help her so that Kathryn was soon placed, as before, on the floor of the room and Tyrell knelt beside her. Mindi again settled next to Kathryn.

When all was in readiness, Tyrell explained briefly to Riznik what she had found—the dark encroachment—while in Kathryn's mind previously. "I want you to remain outward, and to channel your strength to me, so that I can set up a barrier to the ebbing of her life force without need for concern about getting 'back.'

Riznik nodded, and they began.

Again Tyrell met the blackness very quickly upon entering Kathryn's inner self, and this time she consciously sought to trace its every inroad, its every blockade. And as she went, she raised a barrier of light against the dark, temporarily preventing its further advance. She drew on the combined strengths of Riznik and herself, feeling the swell of power from the other, idly noting in another part of her consciousness how much his strength had grown since last they had been intimate.

When done—when every thread of the blackness had been sought out and encircled with light—Tyrell gratefully seized upon her grounded companion's beacon and dragged herself out of Kathryn's mind and back into her own containment. Her hands dropped, of their own volition, as Riznik dropped his from her. She sighed deeply, feeling her exhaustion, but welcoming it as one does for a task well-completed.

In a moment, she opened her eyes to the dimness of the room. Riznik sat on the edge of a chair by the door, watching her. She boosted herself to her feet and he stood with her.

"We can rest in my quarters," she said quietly, stepping toward him. Then, taking his hand for a moment, she looked up into his grey eyes, seeing his pale face as a soft glow in the dim light. "Thank you, my friend."

Riznik simply smiled to her, and together they walked into the evening-illumined corridor. Tyrell realized it had been another very long day.

28

Csatlós had set and dawning paled the brilliance of the starry night sky. Kyril prowled the paths of the deserted park near the apartment, oblivious to the rousing of its non-oupirian inhabitants as they met the new day. Her disquietude was due to the results of the tests she and Taddéos had spent all of the previous day and night running.

Both their computer simulations and their laboratory efforts had yielded the same conclusion: the human body and oupirian blood were incompatible. Without extensive forays into inter-species biochemistry and genetics, it seemed that Kyril's hope for infusing Kathryn's body with oupirian blood was nullified.

As she walked, Kyril mentally reviewed their logic, but could find no alternatives to returning Kathryn to her own dimension. Kyril stopped, jamming her hands deep into the lab coveralls she still wore, and contemplated sunrise on the placid lake before her. A slight breeze riffled the glassy surface here and there. Waterfowl stretched, flapped their wings, and preened in preparation for taking to the water for the morning feed. Abruptly, Kyril realized that tears were streaking down her face. She wiped at them wonderingly, as if they had come from outside her.

The act of acknowledging the tears brought the piercing pain of impending loss to the surface. Folding her arms across the ache, she sank to the still moist earth, her legs curled under her. From some deep level, the urge came to give in, not fight, the pain.

She submitted, and felt her innards convulse as the agony that had threatened to erupt, even if she were to continue to resist, was unbound. Her legs unfurled, and she sagged onto her side. She was conscious of the dampness of the grass, cool against her heated cheek. Sorrow at all her losses strangled her, was a physical ache knifing her, became a giant's hand that shook her mercilessly. She coughed, struggling for air.

As her body shuddered and heaved, Kyril sank to a psychic stratum beyond the loss of Kathryn, to Lanaea's death and their sundering. Then the image of Lanaea she carried within was suddenly replaced by the unsummoned face of her mother, Kolayna. Caught unawares, she lay paralyzed at beholding in her mind's eye a face she had been unable to recall for nearly seventy-five Cycles. She rolled onto her back, her fingers clutching at the ground. Lamentation finally burst from her, echoing across the still water, rousing the waterfowl from their quiet feed. The birds took wing and Kyril heard it as a roar, an explosion of noise that paralleled the explosion of the long pent-up anguish to which she had at last yielded.

Cradling herself with arms and knees, she rocked, grieving, giving way now to the inner child who had never allowed itself to feel the devastation of the mother's death, and the terrifying emptiness that had followed.

As the sun slowly inched toward its zenith, the torrent of anguish gradually diminished to a quiet trickle, the lamentation to a soft moan. Again, Kyril lay on her back. She drew her knees up and rolled onto her side. Restorative blankness overtook her.

When she finally came to herself, the sun stood high and the morning dew had dried against her face. She opened her eyes to a pair of feet and legs squatting in front of her. Dimly, she realized someone was speaking to her. She concentrated on the words, and recognized her name. Stiffly, awkwardly, she turned her head enough to see the face that went with the legs and feet.

"Ta—Taddéos," she rasped. Her lips seemed formed of clay. She tried again, not sure that he could have heard the first time.

His hand cupped her cheek, brushed gently at the dirt. She tried to hear the words he crooned.

"Shhh—no need to speak." He touched her face tenderly. "I thought I might find you here—I knew you would want some time alone." He smiled softly. "But I did not want you lost and alone."

"How long?" she rasped.

He smiled gently. "A while—I've been here a while."

Kyril studied him, saw understanding in his eyes. She reached out with her mindself. *Hold me,* she implored. *Please, hold me.*

Although surprised by her silent, emotional plea, he slid down beside her, lifting her rigid body to him, and cradled her in his arms. They sat while he stroked her hair and cheek, comforting her against the beating of his heart.

The heat of the mid-day sun was warming, and coaxed the stiffness from Kyril's body. When she had had what she needed, she roused herself and sat up, separating from him with gratitude. She attempted with her eyes to convey that, and he nodded silently, his eyes accepting what she offered.

Open as she was emotionally, Kyril detected a sudden flicker of what seemed to be desire—abruptly shielded—and she gazed at him in startlement.

Dismayed at having had his feelings apprehended, Taddéos cringed inwardly, then quickly realized that she had misinterpreted him. "No," he said. *"That* is not what I was feeling." He paused. The intimacy between them was brand new. He had little knowledge of Kyril in the personal realm. Sighing, he forged ahead, forcing his grey eyes to meet hers. "What I wished to share was that. . .my mate. . . ." He felt his throat tighten, but kept on. "She left me, last winter. We had been bondmates since childhood. . . . I— She changed. I do not know why she left. . .but she is gone." He swallowed, looked away, then back. "I understand something of your grief." He closed his mouth hard, biting back deeper sorrow.

Kyril saw the ravages of Taddéos' bereavement in his eyes, in the lines around his mouth as he struggled with bewilderment and pain. Regret swelled within her that she had known nothing of this personal tragedy, that she had been too absorbed in her own struggles to notice any change in him since she had returned from the Other dimension.

She reached out a hand, touched his face experimentally. He closed his eyes and bowed his head. She slid her fingers to the psi points on his temples and opened herself to what was there.

His grief flowed across the connection and she saw that it was, indeed, akin to her sorrows, and she welcomed the sharing for his release and her comfort.

When she dropped her hand, their eyes met and both knew that each had acquired a friend in the other.

29

Once again, Kyril sat in a darkened room, holding the hand of her beloved. She spoke softly to Kathryn, telling her of what must be done. Her voice, sibilant in the silence, carried a note of repressed anguish, even though she maintained an outward calm. As she spoke, she could not help staring at the pale, listless face that Kathryn turned toward her while she hung on every word. Kyril felt herself a marionette, guided by forces she could not control, mouthing words she had no real desire to say. Her monologue ran out, and she drifted into silence, her eyes losing focus.

"How long?"

Kyril glanced quickly at Kathryn's face. Had the question been spoken aloud or apprehended silently?

The pale lips moved. "How long. . .before I must leave?"

Kyril clutched fiercely at the hand she held. "A few more days— when the moons are full." Her face was set in an expressionless mask. If it were to change, the brittle thing would shatter and fall to the floor. She knew that to be an irrational thought, but was helpless against it.

A tear formed in the corner of Kathryn's right eye and trickled slowly onto her cheek. "I don't want to leave you," she pleaded.

Kyril could see pain in the hazel eyes. "Kathryn, you *must*. To stay is sure death," she reiterated.

"Come with me."

Kyril shook her head. "I cannot. I—I am forbidden to leave Kornägy." She had never told Kathryn of the outcome of her meeting with the Security Council, and did not wish to explain now. "And besides, I must continue with the research." She paused, willing herself to remember. "It *was* the reason we came here in the first place." Her eyes found Kathryn's again. "I am truly sorry, my love. I do not *want* you to leave without me." The mask shifted then, and was replaced by genuine sorrowing. "We can only hope that it will not be too long before I am able to join you in your world." Her throat constricted with unexpressed feeling. Lifelong habits were not easily supplanted. "I shall be with you as soon as it is possible. I promise you."

Kathryn accepted that there was nothing more to say. She held Kyril's hand with as much strength as she could muster, and both lapsed into silence.

Some time later, Tyrell arrived for the second of her twice-daily healing sessions. She knocked softly, having been told by Federic that Kyril was with Kathryn. Without pause for reply, she pushed the partly-open door wide enough to admit her and entered the room.

Kyril greeted her with a silent nod of her head and gently disentangled her fingers from Kathryn's. She motioned Tyrell into the hallway with her.

"Why," she asked in a whisper, "is she still so weak?"

"I have been able to keep the blackness at bay," Tyrell replied, "but I cannot restore what has already gone." She apprehended Kyril's suffering and anxiety. "She *will* be well enough until she can return to her own dimension," she assured, pressing Kyril's hands with her own. Kyril's gratitude went into her quietly uttered, "Thank you, Mother," and then she left her spiritual Mother to do her healing work.

Mindi—who in Kathryn's disablement had been adopted and tended to by the clinic staff—trotted out of the room and followed Kyril down the corridor.

Hearing the dog's nails on the floor, Kyril turned curiously to her. It was not like Mindi to leave Kathryn's side. She squatted and waited for Mindi to catch up with her. Then, placing her hands on the dog's head, she reached for Mindi's thoughts.

What she read was a mixture of assurance that she, Mindi, would continue to care for Kathryn and preside over her well-being, along with a desire to remedy Kyril's sorrow.

Stunned by the complexity of this non-humanoid creature, Kyril went to her knees and embraced Mindi, taking comfort in the unconditional love and acceptance that Mindi offered.

Mindi, in order to be closer, tried to climb onto Kyril's lap and succeeded in knocking her over onto her buttocks.

Laughter and tears mingled as Mindi licked at Kyril's face and pushed hard against her, giving of her canine all.

❰ ❰ ❰

Kyril later sought solace in Tyrell's nearness. The apartment she and Kathryn had been sharing was too empty and quiet, and working after-hours at her office presently seemed intolerable.

While Tyrell meditated, Kyril tried to put herself into a light healing trance. She knew she needed its restorative benefits, but was unable to muster the discipline required. With a quiet exclamation of frustration, she gave it up. Rising from the couch on which she had lain, she went to Tyrell's computer and entered a code that would allow her to access the computers at the biosciences facility. When she was on-line, she requested a print-out of the last two days' work on the AIDS virus. *I may as well apprise myself of what I have missed while concentrating on Kathryn,* she reasoned.

Sighing, she stepped away from the terminal and clicked on the printer. Her arms folded, she waited restlessly for the first pages of data to be transmitted. When the printer hummed to life, she moved forward and started to read.

As she haphazardly scanned a few lines of information, she began to realize that one of the teams—she checked the I.D.; it was Doria's— was on to something. Eagerly now, she went back and became totally absorbed in reading the report line by line.

It seemed that the team had taken the hypothesis that a chemical might be derived to block the virus's docking with immune cells and come up with a reasonable twist: They had discovered a protein that formed on the surface of infected cells, but that would not bind itself to un-infected cells. They had dubbed the protein AIP, for AIDS-infected protein.

Using AIP, they were now in the process of testing its ability to bind with other chemicals in hopes of finding one that would be toxic— or could be made to be toxic—to the AIDS-infected cell. Because Evgeny's team had already selected several naturally occurring substances as being promising in this regard, their job was easier and both teams had begun testing the substances Evgeny's team had isolated.

The printer ended that report and ejected a page before beginning the next one. Elated, Kyril snatched the completed report up and went to Tyrell's com-unit. Hurriedly, she tapped out Taddéos' home signal, then waited impatiently for his form to materialize on the small vidscreen. When there was no response, she concluded he might still be at the laboratory suite. She tried his office there. Again, nothing. Not even his answering programs were functioning. In exasperation, she signalled the main desk at the clinic.

The night tech's image greeted her quietly, and she made an effort to match the other's demeanor. "Sara—I am trying to locate Doctor Orosziány. Is he there?"

Sara shook her head. "I have not seen him since—" She paused, frowning. "Actually, I do not recall when I last saw him, but it was several hours ago. Have you tried his home?"

"Yes, and his office. Neither of his answering programs was activated, so I could not even leave a message. If he should come in, please have him contact me at once." Frustrated that she could not reach him with her news, she punched in the return code for Tyrell's terminal and signed off.

Still clutching the report, she stared fixedly at the blank screen, trying to think what to do next. There was little point in going to the clinic—her staff obviously had things well in hand—and there was nothing she, alone, could achieve. It would have been *so* nice to have shared the new results with Taddéos. *Damn! Of all times for him to be out,* she grumbled silently.

She had not noticed that the printer had ceased its whirring, but she did hear Tyrell enter the room. She turned to greet her, glad of the chance to tell someone of her good news. "Tyrell!"

The other woman, who had donned her sleeping garments, paused and raised her brows in surprise. "Yes?" When Tyrell had left her, Kyril had been in a restless state. She now wondered what could have accounted for the obvious change in energy.

Kyril moved toward Tyrell, unable to contain her excitement completely. "They're on to something!" she said, holding the report out to Tyrell.

"Who is 'on to something'?"

"The research teams— While Taddéos and I were trying to figure out how to put oupirian blood safely into the human body, two of my teams have developed a promising lead against the AIDS virus."

"I am pleased to see you in better spirits than earlier," Tyrell commented with an affectionate smile.

"Oh, Mother," Kyril said, her exultation suddenly quieted, "this could mean a significant gain in the time required to defeat this terrible disease complex."

Tyrell nodded, understanding that, for Kyril, that also meant she might be freed to join Kathryn sooner than she had originally anticipated. Tyrell sought to interject a note of caution. "Do not forget that you are under an injunction to remain here," she said gently.

Kyril nodded. "I know. But if we can devise a solution to this threat, I am sure the Security Council will relent and allow me to transit again."

Tyrell studied her soberly. Doubt clouded her ebony features. "I hope you are right, Daughter. Your disappointment in this matter would be extreme."

Kyril, her enthusiasm tempered, returned her gaze. "Thank you for your concern. I shall endeavor to restrain my hopes until this is all resolved."

"Not your hopes, my dear—your expectations. One must always hope—but never allow unfounded expectations to eclipse your assessment of reality."

Kyril could find no further response, but Tyrell obviated the necessity by announcing that she was going to retire. "Your former sleeping quarters are in readiness, should you wish to remain overnight." She stepped forward and embraced Kyril briefly. "Rest well, Daughter. I shall look to see you in the morning."

Kyril nodded and watched Tyrell leave the study. Slowly, she turned and went back to the printer. She cut the power and gathered the remainder of the data she had requested. Then, reading material in hand, she headed for the room where she had slept as a child in Tyrell's home, darkening the study as she went.

30

K yril and Kathryn lay together under Kornägy's lavender sky, a briny breeze caressing them, the susurration of the surf lulling them. Kyril had decided to spend Kathryn's last two days in Kornägy with Kathryn, and had arranged to have them flown to one of her favorite seaside retreats. They now lazed in its healing ambience, one day already gone.

Mindi was fully recovered from her injuries and alternately roamed the beach and lay beside them in the buff-colored sand. Just now, she was curled next to Kathryn, whose hand rested on the back of her neck.

Kathryn was still feeling tired and washed out, but had maintained her strength sufficiently well that Taddéos had deemed it safe for her to be away from Tyrell's support for the short while until her departure.

Lacking the energy for swimming, Kathryn had nonetheless immersed herself in the tepid sea, and they had, together, been basking in the warmth of Kornägy's pale sun. During the night, they had even made love, languidly. Afterwards, Kathryn had slept heavily, then dozed intermittently throughout the day.

With Kathryn near, Kyril had found herself able to relax and sleep restfully. The nights she had passed alone had been fitful ones for her. She did not look forward to the stretch of lonely nights that lay before her, when Kathryn had been returned to her own world.

Her eyes now closed against the sunlight, Kyril allowed her awareness to drift inward, to the newly gained recognition of the changes that had been wrought through this latest crisis. There was an inner stillness where before there had been a terrible, aching nothingness. She retained the picture-memory of her mother's face, felt finally at rest with the fact that Tyrell had filled that place in her life after Kolayna's death. And now there was a weary acceptance of Kathryn's leaving.

She sighed and turned her head to look at Kathryn's profile where she lay next to her. With her eyes, she traced the lines of Kathryn's face, seeking to etch that vision in her memory next to that of Kolayna's. She felt sure now that she really *had* Kolayna's face, along with Lanaea's and Tyrell's. Her fondness for Mindi had grown and was firmly linked within her to the psychic bond she had forged with the loving creature. But she and Kathryn had not yet mated, and that was the hardest of all— Her gaze drifted to the cloudless sky.

"Kyril." The word was spoken softly, an inquiry.

Kyril swallowed hard. She felt the burning in her eyes as she turned them back to Kathryn.

Kathryn's gaze was on her, filled with concern. "What is it?" she asked after a moment's silence. Her voice was yet so lacking in force it was nearly lost in the noise of wind and surf, though they lay but an armspan apart.

Kyril hesitated, pondering how Kathryn had caught her mood. "I—I felt regret—your regret. . . ." Clearly, Kathryn understood nothing more than that she had been aware of the regret.

Still, Kyril hesitated. *Am I so open to her, now?* She swallowed again, seeking the words she needed. They were not in her mind. She looked at Kathryn, saw that she simply waited. Closing her eyes, she delved deeper, found the feelings she wanted to express and dragged them upward, toward the level of language. She turned, lifted herself on her elbow, reached out with her other hand, took Kathryn's where it lay, on the blanket between them.

"I am going to miss you—" She faltered. That was not it. She tried again. "If we were bonded, it would be easier to. . . ." Her throat constricted. How to put into words the nakedness of her soul without its mate?

Kathryn rolled onto her side. The hazel eyes offered encouragement, said she was willing to give whatever time Kyril needed. Her hand turned; she clasped Kyril's fingers in both hands.

"Kathryn—when oupirian babes are still *in utero,* they have a conscious bond with their mothers, beginning in the fourth month of gestation. That bond survives and strengthens through the transition of birth. It deepens to unconsciousness during the years of early childhood, and it is only when we become adults—sexually matured and capable of reproduction ourselves—that another bond on that order of intimacy is formed. And that occurs when we choose a mate." She paused, looking out at the surf, amethyst and foaming white under mauve skies. "My mother died when I was seven. Except for the spirit-bond with Tyrell, I accepted no one into that inner level until I joined with Lanaea. When she died, there was a gaping hole—again—where *she* had been, within me."

Her gaze returned to Kathryn's. "I want you to be in that inner place with me—it is all I have wanted since. . . ." She searched her memory, unable to determine now when first she had come to that place of wanting with Kathryn. She sighed, giving up the effort. "When Lanaea and I were apart physically, I was still *with* her, because we were bonded. I will not have that connection with you—" Her throat constricted, made her unable to go on. She sought understanding with her eyes.

Kathryn sensed Kyril's pain and moved across the blanket to take her in her arms. Cradling Kyril's head against the hollow between her neck and shoulder, she stroked the raven hair, murmuring soft words of comfort. She knew she was not yet able to share in the bonding ritual Kyril had told her about. But she knew she loved Kyril deeply enough that she was not willing to let her go; knew that mere distance could not change what she had come to feel for her. She pushed back from Kyril a little, brought Kyril's chin up gently, so she could see the night-dark eyes.

"I will be in my world and you will be in yours—but I am *not* going away from you." Kathryn tilted her head to the side. "I *love* you— and I need you and want you in my life. I think, somehow, I knew *that* the very first time I ever saw you." She smiled a little, a melancholy loving smile. "We both needed time, then. I need a little more. When you come to me, I promise, I'll try to be ready for you."

Kyril's heart lurched and thudded in her chest. She believed Kathryn, believed that time *was* what she needed now. She leaned up to kiss her, and her hand went behind Kathryn's neck, pulling her down onto the blanket with her.

Their lips met and the fire ignited between them again, smoldering in their eyes, leaping from their hands to each other's skin. Except for Mindi and the seabirds, they were alone on the beach. In abandon, they made love with an intensity like unto their first nights together. And when they lay spent, and Kathryn's body blanketed Kyril's with its warmth, both felt that a commitment had been made, a betrothal, wherein each promised to reserve herself for the other, until such time as they could complete their bonding in the manner of Kyril's people; could, in the manner Kathryn had always dreamed, become one.

Spring 1985

Epilogue

Kathryn sprawled on the floor of her living room, listening to a tape of movie-soundtrack music she had made. Mindi lay beside her, stretched on her side to her full length, pressed against Kathryn's thigh and hip. Candles burned low in holders on the bookcase and stereo unit, and on the coffee table where the remnants from her earlier dinner with Megan and Joel Kastner remained.

Joel had recently been released from the hospital for the third or fourth time, and everyone knew the thread of his life was running out. Megan had tested positive on the recently developed screening instrument for HTLV-III antibodies. So had their baby, Aaron, now a year old. In spite of the cloud of doom hanging over all their futures, Megan and Joel had managed a kind of acceptant peace, and were able to enjoy their friends and their son, who, for the time being, remained asymptomatic.

Upon her return from Kornägy, Kathryn was saddened to find that Rob had died in her absence and that Kent, inconsolable in his loss, had moved out of her house, appointing a reliable caretaker in his place. Shortly after Kathryn's return, Kent had developed Kaposi's sarcoma and moved back to New York City to be with what remained of his family and his boyhood friends.

Kathryn sighed, expelling the sadness that had come with these memories, allowing the strains of "Chariots of Fire" to take her deeper into her feelings.

Suddenly, Mindi's head raised and she came alert, startling Kathryn. Slowly, Kathryn sat up. Realizing she had not pulled the shades down over the windows, she felt exposed. She watched Mindi, a prickle of fear running over her at the thought of someone watching her through the naked panes. Mindi, however, was looking around the room, as if expecting to see someone there, in the room with them. Kathryn's anxiety gave way to curiosity—she had never known Mindi to behave this way before.

Keeping her eye on Mindi, who settled into an attitude of watchful waiting, she rose and began closing the shades, pointedly avoiding looking out into the dark. As she drew the last one, a candle guttered out, sputtering and flaring as it died. Kathryn jumped, letting go of the shade, which flew up and spun around noisily, completely rattling her. Shaking, she cursed under her breath and drew the offending device down to cover the window again. Mindi seemed unaffected by Kathryn's sudden case of nerves. She remained alert but calm in her place on the floor.

Kathryn let out her breath in a nervous rush and went to flip the tape, which had cut off about the same time the candle had burned out. Before she could push the PLAY button, the doorbell rang. Quickly, she looked again at Mindi, who, upon hearing the bell, trotted eagerly to the front door and set about scratching busily at it, whining softly.

Gathering her composure, Kathryn walked over and unlocked the deadbolt. Restraining Mindi, she twisted the door handle and pulled it open. Standing on the stoop, backlit by the streetlamps, was a tall figure in dark clothing. The face was in shadow, but light from the living room glinted softly on an elliptical pendant suspended on the figure's breast.

Kathryn's free hand went to her throat, where her heart seemed to have lodged. *Oh, my God!* Her mind continued to function, but her body refused. Mindi was wagging her tail and barking, tugging at the hand which was locked woodenly on the dog's collar. Abruptly, the rigid fingers gave and Mindi jumped against the dark form even as Kathryn's voice finally animated her lips.

"K-Kyril?"

The figure stepped across the threshold, laughing with pleasure at Mindi's greeting, then turned back to Kathryn where she stood, frozen in place.

"Hello, Kathryn." Kyril allowed the joy that filled her heart to light up her dark eyes and infuse her words with warmth.

The sibilance of the well-remembered voice freed Kathryn from her paralysis. She threw herself at Kyril, whose arms came up to embrace her.

They stood for a long moment, holding each other tightly, Kyril savoring the warmth of Kathryn's body, Kathryn trying to believe that what she held was real and not another dream. When they leaned back and regarded each other, both women had tears in their eyes.

"I've missed you so," Kathryn whispered, drinking in the features that, tonight, had some color in them: the high cheekbones, the finely chiseled nose, the ebony eyes, and the crimson lips.

"And I you." Kyril saw health written on the countenance where last had been malaise.

A brief contemplative silence was followed by a hesitant kiss. A shyness that came from their long separation overtook them. They stood, uncertain, their hands clasped loosely between them.

Suddenly, Mindi barked demandingly from where she sat in the open door, causing both women to laugh. While Kyril knelt to Mindi and greeted her at more length, Kathryn secured the door. When Mindi seemed satisfied with the attention she had received, the two women again regarded one another with uncertainty.

Kathryn motioned Kyril to the couch, and they sat, eyeing one another in silence, unwilling to make small talk, while Mindi leaned against Kyril's leg, enjoying the hand that absently stroked her.

Finally, awkwardly, Kathryn reached out, taking Kyril's free hand in hers, and stood. She inquired with her eyes. After a moment, Kyril stood. Kathryn led Kyril, each with an arm around the other, into her bedroom. There, in the stillness, they began to undress one another, each keenly aware of when they had last been together sexually, building from that encounter, across the many months that had separated them, to the present. The hunger each woman felt was more than a hunger of the flesh: It was also the craving to see, touch, taste, and *remember* the one for whom each had longed so deeply, and for so long a time.

Their lovemaking, once begun, was intense, long and drawn out, an act of re-acquaintance, a re-affirmation of their relationship. When it seemed that, at least for the moment, the hunger and yearning had been satisfied, they began to speak of their time apart.

"Are you here to stay?" Kathryn asked quietly, prepared for any answer she might receive. She lay propped on one elbow, her leg across Kyril's, her hand at rest in the hollow below Kyril's breastbone.

Kyril looked deep into the hazel eyes, perceiving the acceptance there. "It was either remain in Kornägy for another eight or so of your years, or. . .come here and agree not to return for the same length of time."

Kathryn tried to sense what Kyril felt about the choices she had faced and made. But she could not read the dark eyes.

"I completed my work—and I came, immediately thereafter. I shall miss Tyrell, and Taddéos,"—she smiled to herself, remembering their still young friendship—" but it would have been *unbearable* to be any longer than necessary without you." She traced the hairline at Kathryn's temple with a finger, noticing grey where before there had been none. "You have started to go grey."

Kathryn heard the surprise in Kyril's voice, saw it on her face. She nodded. "Yes, after I returned from Kornägy."

Pain leapt into Kyril's eyes. "That journey took its toll on you," she said, regret—or was it guilt?— coloring her words.

Kathryn placed the palm of her hand forgivingly against Kyril's cheek, then dropped it to Kyril's chest again. "Have you *finished* your work, then?" Kathryn asked. Kyril nodded, willingly distracted. "You've found a cure for AIDS?" Excitement crept into Kathryn's voice and manner.

Kyril moved her head in qualification. "For oupirs—not human beings."

"But that's wonderful! Your people are safe!"

Kyril was gratified at Kathryn's response. She had not been sure that Kathryn would still have reason to care about the fate of oupirs in their own dimension. But grief overrode gratitude as she replied, "Most. It was not soon enough for some."

Kathryn hesitated, not wanting to ask but needing to know. "Orlov?"

Kyril shook her head, saw the sorrow on Kathryn's face, and hastened to reassure her. "But his life was prolonged by the work that you did, and we have incorporated what was efficacious into our treatment program. We still cannot *prevent* oupirs from getting AIDS, but at least we can cure those who do."

"Then, is your work truly done?" Kathryn's voice was tentative. She wanted to believe that Kyril was here to stay, but—

"My work is completed. I set a goal of cure or preventive. Taddéos continues the work on prevention. I have brought with me what is needed for the preliminary treatment of those of my kind who reside in this country, who are infected—and it has been disseminated to others in other countries. I also intend to resume my research in this dimension. I hope to adapt what we have learned about AIDS in the oupirian body to defeating AIDS in the human body."

It was Kathryn's turn for surprise. She had never been privy to the full depth of Kyril's previous contempt for humanity, yet sensed that, in this also, Kyril had changed. "You know that a test for the presence of the HTLV antibody has been developed?"

Kyril nodded. "Yes, and we developed a similar device for screening oupirian blood."

Their eyes met for a moment while Kathryn wondered whose test had come first. Then Kathryn lowered hers.

"Kyril, does your staying here—and others of your kind—mean that you will no longer feed on human beings?" Her gaze again met Kyril's, waiting.

Kyril sensed that Kathryn's former revulsion had been replaced by a mild apprehension at her possible response. "An oupir cannot survive long on bottled blood—we *must* have the blood of the living, eventually." She paused, measuring Kathryn with her gaze. "I am fairly certain that the safest way for any of us to feed here—at least for now—is to use non-human species. There *are* ways of preventing the death of the one whose blood sustains me. . . . I will seek those ways."

Kathryn released a breath she had not realized she held. "Kyril, how are we ever going to resolve our differences?"

"Perhaps with an agreement—at least in some areas—to disagree."

Kathryn pondered that, her eyes on Kyril's face. "Perhaps," she conceded, stroking thick waves from Kyril's temple. "It's just that. . .this is such an important thing to me. I—I know I promised I'd try to be ready for you when you came. . .but I haven't been able to fully resolve the issue of the death of one of my species in order that you may survive."

Kyril touched her face gently. "Kathryn, I have said I will seek ways *around* death—and that, for now, I will not feed on human beings."

Kathryn dropped her eyes again. "I guess it's not just the death." She raised her eyes to Kyril's. "There's something atavistic in my reaction to the idea of your feeding on human life. . . I'm sorry," she finished softly.

Kyril nodded. "I think I understand. I've felt something similar in contemplating the killing of one member of your species by another."

Kathryn looked away, thinking that it was not the same thing, but knowing she could not articulate it any more clearly right now. *Perhaps,* she thought, *it's a non-issue—at least as long as we have to worry about AIDS.*

With deep love and acceptance, Kathryn's eyes once more sought Kyril's.

They made love again, and when at last they lay quiescent, and Kathryn dozed in Kyril's arms, Kyril lifted her heart in thanks to the Goddess. Reminding herself that initially she had been prepared to remain here, had she been unable to solve the riddle of Lanaea's death, she reflected that now, it was no real punishment for her to agree to an extended stay in this dimension. She felt sure that not only was there much she could do in Kathryn's world, professionally, there was also much she would be learning: about herself, about Kathryn—and certainly about their relationship.

And one day, she must believe, they would engage in the ritual of *lélek bizalmas.* Until then, she was content.

The End

If You Liked This Book...

Authors seldom get to hear what readers like about their work. If you enjoyed reading **Shadows After Dark**, why not let the author know? Simply write the author:

Ouida Crozier
c/o Rising Tide Press
5 Kivy Street
Huntington Station, NY 11746

ABOUT THE AUTHOR

Ouida Crozier was born and raised in Florida, lived in South Carolina for ten years, and now resides in Minnesota. She has worked as a teacher, a psychologist, a computer programmer, and sundry other things. She lives with her dog, Idgie Threadgoode, in Minneapolis. She believes in vampires. This is her first novel.

MORE EXCITING FICTION FROM
RISING TIDE PRESS

ROMANCING THE DREAM
Heidi Johanna

This imaginative tale begins when Jacqui St. John leaves northern California looking for a new home, and cruises into the seemingly ordinary town of Kulshan, on the Oregon coast. Seeing the lilac bushes in bloom along the roadside, she suddenly remembers the recurring dream that has been tantalizing her for months—a dream of a house full of women, radiating warmth and welcome, and of one special woman, dressed in silk and leather.... But why has Jacqui, like so many other women, been drawn to this place? The answer is simple but wonderful—the women plan to take over the town and make a lesbian haven. A captivating and erotic love story with an unusual plot. A novel that will charm you with its gentle humor and fine writing.

ISBN 0-9628938-0-3;   176 Pages; $8.95

YOU LIGHT THE FIRE
Kristen Garrett

Here's a grown-up *Rubyfruit Jungle*–sexy, spicy, and side-splittingly funny. Garrett, a fresh new voice in lesbian fiction, has created two memorable characters in Mindy Brinson and Cheerio Monroe. Can a gorgeous, sexy, high school math teacher and a raunchy, commitment-shy ex singer, make it last, in mainstream USA? With a little help from their friends, they can. This humorous, erotic and unpredictable love story will keep you laughing, and marveling at the variety of lesbian love.

ISBN 0-9628938-5-4; 176 Pages; $8.95

EDGE OF PASSION
Shelley Smith

The author of **Horizon of the Heart** presents another absorbing and sexy novel! From the moment Angela saw Micki sitting at the end of the smoky bar, she was consumed with desire for this cool and sophisticated woman, and determined to have her...at any cost. Set against the backdrop of colorful Provincetown and Boston, this sizzling novel will draw you into the all-consuming love affair between an older and a younger woman. A gripping love story, which is both fierce and tender. It will keep you breathless until the last page.
ISBN 0-9628938-1-1;   192 Pages; $8.95

RETURN TO ISIS
Jean Stewart
The year is 2093. In this fantasy zone where sword and superstition meet sci-fi adventure, two women make a daring escape to freedom. Whit, a bold warrior from an Amazon nation, rescues Amelia from a dismal world where females are either breeders or drones. Together, they journey over grueling terrain, to the shining world of Artemis, and in their struggle to survive, find themselves unexpectedly drawn to each other. But it is in the safety of Artemis, Whit's home colony, that danger truly lurks. And it is in the ruins of Isis that the secret of how it was mysteriously destroyed waits to be uncovered. Here's adventure, mystery and romance all rolled into one.
Nominated for a 1993 Lambda Literary Award

ISBN 0-9628938-6-2;   *192 Pages;*   *$8.95*

FACES OF LOVE
Sharon Gilligan
A wise and sensitive novel which takes us into the lives of Maggie, Karen, Cory, and their community of friends. Maggie Halloran, a prominent women's rights advocate, and Karen Weston, a brilliant attorney, have been together for 10 years in a relationship which is full of love, but is also often stormy. When Maggie's heart is captured by the young and beautiful Cory, she must take stock of her life and make some decisions.
Set against the backdrop of Madison, Wisconsin, and its dynamic women's community, the characters in this engaging novel are bright, involved, '90s women dealing with universal issues of love, commitment and friendship. A wonderful read!

ISBN 0-9628938-4-6;   *192 Pages;*   *$8.95*

LOVE SPELL
Karen Williams
A deliciously erotic and humorous love story with a magical twist. When Kate Gallagher, a reluctantly single veterinarian, meets the mysterious and alluring Allegra one enchanted evening, it is instant fireworks. But as Kate gradually discovers, they live in two very different worlds, and Allegra's life is shrouded in mystery which Kate longs to penetrate. A masterful blend of fantasy and reality, this whimsical story will delight your imagination and warm your heart. Here is a writer of style as well as substance.

ISBN 0-9628938-2-X;   *192 Pages;*   *$9.95*

DANGER IN HIGH PLACES: An Alix Nicholson Mystery
Sharon Gilligan

Free-lance photographer Alix Nicholson was expecting some great photos of the AIDS Quilt— what she got was a corpse with a story to tell! Set against the backdrop of Washington, DC, the bestselling author of **Faces of Love** delivers a riveting mystery. When Alix accidentally stumbles on a deadly scheme surrounding AIDS funding, she is catapulted into the seamy underbelly of Washington politics. With the help of Mac, lesbian congressional aide, Alix gradually untangles the plot, has a romantic interlude, and learns of the dangers in high places.　　　　*ISBN 0-9628938-7-0; 176 Pages;*　　　　**$9.95**

CORNERS OF THE HEART
Leslie Grey

This captivating novel of love and suspense introduces two unforgettable characters whose diverse paths have finally led them to each other. It is Spring, season of promise, when beautiful, French-born Chris Benet wanders into Katya Michaels' life. But their budding love is shadowed by a baffling mystery which they must solve. You will read with bated breath as they work together to outwit the menace that threatens Deer Falls; your heart will pound as the story races to its heart-stopping climax. Vivid, sensitive writing and an intriguing plot are the hallmarks of this exciting new writer.
ISBN 0-9628938-3-8;　　　　224 pages;　　　　**$9.95**

ISIS RISING
Jean Stewart

The eagerly awaited sequel to the immensely popular **Return to Isis** is here at last! In this stirring romantic fantasy, Jean Stewart continues the adventures of Whit (every woman's heart-throb), her beloved Kali, and a cast of colorful characters, as they rebuild Isis from the ashes. But all does not go smoothly in this brave new world, and Whit, with the help of her friends, must battle the forces that threaten. A rousing futuristic adventure and an endearing love story all rolled into one. Destined to capture your heart. Look for the sequel.

ISBN 0-9628938-8-9;　　　　192 Pages;　　　　**$9.95**

How To Order:

Rising Tide Press books are available from you local women's bookstore or directly from Rising Tide Press. Send check, money order, or Visa/MC account number, with expiration date and signature to: Rising Tide Press, 5 Kivy St., Huntington Sta., New York 11746. **Credit card** orders must be **over $25. Remember** to include shipping and handling charges: $4.95 for the first book plus $1.00 for each additional book. *Credit Card Orders Call our Toll Free #* **1-800-648-5333**. For UPS delivery, provide street address.

Our Publishing Philosophy

Rising Tide Press is a lesbian-owned and operated publishing company committed to publishing books by, for, and about lesbians and their lives. We are not only committed to readers, but also to lesbian writers who need nurturing and support, whether or not their manuscripts are accepted for publication. Through quality writing, the press aims to entertain, educate, and empower readers, whether they are women-loving-women or heterosexual. It is our intention to promote lesbian culture, community, and civil rights, nationwide, through the printed word.

In addition, RTP will seek to provide readers with images of lesbians aspiring to be more than their prescribed roles dictate. The novels selected for publication will aim to portray women from all walks of life, (regardless of class, ethnicity, religion or race), women who are strong, not just victims, women who can and do aspire to be more, and not just settle, women who will fight injustice with courage. Hopefully, our novels will provide new ideas for creating change in a heterosexist and homophobic society. Finally, we hope our books will encourage lesbians to respect and love themselves more, and at the same time, convey this love and respect of self to the society at large. It is our belief that this philosophy can best be actualized through fine writing that entertains, as well as educates the reader. Books, even lesbian books, can be fun, as well as liberating.

WRITERS WANTED!!!

Rising Tide Press, Publisher of
Lesbian Novels,
is Soliciting Quality Fiction Manuscripts

Rising Tide Press is interested in publishing quality Lesbian fiction: romance, mystery, and science-fiction/fantasy. Non-fiction is also welcome, but please, no poetry or short stories.

Please send us the following:

- One page synopsis of plot
- The manuscript
- A brief autobiographical sketch
- Large manila envelope with

sufficient return postage

RISING
TIDE
PRESS

5 KIVY ST.
HUNTINGTON STATION,
N.Y. 11746